Also by Jessica Lawson

The Actual & Truthful Adventures of Becky Thatcher

Nooks & Crannies

Waiting for Augusta

Jessica Lawson

Simon & Schuster Books for Young Readers

NEW YORK   LONDON   TORONTO   SYDNEY   NEW DELHI

SIMON & SCHUSTER BOOKS FOR YOUNG READERS
An imprint of Simon & Schuster Children's Publishing Division
1230 Avenue of the Americas, New York, New York 10020

SIMON & SCHUSTER BOOKS FOR YOUNG READERS is a trademark of Simon & Schuster, Inc.
For information about special discounts for bulk purchases, please contact Simon & Schuster Special Sales at 1-866-506-1949 or business@simonandschuster.com.
The Simon & Schuster Speakers Bureau can bring authors to your live event. For more information or to book an event, contact the Simon & Schuster Speakers Bureau at 1-866-248-3049 or visit our website at www.simonspeakers.com.
Jacket design by Lizzy Bromley
Interior design by Hilary Zarycky
The text for this book is set in Adobe Caslon Pro.
Manufactured in the United States of America
0416 FFG
First Edition
2 4 6 8 10 9 7 5 3 1

Library of Congress Cataloging-in-Publication Data
Names: Lawson, Jessica, 1980– author.
Title: Waiting for Augusta / Jessica Lawson.
Description: 1st edition. | New York : Simon & Schuster Books for Young Readers, [2016] | Summary: In early 1970s Alabama, eleven-year-old Ben, carrying an urn with his father's ashes, sets out on an eventful journey to the Augusta National, "the Sistine Chapel of golf courses," to make peace with his father.
Identifiers: LCCN 2015026346| ISBN 9781481448390 (hardback) | ISBN 9781481448406 (trade paper) | ISBN 9781481448413 (eBook)
Subjects: | CYAC: Grief—Fiction. | Fathers—Fiction. | Runaways—Fiction. | Golf—Fiction. | Southern States—History—20th century—Fiction. | BISAC: JUVENILE FICTION / Fantasy & Magic. | JUVENILE FICTION / Action & Adventure / General. | JUVENILE FICTION / Sports & Recreation / Golf.
Classification: LCC PZ7.L438267 Wai 2016 | DDC [Fic]—dc23
LC record available at http://lccn.loc.gov/2015026346

For my husband, Christopher
I've got gaps, you've got gaps, together we fill gaps

Rural Alabama, 1972

The Lump

Last month Mama caught me rubbing my neck. Even though I told her what I guessed was wrong, she snatched me over to Dr. Landry, Daddy's tumor doctor before he died, who said there wasn't a thing the matter with me. When I told *him* what I thought the problem was, he gave me a funny look and told Mama maybe I should "go see a different kind of doctor."

Next Mama took me to Dr. Temple, who I'd been going to my whole life for checkups. He was Daddy's and Uncle Luke's doctor when they were young and said maybe it was that awful Adam's apple of the Putter boys, gurgling around before it got ready to spring itself on the world during puberty. "Putter boys might end up small," he told me, "but they've got overzealous larynxes to make up for it." Then he snatched my drawing pad away and said I needed to get outside more.

Then Mama took me to Dr. Bartelle, a head doctor who

goes to our church, who said with a whole bunch of head nodding and chin stroking that my neck rubbing was a cry for help. "You're too quiet for an eleven-year-old boy, living in your head too much. You better work through whatever feelings are rattling around up there or you're liable to go crazy like my sister Bernice did over her no-good boyfriends." Then he told me that I wouldn't be able to let Daddy go until I'd had a good cry about it.

"Yes, sir," I'd answered. I didn't have the heart to tell Dr. Bartelle that when it came to Daddy, it was like me holding a golf club. I'd never really gotten the grip down, and it was hard to know the proper way of letting go of something when you were never holding it right in the first place.

After the appointments, I didn't tell a soul about the lump in my neck, even though I knew by then exactly what it was. Nobody would have believed me anyway. In the month after Daddy passed, everyone except Mama seemed to be going about their business, sucking down the sky like it was a glass of strained lemonade. Nice big lump-free gulps. Sure, every now and then I'd get a pat on the head and someone saying "You poor, poor thing" or "You poor, poor boy," but that wasn't gonna help a thing. Plus, it didn't seem too nice to rub in the fact that Daddy never made much money and any extra he had mostly went toward hitting balls at the driving range and walking rounds of eighteen holes.

So I didn't say another word about the lump, but there

was no doubt in my mind that I had a golf ball trapped in my throat. Maybe it didn't show up on any X-ray, but I knew it was in there. Hiding inside me like it was waiting for something.

And you know what?

I was right.

ROUND ONE

Honey Air and Lightning

Alabama's heat started waking up and stretching around the same time Daddy died, and by the first full week of April it'd gotten good and dressed. Overdressed, I'd say, with the golf club thermometer stuck to the hog shed filled up just past the ninety line. A record high, the radio had declared, the afternoon announcer saying that if he were still a boy, he'd have ditched school for the pool on this steaming pot roast of a Tuesday, and thank goodness a battalion of storm clouds was heading our way to cool things down. Between the heat and the thunder grumbling and the lightning flashing on the horizon, it wasn't the best of evenings for running away, if a person was thinking about doing that sort of thing. Which maybe I was.

With a heave, I hauled open the iron lid of the backyard smoker and caught a blast of fiery air and sizzling pork scent. Eyes stinging, I turned and shook my left arm's day-old burn, trying to ignore the way the raw spot flared and shouted *Hey, you! Watch it this time!* when it neared the burning coals. Grabbing the metal grabbers, I loaded up our double-deep pan with good hunks of pig and waded down the side yard through air thick as honey, careful so I'd spill nothing more than a little of the juice. House rent was on that tray—might as well have been bundles of money instead of meat.

Even though our barbecue didn't compare to when Daddy manned the big pit, and even though we had to set up business in the front yard when we were short on a café payment after he died, we still got a steady set of regulars and word-of-mouthers right at our house between noon and seven or so at night. The bank may have taken back the café property, but it couldn't take away our barbecue. Sauce and sympathy were keeping us afloat.

I plopped the pan on the wooden saucing table tucked off the front porch near the side hose, where we'd taken to finishing the meat before putting it in the public eye, and swiped my arm across my forehead. Salty sweat got into my burn, but I held off hollering. Mama was already worried that she left me alone with the smoker too much, and she was close by on the porch, cutting pieces of sheet cake while she minded the cash box and her long table of side dishes.

"Benjamin, you hurry up now and slather those good!"

"Yes, Mama." Dipping a paintbrush into a bucket of ketchup, chili powder, vinegar, paprika, crushed mustard

seed, little bit of cayenne, chicory, and brown sugar, I slath-
ered those ribs up and down like I was painting a fence,
which was the only kind of art Daddy ever approved of. He
was a golf and barbecue man through and through. Both
took plenty of time and focus, he said.

"Get 'em nice and red," someone called from one of the
four picnic tables set up in the front yard. "Sure is fine, your
mama's sauce."

"Sauce was Daddy's," I muttered to the ribs, even though
they knew it already. We were almost through his supply
and he'd never bothered to write down his exact recipe, so
the Putter flavor was bound to change. I dipped two more
brushfuls and took my time making the color nice and even.

Poking into my eye corners were the orange and yellow
from our neighbor's tulip poplars and white from her magnolia trees that hung over into our yard. Flower colors in
Mrs. Grady's yard were always better and brighter than anything in my art box, but I wasn't much impressed by flowers
lately. Didn't even care about the ones that smelled like Erin
Courtney, who sat in front of me in class and had the nicest
hair I'd ever seen.

No, today those petals and leaves whispered together in
the hot wind, saying *There's Ben Putter, he's got a golf ball right
in his throat, see him rubbing at it with his free hand, do you see
him, he's got no friends, no he doesn't, yes, I see him, how about
you, why yes, I see him, too . . .*

"You all hush," I told those leaves and petals, picking up the pan and walking past the tables to Mama. The ribs were heavy, and I was glad to set them down next to bowls of Mama's beans and potato salad. I wondered who'd help her with everything if I went running. I rubbed the lump in my throat and wondered who'd help me get back to normal if I didn't.

"Lemonade, Benny," Mama told me, her elbow digging into my side and her head jerking toward the road. "Get a glass for Mr. Talbot and May when you're done filling at the tables, won't you?" She pointed to the brown truck coming down our dirt street. "And tell Mr. Talbot that I've got a big package of pork made up for his family." Her eyes drifted to the top of the house. "It was beyond kind of Rudolph to fix that roof leak."

When I saw the distant, approaching outline of May Talbot sitting beside her daddy in the passenger seat, I swallowed hard and felt the golf ball lump rotate in my throat. I wondered if she'd asked to come along. My chest went tight and the banging inside it sped up, from nerves or hope. Both maybe. "Yes, ma'am."

"I put your paint pad and drawing book on the kitchen table, in case you were looking, sweetheart," Mama said, lowering her voice, though the twelve or so customers were out of earshot, scattered among the tables down in the yard, eating and talking and fanning themselves with hats or what-

WAITING FOR AUGUSTA / 13

ever was handy. "You know you don't need to hide them in the sofa cushions." *Anymore*, she didn't add, but I still heard it. "And that art teacher of yours called again. Miss Stone, right? You really need to call her back, okay?"

Clearing her throat, she called out, "I declare, it's hot as Georgia out here. Who wants more lemonade? Quarter a cup with a refill, good and fresh, coming right up." She waved and smiled at Mr. Talbot as he drove up our long driveway that circled around back to the hog shed, hauling the pig we'd ordered. A few customers turned toward the vehicle, and I watched their faces, saw eyes narrow or drift back to plates, saw lips get tight while they stared or looked away fast, saw within moments what kind of difference, if any, it made to them that the Talbots were colored.

By the time I looked at the truck, my hand ready to jump up in a careful wave, May's eyes were aimed straight ahead. They'd been aimed straight ahead for the last four months. I didn't know what I could do to get my friend back. I just knew that things weren't the same, and a glass of lemonade wasn't gonna change that.

After I'd mixed two new batches, I walked the picnic tables and tipped the lemonade pitcher for two men I knew from town and four dusty-clothed workers who looked to be from the railroad yard. Hobo workers, Grandma Clay had called them, back when she was alive, though Mama always hushed her and said traveling railroad hobos died out long ago.

"Hey, son."

"You sure are looking like your daddy."

"Thank you, kindly, boy."

People knew I hadn't said much at all since Daddy passed, so I felt fine letting one nod do for answering all their chatter. All those men loved him. He'd always been there at the end of their work days, handing them good food to make the body aches fade, listening to their talk and then cracking enough jokes to make their troubles disappear just a little.

My eyes wandered around the side yard to see Mr. Talbot heaving the pig off his truck bed, then I refilled the paper cups of two men, a woman with tired eyes, and a dirty-looking kid who didn't appear to be with anyone in particular. Maybe she was one of the railmen's daughters.

The girl was around my age, maybe a little younger. She looked up at me with sauce all over and big mean eyes like I'd spit in her drink. I refilled it anyway.

Pouring two fresh cups, I kept my feet moving, my gaze grazing the fence that separated our front yard from Mrs. Grady's. The same kind of fences were just about everywhere in Hilltop, lining the roads and splitting yards, but they weren't proper barriers. They were nothing more than a post every twelve feet with two lengths of raw wood between and didn't keep a thing in or out.

The Talbots were both waiting outside the shed. Looking in the open doors, I saw the hog had been placed on the three-foot-high cutting station that had catch drains all around it. "Thanks, Mr. Talbot." I handed him the lemonade.

He took the cup and squinted sweat out of his eyes. "You're welcome. You need help cutting him up?"

It was the same question he'd asked since Daddy died. "No, thank you. Mama has a package of pork for you." I looked at May's shining shoes and passed her the second cup, feeling her fingers brush against mine as she took it and thanked me. It was a polite but faraway kind of thank-you— the kind I'd heard her use with the teachers at school who'd made it clear they didn't want her there.

"That's fine. You and May catch up for a minute."

Mr. Talbot's tall form walked around the side of the house, and May and I were alone. She was dressed real nice, like she always was, and I was suddenly shy of my ash-stained clothes. Don't know why I felt that way. She'd seen me like that about a million times. "Hot today," I said.

"Mm-hm."

"You draw anything lately?"

"Maybe," she said, tugging at one ear.

May was good at art. The first time we'd met was when we were both five years old and Mr. Talbot had brought a hog over to the café. I was around back, trying to make watercolors from a load of Popsicles that hadn't made it to our freezer in time and were too melted to sell. She sat right beside me, and I handed her a stick brush and a piece of paper. She took them, and that was that.

Since then, we'd seen each other at least twice a month during deliveries. As her daddy and my daddy had gotten to know each other, the deliveries had turned into short visits, and May and I had worked our way up from making Popsicle paintings to taking walks and tossing rocks in the nearby streambed. We even made plans to meet at a spot at the creek on some Saturdays.

We'd sit and draw. We'd talk or not talk. Sometimes she'd write words beside her sketches and paintings, cross some out, leaving just a few to make the picture into a story. *Water, rock, hand, splash. Pecans, trees, basket, pie. Crane, frog, dive, dinner.* She was the best friend I had in the world, and the day I told her that, she'd said I was hers, too.

But all that had changed over the last year. I wished there was a way of going back to before.

"I'm thinking about running away for a time," I told her, the words spilling out before I could remind them that May and me weren't the same anymore.

A hint of light hit her eyes, and they flashed. "What problems could you have to run away from?" Her tight mouth burst open and formed a delicate O. One of her hands lifted to cover it. "I mean . . . well, other than your daddy passing. Never mind. I'm sorry about your daddy."

I shrugged. The truth was, I felt squeezed. Hilltop felt a

whole lot smaller with Daddy gone. Seems like some space should've cleared up with one less person, but I felt tight all over. That darn lump needed to bust outta my throat, darn toes wanted to bust outta my shoes. Seemed like my whole self wanted to bust out of my insides altogether. I didn't want to run away forever. Just for now. Something had been pulling on me since Daddy died, and whatever it was, it wasn't in Hilltop.

She frowned at my neck. "Why do you keep scratching at your throat like that?"

I dropped my hand as Mr. Talbot came around the house corner. We had maybe a few more seconds when it was just us. Sweat was dripping down my forehead and back, and whatever pressure was bubbling inside me couldn't hold back any longer. It had to come out somehow, and it came out with—

"I don't know what I'm supposed to do. It's like everything's changing and I . . . I just don't know what to do." The ground was a comfortable place to look, so I shoved what felt like my whole self in that direction. I raised my head a couple of feet to meet the answer halfway.

"Well," she said, arms wrapping around her waist as her father approached. "Maybe you changed, too."

My ears got hot first, then my cheeks and neck.

Mr. Talbot's hand squeezed my shoulder on the way to his truck. "'Bye, now, Ben. May, let's go, honey."

She stared me in the eyes while Mr. Talbot opened the driver's door and motioned her around the other side. Then she walked away.

I lifted my chin and blinked at the gray-whites and dark blues smeared rough across the sky like brushstrokes being blown straight into Hilltop. Straight into me.

"'Bye," I finally said, staring at the side of May's face as the truck passed by me. She turned in her seat and watched me, her brown eyes soft and wanting, mad and sad and disappointed, and I think that maybe she looked through my body and saw my insides as the Talbots drove away. She was the only one who'd always seen me, and she was leaving.

I decided right then, for certain, that it was time for me to leave, too.

HOLE 2

A Familiar Voice

The rib pan was half-empty by the time I got back to the porch. Mama wiped her hands on her apron and tilted her head toward the side yard. "Ben, you go inside. Take a break and do your schoolwork, all right, honey? I believe I'll finish with these three coming down the road." She looked bone-tired, but was holding on. Her crying time wouldn't come until everyone'd left.

"Yes, ma'am." I walked to the side door next to the hose and dinged the café sign with my foot. Mama refused to put the sign up, but she couldn't seem to bring herself to throw it away either. She'd always hated the name "Putter's Pork Heaven" and the slogan Daddy came up with when he'd taken over the Clay family business: *Where the Best Pigs Come to Pass.*

It was humid inside our house. Everything looked and felt sweaty. Daddy's seven iron was getting a little grimy, leaning against the wall next to the pantry. He kept the old club in the house "in case of intruders," but mostly used it to take practice swings in the living room and to scratch his back. It hadn't moved from its spot since the night he went to the hospital for the last time. I touched the grip and jerked my hand away when it shocked me with a sharp stab of static electricity.

I let out a Daddy word while jitters traveled up my arm and lingered. I felt buzzy all over, like even my eyebrow hair was reaching for the ceiling. Shaking out the tingles, I poured a glass of water and settled at the kitchen table to think more about running away.

I stared at nothing for a good half minute before my hands took over and reached for my thick watercolor paper, brush, and paint pad. I started with the paints, but a minute later, ditched the brush and picked up a pencil, scrawling five letters underneath the mess of color I'd painted. I stared at the greens and blues and light brown and purple and the lone word.

where

I'd made a decent point. You can't do a good job of running away if you don't know where to go. Flipping to the third-to-last page on my drawing pad, I let a finger outline the pencil portrait there. It had been coming along when I'd stopped working on it. The eyes were perfect. Best eyes I'd ever done. "Daddy might have actually liked this one," I told the kitchen.

Maybe not, though. He'd always wanted a boy who loved to inhale barbeque smoke and butcher pigs and play golf, not one who squeezed extra ketchup and mustard on the side of his dinner plates and tried to make sunset colors.

"Sure is hot," I said to the drawing, then caught sight of Daddy's urn settled on its special-built shelf next to the pantry door. He'd been burned up in the cremation place, which had to be even hotter than Alabama.

Instead of spending money on a casket and cemetery plot, Mama'd hired a furniture maker from Mobile to put a small, hand carved platform right in the kitchen, Daddy's favorite room. She said he wouldn't want to be over in the churchyard, so his ashes sat there on the shelf, nice and quiet, which still didn't seem right. He never liked being quiet, and I didn't like seeing him cooped up like a jar of powdered lemonade.

Between the ten-inch-high pewter urn and the ashes inside, Daddy didn't weigh much more than a brand-new baby now, the crematory man had said. It seemed like a strange and awful thing to say, but somehow there was a niceness to it, too, and I noticed later how Mama had cradled Daddy in her arms on the walk to the car.

Feeling the weariness of the day, I leaned forward and let my eyes shut for a second. Maybe a little longer.

"Hey, Ben, that you?"

Jerking up, I looked around the room. Nothing and no one, but the voice had sounded familiar. Eerily familiar. I stepped out the side door and peeked around to the front. Saw Mama waving goodbye to folks. Saw a few men talking to one another in between bites. Saw that big-eyed girl looking at me, her glare lessened to a stare. Girls had all sorts of things going on in their heads at this age, Mama said, so I didn't pay her much mind.

"Mama, did somebody out there call for me?"

She turned, letting her smile for the customers fade into sadness for us. "No, but I'll need you to cut up that pig Mr. Talbot brought by sometime tonight."

"Okay, Mama."

I let the screen door close, sending a cool breeze through the sleeve of my shirt just as the same voice rang out.

"Benjamin Putter, where the heck am I?"

My paintbrush dropped to the floor and made a soft spray of green. I didn't even know I'd still been holding it. All I knew was that the voice sounded exactly like Daddy's extra-thick Alabama accent. And it wasn't coming from outside at all.

It was coming from the urn.

It was hard not to panic. My fingers reached for the fallen brush while I considered the best approach to imaginary voices of used-to-be-real people. Colors. Colors would set me straight. I tried to move, but only managed to twitch a little and sink back into my chair while the room spun and the wall's white blurred with swatches of the countertop's blue, the golf club's silver, and wood floor's brown. *Ben Putter's gone dizzy*, the room whispered. *His ears have gone bad, and all he can do is rub his throat and try to swallow, swallow, swallow that darn golf ball.* "Quiet, you," I whispered back.

"I said, where the heck am I?" Daddy's voice boomed again.

There's something in barbecue circles called the meat sweats. I'd seen full-grown men sit down at our picnic tables on a weekend: pulled pork, ribs, loose pork, shaved pork. A pound past their limit and their eyes would glaze over. A half pound more and the sweat started rolling. But the sauce made it go down so nice that they'd keep going and, once in a rare while, we'd get a crazy on our hands who would get the meat sweats, then see and hear things that weren't there. Voices, people. But I'd only had a peanut butter sandwich in between serving folks, so the meat sweats were out.

Through the screen door, I saw two more flashes of lightning, followed shortly by cracks and grumbles. The storm was getting closer. I eyed the urn. "Daddy . . . is that you?" I asked, feeling scared and confused and half crazy, or maybe whole crazy. "You're in the kitchen. You died, remember?"

He didn't talk again for a full minute, and then he said one more word. He said it slow, like it was the most beautiful, perfect word in the world and I needed to understand how much it meant to him, which I did.

Imaginary or not, my dead Daddy'd given me permission to run away.

And he'd told me exactly where to go.

Runner

Now, I'd been hearing imaginary voices all my life. Mamas and uncles and neighbors think it's cute when you say you hear things talk until you're about six, and then they start looking at you funny, so you either give those voices the boot or keep them to yourself. I kept mine around because they weren't doing any harm and, besides, it felt rude to ignore them just because I was growing up. I knew the voices weren't real—the salt shaker voice and the spatula voice and the dishwater voice and the faucet voice and the paintbrush voice and the pit voice. I knew those were only *me*. But this voice was different. Sounded different. Felt different. Like a memory come back to life.

I wrote down what Daddy'd said, then traced the word with a finger. *Augusta*. Augusta, Georgia was more than four hundred miles away from Hilltop, practically in South Carolina. Might as well be in China. Standing on my tiptoes, I reached for Daddy's urn. I pulled him into my lap and felt the coolness of him. "This can't be real. You're gone forever."

"Could be," Daddy said. "Hope not."

The sound of men laughing drifted in through the screen window. I closed my eyes, inhaled charred oak blocks and hickory chips stocking the smoker, and saw Daddy laughing and pounding backs at the café. Chopping wood that'd burn down to coals. Hauling hogs and ash-burying them in the pit. Swinging a golf club at nothing and saying he was shooting for heaven.

"I hope not, too," I whispered.

Daddy always said that when he died, he wanted to be cremated and have his ashes scattered on the eighteenth hole of Augusta National, the most famous golf course in the world, founded in the 1930s by the most famous golfer of his time, Bobby Jones. It was private, but opened its gates once a year for the Masters, a tournament that was legendary.

When Bobby Jones died last December, it cut a hole in my father, and I think maybe that's when the cancer first snuck back in him. Daddy was quiet for most of a week after news of the death came, finally breaking his silence by reminding Mama and me of his final wishes over his turn at dinner grace one night. He'd clasped his hands together, looked to the ceiling, and then said,

"Dear Family, it's best you know that a piece of my heart has departed along with Mr. Bobby Jones's spirit. As you're both aware, I'd like nothing more, when my time comes, to be spread on the eighteenth green at his magnum opus, Augusta National Golf Club, the place that has brought men to glory and let them know that somebody or something had faith in them." He looked over the spread on the table, then nodded at Mama. "Holly, I believe you may have outdone yourself tonight. That meat loaf looks divine, those potatoes smell like heaven, and Lord knows I love a green bean casserole. Amen to you and the Ol' Creator, let's eat."

Still, nobody took his request seriously. It was an impossibility—just something he liked to say, that's all. But he loved golf that much.

Daddy would smack balls toward Mr. Perry's cotton field every morning with his driver after getting the café pit stoked, one slipping through his homemade baling wire net now and then. He'd hit short strokes on the makeshift green behind the café during the day. And Pork Heaven was closed until four p.m. on Sundays so he could drive to PJ Hewett Municipal Golf Course and play a full round. Church, he called it, and Augusta National was the Sistine Chapel to him. Mama hated that he never came to Sunday services with us, but Daddy told her that he and God heard each other the clearest when neither of them were walled in with a questionable interpreter. He only owned one book in the world, and it wasn't the Bible. It was full of photographs and facts about Augusta.

I set the urn on the table and walked straight out of the kitchen to consult with the grandfather clock in the hall. "Now," I told the second hand, "there are two possibilities for me to believe here."

Go on, the clock told me.

"Number one, my daddy's spirit has come back from beyond to settle some unfinished business. Ghosty style."

And number two?

I looked back toward the kitchen and eyed the seven iron. Maybe it had shocked the crazy into me. Or maybe I'd been crazy all along. I'd already told people about the golf ball in my throat. Was the ball the first step toward me turning into a man who thought underpants should be worn on his head and barbecue sauce went inside shoes? I felt my throat again and swallowed. No. It was in there. The golf ball, at least, was real.

"Number two, Daddy's come back from beyond to help me run away. And help me get rid of this ball in my throat. So, which is it?"

Are you expecting an opinion? the clock asked. *I'm a clock. Believe whatever you want. You want to get out of Hilltop or not?*

"Fine." Straightening my shoulders, I gave the clock a nod and stepped back into the kitchen. *If you're gonna try a new swing in life, you better be all in*, Daddy once told me. "Okay," I said to the urn. "We'll go to Augusta."

Before Daddy could answer, the screen door slammed open, knocking against the wall in a way Mama hates. Standing there was the big-eyed, mean-glared girl, holding a stack of orange-red-smeared plates. "Who's going to Augusta? And where do I put these dishes? Your mama wants pie out there."

"She does?"

The girl rolled her big eyes, and I got the idea that if her hands weren't full, they'd go straight to her hips. "Fine, I want pie. Gimme a bunch and maybe those others'll buy some. So, who's going to Augusta? And who were you talking to in here?"

My face got red as our special sauce. "I wasn't talking to anyone."

The girl didn't seem to mind the lie. She took a quick inventory of the room, which didn't take long. There was the stained oak eating table, blue countertops along one wall with our big white sink and low cabinets set beneath, an old wooden icebox where Mama kept her needlepoint basket, the pantry with its open door showing a line of dented canned goods, a tall refrigerator Daddy'd ordered for Mama from a Sears catalog instead of the ladies' hat she'd asked for, and an electric oven that Mama insisted be pushed right under the window to the side yard, to try to trick the heat into going outside where it belonged. Every piece could speak if I let it, reminding me of good times and bad ones.

"Don't mind me," the girl said. "I'll clean these dishes for you and collect a favor later. You can start by digging up some pie." She walked the plates to the sink, turned on the faucet, and grabbed a dishcloth. Started washing like she owned the place.

Her sureness didn't match her jeans and Coca-Cola shirt, which were wrinkled and caked here and there with dried mud. The long-sleeved shirt tied around her waist looked like it belonged to a grown man, and it wasn't any cleaner. Freckles sprinkled her face, and one side of her long, straw-straight ponytail had a piece of moss in it. There was a dark bruise on her elbow, and her sneakers looked like they'd already been used for a lifetime. There was old dirt on her neck, the kind of dust that could come from working in a windy field or from driving down the roads of Hilltop with car windows down. She was filthier than the plates she'd just washed.

"Say, you look like a runner," she said without turning.

"How's that? And what kind of pie do you want? Apple or lemon cream?"

"Apple." The back of her shoulders shrugged at me. "You just look twitchy. Plus, you told that girl you were thinking about running away."

I'd been over a hundred yards away when I talked to May. I would have been barely visible from where she'd sat.

"You couldn't have heard me."

She sneered and raised a dusty eyebrow easy as anything, in a way I'd tried to do in the mirror a few times because it was one of Daddy's signature moves. Eyebrow raise with a chin tilt and a head raise meant he'd caught me drawing or painting. Eyebrow raise with a wink and a back slap meant he was telling a joke to a barbecue customer.

"I wandered over by one of those big trees," the girl said. "Felt like a walk."

"You felt like spying."

"I'm running, too. Wanna know why?"

"No." I reached in the refrigerator and pulled out two full apple pies with crisscrossed crust. They clanked on the counter, then settled while I took off the clear wrapping.

"All right. Respectful of privacy. I appreciate that in a partner." Finished washing, the girl wiped her hands and threw the cloth on the counter.

"I'm not running away. Not with you, anyway." I remembered her stink face at the picnic table. It hadn't improved much. She was prowling back and forth like a cat in the early stages of rabies. "Besides, you looked mad outside. You look mad now."

"Was sizing you up, that's all. Still am." She pawed at the edge of my watercolor. "Whatcha got there? Looks like a big smush of green and purple. Bushes?" She turned her head sideways. "Flowers maybe? You paint, huh?"

I covered the paper, and she grabbed my drawing pad,

flipping through to a page near the end. "Nice eyes on that one. So we should get this pie out to your mama. Then we should do some planning. Not now, though. Tonight. I found a sheet along the tracks and stashed it for making a tent. It's too nasty to last more than a night, but it'll do. You got a tent?"

I shook my head. Daddy'd had a tent that he used to take fishing with his buddies, but Mama'd thrown it out because it stunk like cigarette smoke.

"I'll set up down by the creek. Saw it running past that big saloon-looking place at the far end of town. I'll be some-where along there. You come find me."

"No, thank you." With a snatch, I got my pad back and smoothed the pages.

"Why you going anyhow?" She jerked her head toward the door. "Your mama seems nice. Got plenty of food here. Heck, I'd run away to a place like this any day."

I didn't answer. I wasn't telling a strange girl that I had a golf ball in my throat and a dead daddy talking to me. And I definitely wasn't taking her with me to the Sistine Chapel of golf courses.

"Why you keep rubbing your throat like that?"

I couldn't help rubbing on it. Since its arrival a couple of months back, the ball mostly stayed still, but over the last week, it'd started twisting around now and then. Tickling at me like it was getting ready to talk.

"Leave your mama a note if you run. She seems nice."

"I'm not leaving forever. I just got something to do."

"That's fine. Now, you take care of money and provisions, and I'll be in charge of the rest."

I couldn't believe my big Putter ears. "What else is there, other than money and provisions? And why would I go anywhere with you?"

She stuck out her lower lip. "I'm a good talker and I'm tough. You don't seem to be either of those things. I'm good at tying knots, and I can sing real well and do magic tricks if we need to make street money. More like why should I run off with you?" She snorted. "Neck-rubbing twitchy boy. But I'm willing to take on a project like yourself because it ain't safe traveling alone. Things happen." She burped. "Name's Noni. I'll be along that creek. Bring some of that barbecue tonight. Password will be, *It's a fine night for a pork sandwich.*"

"That's not a word."

"Well, use your imagination. Must have a decent one since I caught you talking to yourself." Plucking the two pies from the counter, the girl did a handy leg swipe to open the side door and disappeared around the corner.

Magic Words

An hour later, the yard was empty and I was eating a pulled pork sandwich at the kitchen table, thinking about May Talbot and how I wished she'd slammed open the back door and demanded to go with me to Augusta instead of that Noni girl. But May'd never been the demanding type, unless it came to peaches, which she wouldn't touch unless I peeled all the skin off for her, or the color green, which she always called dibs on when we used my paints together, only letting me use it when she was done. She was always making me run out of green.

Mama came in full of sighs, putting a hand on my head. "I'm worn out. Think I'll lie down for a spell, but I may fall asleep for the night. I've got those meetings in Bridger tomorrow, and then I have to talk to the bank. I have to leave early, so I won't wake you. You get yourself some cereal. I won't be back until around six o'clock, so we'll be closed. If anyone stops by after school, you can sell them leftovers, but that's all."

"Mm-hm." Mama'd set up meetings with a few farmers to see if we couldn't afford to add chickens to our menu. They were cheaper than pigs and the occasional beefsteaks we bought, and less hassle. If the prices were right and the bank loan was approved, we'd get the café back.

"That your dinner?"

I nodded, wiping sauce from my cheeks. "Had broccoli and slaw earlier. I'll take care of the cleanup."

She hung up her apron, cracking her neck and moaning while she stretched her back. Then she smiled the best she could and cupped my chin. "Good boy, Bo."

Bo. Bo was Bogart and Bogart was Daddy. She'd accidentally called me Daddy's name even before he died. It was a joke back then and, boy, how we poked fun and laughed. But it wasn't funny anymore and I wasn't about to mention the slip.

"Mama, what day is it?"

She glanced at the golf course calendar I'd bought Daddy for Christmas. "Tuesday, April 4th."

I cleared my throat. "The Masters starts this week. Remember how Daddy used to say he wanted to end up at Augusta?"

The tiniest raise of her lips was canceled out by the way her chin was shaking. "Yes, I do." She poured herself a glass of water.

"You think we should take him there?"

She pushed against the counter with both hands, stretching. "Oh, Ben. Even if the truck wasn't begging for the junkyard and even if I didn't need to keep up with the business, we don't have the money to go anywhere right now. Sometimes life doesn't give you everything you want, but if you're lucky you have most of what you really need. Your daddy knew that." She took a sip of water and looked at the wall like maybe it had something to say. Turning her face back to me, she lifted a hand to my cheek. "Goodnight, sweetheart."

I went back to the shed and dealt with the hog. It wasn't a particularly big one, which I was glad to see. Daddy'd taught me careful, telling me to watch when I wasn't more than five and having me take a knife on my seventh birthday. Not a pretty sight, he'd said, but everything worth having in life starts messy. *Like your golf game*, he'd joke. *Heck, like my golf game*.

Mrs. Grady was just visible over her backyard fence. It was close to eight o'clock, and she was wearing a nightgown and special socks that kept her leg veins held in, holding a rake and hacking away at the Spanish moss hanging from her trees. She hated that stuff. Crazy Grady was somewhere in her eighties and thought her husband was still alive.

Mama sent me over there once a week or so to bring her a plate of barbecue and visit for a while, which I didn't mind at all. I usually just sketched or painted while she served walnut bars to me and talked about Mr. Grady's arthritis. I thought about calling a hello to her, but decided the pig needed to be butchered more than Mrs. Grady needed to have another long conversation about joint pain.

The cuts came easy and the hog had been delivered good and blood-drained, so there wasn't much mess. Mr. Talbot used to run a barbecue pit over in the colored part of Hilltop and knew hogs better than Daddy, but his place caught fire in the middle of the night last December, just a few months after May started going to our elementary school along with six other colored boys and girls.

The closest high school, over in Woodard, had been integrated for a few years now, but none of the colored parents had sent their younger kids to Hilltop Primary until this school year. May was in my class, and before her first day, she'd seemed nervous but pleased. She told me that she'd heard everything was better at our school, from the desks and books to the toilet paper. Neither of us thought the things we'd heard about the high school would happen.

But soon she was near silent at school, even after most of the boys and girls who'd yelled things and spit in her food were gone, transferred over to the newly built white-only private school, Hilltop Christian Academy.

I divided the hog into spare ribs, loin, shoulder, butt, bacon, chops, and ham cuts. Mama would pickle the ears and feet, so those came off, too. The organs had already been taken out by Mr. Talbot, who made sausage, and I saved the head for a church lady who boiled it for head cheese.

Butchering was always hard for me, even after I got handy with the cuts. I hated taking something whole and cutting it to pieces and throwing some of those pieces away. *Good, good, good, bad.* It wasn't the pig's fault that some of it wasn't worth keeping for barbecue.

After the meat was packed into the shed cooler and freezer, I picked up the lemon sacks and peeled until my hands smelled like a citrus orchard and white pith was pushed up under every one of my fingernails. I put them all in our large plastic bin and stuck the whole thing in the big fridge, knowing I'd saved Mama from the hardest part of lemonade labor. It was ten o'clock by the time I finished and sat at the kitchen table to write a note.

Dear Mama,

I know you worry about me, but don't this time. I got something that needs doing. I'll try to be back by the time you run out of pig. Please don't be mad. I love you.

Ben

People always said how much I looked like my daddy, right down to those unfortunate Putter ears. Maybe a few days apart would do both me and Mama good. I'd get rid of my neck lump and get Daddy to rest and then everything would be fine.

Daddy coughed. "Ben, you there?"

The pen in my hand scrawled across the table's wood. Hearing a dead man's voice, even if it's related to you, takes some getting used to. "Yes, sir, I'm here." I licked my finger and tried to spit-scrub out the stain I'd made, but the rubbing just made it worse. I'd throw a tablecloth on before I left.

"Listen, we need to get going. It's Augusta or nothing, Ben. You understand? It's where I belong. Otherwise, I'm never gonna get any peace. Now, I know you aren't the kind of boy—" He stopped himself. "I know that journeys like this aren't your strong suit, son. I'm asking you to be . . . what I need. Can you do that?"

"Yes, sir, I can," I said, wondering what kind of boy I was and what kind of boy I should be and how to color in the empty space between.

He sighed, relieved. "Good boy."

"I've never ditched school before." I didn't add that I'd dreamed about ditching nearly every day that year. Having a reputation for being the only boy who tried hard in art class and smelled like pig smoke hadn't made it the friendliest of places. And things with May, the one person who didn't care about all that and who was right there in school with me, weren't the same.

"What, never ditched school?" Daddy let out a phlegmy cough so real that I wondered if he was spraying spit-snot or ash inside his urn. "Well, never mind, I could have guessed that. When I was your age, I was skipping school once a week to caddie or go fishing. Both sometimes. No better feeling than missing class and bringing home money and dinner."

I picked up the kitchen club, half expecting to get zapped again. When I didn't, I settled my grip and took a light swing. "Daddy, the Masters starts two days from now."

"The Masters?" I swear, I heard my father smile inside that urn. "Hot *dog*, isn't that a trick? Fate or the Ol' Creator or Mama Nature or Whatever must have waited a month to send me back so I could go to the Masters. And so you could take me."

I saw him rub his hands together like he was excited to bite into a batch of twelve-hour pork butt. "I'll finally make you fall in love with the greatest game ever played. We'll watch most of the tournament together, and then you shake me outta this can by Sunday morning, so I can be right there on the last day of play. Front and center, eighteenth green. You pull this off and I can't tell you how much it'd mean. That's the plan, okay?"

I couldn't answer. My daddy'd come back from the dead so I could skip school and sneak him into a golf tournament.

Sounds about right, the club head said.

Maybe you can change his mind about scattering him there—make him want to stick around for a while, said the golf calendar.

I shook my head at it and let my eyes drift over to the counter, where golden pie crust crumbs lay like sprinkled ashes. *Maybe while he's trying to make you finally love golf, you can finally make him pay you some attention,* said the smallest crumb.

"I don't know about that," I said.

Fine, then, the crumb said. *You could make him proud.*

"Please, Ben." Daddy coughed. "I need you."

I need you. Those were magic words. Soft, warm, hickory-smoke words that wrapped around me and gathered me close, until I sank inside and belonged only to them. "Okay."

Today was Tuesday. The Masters tournament lasted four days, starting Thursday and ending on Sunday. If he needed to put his soul to rest by the time the players took the course on the final day, that didn't give me long to go over four hundred miles, sneak onto private property, let my father watch the greatest golf tournament in the world, and commit what I suspected was a crime of some kind. "I'll try. But you know this is impossible, right?"

"Lots of things are, right up until they're not. Now, listen here . . ."

Filled Up

My runaway bag was Daddy's old canvas camping pack, the one that still smelled of his cigarette smoke and had Marlboro patches all over it. It was wide as Daddy's shoulders and deep enough to hold a water bottle, a flashlight, a big plastic container packed full of pork, a bag of pretzels, a ball cap, a change of pants, two shirts, three pairs of clean underwear, a framed photo of Mama so she'd be with us, Daddy's Augusta book, our nearly untouched Rand McNally road atlas, my lucky quarter, and my box. The box had my paint pad, drawing pad, color set, brushes, and pencils.

Daddy'd told me to take my dress pants and my one golf shirt for walking around the tournament, so I grabbed those. Then I picked up a year-old picture of him and me from my dresser.

In the photo, we're standing side by side at the municipal golf course and he has his arm around me right at the first hole's tee box, both of us smiling. It was taken just before the last round we shot together. Two rounds, actually. We played thirty-six holes that day, since the first eighteen hadn't gone well for me. There hadn't been many times when Daddy'd asked me to come along, and I was excited and fidgety enough to miss the ball the first two times I swung that day.

He'd handed over his lucky quarter to be my ball marker, my placeholder in case I needed to pick up my ball on the green so that the golfers could putt in the right order, farthest away from the hole to closest. That's how it went in golf. Once you got on the green, it was the people who had the longest distance to putt who got to go first. Didn't quite seem fair to me that the closer you were, the longer you had to wait.

Daddy'd dug that quarter out of a low pocket on his golf bag and told me to keep it. It was dated the year I was born, he said, which had been a good year. He looked so happy in the picture, and I closed my eyes for a second, inhaling the memory of the sweetgum trees and holly bushes that dotted the course.

The last thing I put in the backpack, right around midnight, was Daddy's urn. I carved out a spot between the pork and my paint box, cushioning it with the golf shirt. Just before I placed the urn inside, I had the sudden sensation that I was putting my daddy to bed, tucking him into a safe spot, about to scoot a chair right beside him and stay there until he fell asleep.

"Don't worry, Daddy," I whispered, folding the golf shirt over the top of the urn and closing the backpack. "I'll keep you safe."

Quietly, I crept to the kitchen and sifted through the cupboard until I found an old flour canister at the back. I stood it in the exact spot where Daddy's urn had been perched, thinking maybe it would buy me some time.

I checked on Mama, who looked awful, but out cold. She'd been crying in her sleep again. Leaving through the back door, I walked between picnic tables and stepped outside the front gate, feeling like the entire world had put its wonder inside me. I felt filled up, but not squeezed. I felt like right after I'd set a watery brush on a color plate and was about to touch it to paper, not knowing what would happen.

When Daddy told me where to get some traveling money, I'd flinched for sure, but there was no way I'd take what little Mama had and this was Daddy talking. I couldn't say no when somebody had given me one last chance to be the boy he wanted me to be. So I was about to do like he said and see how it turned out.

I was about to go to the local bar to steal travel money from its mascot, Mrs. Clucksy, the most famous chicken in Hilltop, Alabama.

Nest Egg

The bar's real name was the Alabama Moon, but everyone called it Pastor Frank's on account of the owner dropping out of the preaching world to take up barkeeping. An old cabin had been expanded and connected to a barn that got loud every weekend. On nights when Mama and Daddy went dancing, I used to sneak over and watch the windows glow with strung-up lights and with the heat from men and women stomping and twirling by in swatches of color and silhouette. Some things you can paint and they turn out better than they really are, but not that sight. I'd tried, but it didn't want to be stuck on paper.

While I walked, I looked up at the sky, which was clear and star-filled as anything. That storm had never hit, though the world still felt full of something brewing. I was grateful it wasn't pouring, but it made me uneasy, too. Like whatever had been pushing and pushing at the clouds might return when I least expected it.

Pastor Frank's was at the far end of Main Street. I lay low and took Cricket Road all the way to where it dead-ended and nearly dipped into Hilltop's favorite fishing creek, then crossed over to Main. *I'll be somewhere along the creek,* that Noni girl had said. I glanced along the water quick, wondering where that girl had come from, but didn't see a sign of her. Maybe she was nothing but a big liar. Or maybe she thought I was one.

Get the money first; think about that girl second, the creek told me.

She's nothing like May, a tree chimed in. *I really don't know what you're thinking.*

"*Shh,*" I whispered. "I know she's not May. And I never said she was coming with me."

The sign hanging over Pastor Frank's porch had been flipped from a blue OPEN to a red GO HOME. Beer bottles littered the wooden floor near several rocking chairs at the entrance, looking empty and lonesome. I picked up a few bottles and turned them upright. *Thank you, Ben,* one said. *Thank you for noticing us.*

Shifting the backpack on my shoulders, I looked at the dark windows. "You didn't go here much in the last year," I said to Daddy.

"Yeah. The doctors didn't think it was good for me, I guess. Told me to cut back."

Maybe you should've cut back on other stuff, too, I wanted to say, but didn't. I also wanted to point out that it was strange how Daddy had died from smoking too much, and now he was a pile of ashes. I must've had that thought a million times over the last month.

I didn't know my daddy's cancer had come back so bad. On the day he died, he told me to stay home from the hospital, saying, "See you in a little bit," on his way out the door. He told me it was nothing at all, just a little tiny scrape of a tumor. Then he'd said something else, probably quoted a golfer, and I didn't even listen because I'd been sick of golf being better company than me.

He knew, a still-fallen bottle told me in an accusing voice. *He knew he was gonna die and you didn't see it. It was in his last words to you and you shut your ears.*

Yep, the porch said. *Same way he shuts his ears when people talk about May at school.*

I looked away from them both. "May Talbot told me that her daddy never goes drinking here."

"Coloreds aren't overly welcome at Pastor Frank's. I'm sure they've got their own places for drinking and dancing."

I crept past the porch and around the side of the cabin. "Could he have come if you'd brought him with you?"

"I wouldn't. I have a heckuva lot of respect for Mr. Talbot, especially carrying on after his place got burned down. And I think that folks who get a stink eye about me buying my pigs from Mr. Talbot should be boiled in their own stupidity.

But buying a man a beer won't change anything. When it comes to that kind of thing, Putters keep their heads down. Can't hit a solid golf drive off life's tee without keeping your eye on the ball."

Shifting gravel and a low scratching noise came from around the cabin's corner, and I slammed myself against a wall. A tail flicked into sight, and I relaxed. Barn cat, nothing more. Probably smelled the meat in my backpack. A window clicked open in the bedroom over the bar, and a grizzled and grumpy Frank stuck his naked torso into the evening air. "Someone there?" I heard another click. It was the safety being released on a loaded shotgun.

I held my breath.

"We're closed, goshdarnit! Get outta here!" Frank slammed the window shut.

A thought occurred to me. "Hey, Daddy?" I whispered. "Even if he quit being a pastor, stealing Frank's money can't be too good for getting you into heaven, can it?" And it wouldn't be too good for me either, if I got caught.

Daddy huffed and seemed to consider the situation, and I could picture one finger going to his lip. That was his Considering look. "It's not stealing," he said finally. "When Frank opened his bar and caught hell from the town for leaving the church, I let him eat free whenever he came to the café. Felt sorry for him at first, and then when I said he'd need to start paying, he always said he'd pay his tab with me when everyone else settled their tabs with him.

"That's at least five sandwiches a week for going on ten years now. That man owes me thousands of dollars in free pig. And Frank used to be a man of God, so I'm sure he'll understand that I need to get myself out of whatever purgatory I'm floating in. Believe me," he added, "he owed me much more money than you'll take. We aren't doing any harm at all."

Doing harm. What made something bad enough that it was harmful? Hard to say. Folks from up north thought Spanish moss was nothing but pretty, but Mrs. Grady wasn't the only one taking a rake to her trees. People got scared, thinking the moss could take over their healthy trees and kill them. Nobody could seem to agree on whether it was a thing of beauty or a tree strangler, but I had a feeling that the moss didn't mean anything. It just didn't know how else to grow.

Gulping back thoughts that shouted how stupid an idea this was, I crept around to Pastor Frank's backyard. Easing the gate open wasn't an option because Daddy told me Frank blocked it from the back with full kegs so that nobody could get in. I'd have to climb the ten foot tall fence.

A finger tapped my shoulder. "*Hey,*" it whispered.

My heart nearly shot outta my chest, and I turned around ready to lie, the excuse dying in my throat when I saw a dirty ponytail. "*You,*" I angry-whispered back. "What are you doing here?"

Noni backed off a step, the hurt on her face switching quickly to annoyed. "What're *you* doing? And who on earth do you keep talking to?" She sniffed the air. "If you're a little nutty, that's fine."

"You've got a poor sense of timing, you know that?"

She eyed the fence, then fixed me with a doubtful stare. "You gonna jump that?"

"Do I look like I've got springs for feet? I'm climbing it. Quit talking and get out of here before you wake someone up. I've got a plan, okay? Now, go."

She stood her ground, studying me. "What's over that fence?"

"Please?" I tried. "If you've gotta know, it's a chicken guarding my traveling money."

She blinked in the moonlight, a goofy smirk fluttering at the edges of her lips, like she wasn't sure if I was joking or just crazy. "*Our* traveling money. We're partners," she said, smacking my arm. "Shake on it."

"Who's that?" Daddy asked.

"*Shh, not now,*" I told him.

"Yes, *now,*" Noni said, thinking I was talking to her. "I'll be down by the creek. Quarter mile, dark sheet. Can't miss it. I'll get outta your way, but you got to shake first, so I don't go waiting for nothing."

"Keep your voice down!" I whisper-shouted. "Just wait a minute. I never said you could come."

"Sure you did."

"Oh? When's that?"

"When you confided in me about our traveling money just now."

"It's not *our* money, it's *my* money."

"Since you're about to hop a fence to get it and you're shushing me like an old lady, I'm guessing it's not your money at all. But I'm offering to share the guilt you're gonna feel about stealing it by saying it's *ours*. I'd say that's pretty generous of me."

Good Lord, she was trouble. "And remind me what I get out of this partnership?"

"I don't know. A friend." She waited with her bottom lip sucked into her mouth. Her arms wrapped around her waist, the same way May Talbot's had done back by the hog shed. "And all those things I told you before—knot tying and stuff."

The girl's arm bruise was clearly visible, and I saw that it circled her elbow the whole way around. It looked bluish purple in the moonlight. I wanted to know where that bruise came from. It looked like it had to hurt, but she wasn't complaining. She'd told me she was tough. I already knew she was stubborn. Tough and stubborn were the sorts of things that might come in handy when trying to do something impossible.

And she seemed to really want to come with me.

It felt good to have someone want that.

Well, shoot. She'd worn me down. I shook her hand, then watched until she disappeared into the trees along the streambed.

"Who was that?" Daddy asked.

"That was our running away partner. Now, keep quiet or you'll distract me."

Daddy snorted. "You sound like me on the golf course."

I smiled at that. A soft light was on in the upper bedroom, but I didn't see any movement. Taking a deep breath, I wedged my shoes between the fence boards and shimmied up to the top. Heaving my body over the side wasn't too difficult, except for the last part. The falling part.

I slipped down the splintered fence, catching on a stray nail. Its edge scratched against my chest, ripping my shirt from waist to armpit before I smacked into dirt dust and sprigs of Alabama crabgrass. I shut my lips tight so I wouldn't cry out and lay there for a few seconds to catch my breath. Then I sat up and got to my feet.

A sign above the henhouse said MRS. CLUCKSY'S PALACE, and it was the goofiest thing I'd ever seen for a pet. More like a garden shed, the wooden structure stood five feet high and eight feet wide. The door was just big enough for me to squeeze through. Twinkly light strands and plastic ears of corn, all with evidence of heavy-duty pecking, were stapled around the entrance. One more check toward Pastor Frank's house, then I poked my head in the chicken palace and heard the familiar snoring that's particular to birds.

"You sure it's under her?" I said to Daddy.

"Heck, yes. There were only a couple of us left one night and someone was talking about security guards at a hunting store in Mobile. Frank started bragging about his security system and how Mrs. Clucksy guards the night's take by sitting on it after she's done with her shift. He even said he puts it in a big plastic egg, so she feels motherly."

I didn't see how Mrs. Clucksy could ever be the motherly type. She spent her nights wearing a cape and strutting along the bar, taking pecks at bowls of corn nuts and sips of the patrons' beer. The new town preacher spoke a whole sermon about her one Sunday, saying how the minions of Satan come in all shapes and sizes, and that beer-drinking chickens were an abomination and were certain to carry disease.

"Okay, Daddy. You stay here." Taking off the pack, I tickled my fingers in the air to loosen up the joints and leaned my entire torso inside Mrs. Clucksy's home. It was cave dark in there, so I backed out, yanked on a strand of twinkly lights, and brought it in with me.

Sweet Sally, "palace" was no understatement. This was a royal castle for chickens. Lengths of red velvet hung like wallpaper, and several shiny bowls were secured by a metal rack that ran the length of one side. Mrs. Clucksy had her pick of corn, wheat, seeds, and what appeared to be bran cereal. Water and an amber liquid were the beverage options, the pee-colored stuff smelling suspiciously like beer.

"Hey! What's going on in there?" Daddy whispered.

I ignored him, advancing on my knees to the throne at the back. Mrs. Clucksy looked to be as out cold as Mama, and I was hoping for a quick steal and getaway. Barely registering the line of rooster pictures posted near her bed, I paused beside the feather pillow nest and gave her the tiniest of pokes.

Nothing.

Mrs. Clucksy's premises and breath reeked. I held my breath while slipping a hand under her chicken bottom. It was there—a smooth shape that had to be the money. Quickly and gently, I reached my other hand out, lifted her body, and pulled on the egg. Sweaty and grinning with excitement, I set her down, backed out, and put on the pack. "Got it."

"She didn't even make a peep. Good work, son!"

And that's when Mrs. Clucksy woke up.

If a bird could scream, Mrs. Clucksy would be the queen yeller of any horror film. The high-pitched squealing was part chicken cluck, part about-to-be-butchered pig, and part angry-female-having-her-baby-stolen. The second she started cackling, another light flickered in the room above the bar. I tucked the egg into my waistband, ran to the fence, and was halfway up when Frank stormed out the back door, yelling, "Mrs. Clucksy? What the heck is going on, sweetheart?"

That chicken was charging down the welcome plank like a crazed, half-drunk animal (which, in all fairness, she was), and she headed straight for me.

"Hold on tight, Daddy." I scrambled over and started running like the wind. Frank must've caught sight of my backside because he gave a holler and scooted for my section of the fence.

"Thief! Stop right there, you weasel!"

Metal clanked as Frank shoved the kegs away from the gate. I dumped the money in my backpack and tossed the empty cash egg aside while I ran into brush cover. Looking over my shoulder to make sure Frank wasn't heading our way, I swear that egg looked like a big version of a golf ball that somebody had hit way off course.

I threaded through bushes down to the creek bed and stopped to catch my breath. "Hey, Daddy, you didn't put this ball in my throat, did you?"

He didn't answer. I waited a few minutes, then dug in my bag for the flashlight and pointed it at him, half expecting him to jerk away from the light like I was shining it in his eyes, not his urn. "Hey, Daddy . . ."

The only answer was a soft sound, like a muffled hog pen, and something ached right in my chest, because it was a sound that I truly didn't know I'd missed until it hit my ears. Daddy was snoring just like Mrs. Clucksy had a couple minutes ago.

"This is the craziest thing that's ever happened to me," I told him.

It's not crazy, the urn's clasp said back. *It's a miracle.*

A Watercolor for May Talbot

A quarter mile down the stream, something hit me on the back. When I turned and traced the blow, I noticed a raggedy sheet on the opposite bank, hanging over a low willow branch to create a makeshift tent. Noni's arm poked out of it.

"*Stop*," I told her. "Quit throwing stuff."

"What's the password?" the center of the sheet called. Noni crawled out of the tent and stood. "Oh, never mind. Anyone follow you?"

"No. How am I supposed to get over there?"

"Try stepping in the water. Isn't any deeper'n your knees right there." She pointed.

I followed her fingers and found the low section, wading fifteen feet to the other bank. Long stream grass and bushes near the willow did a nice job of hiding a tiny clearing. She'd used rocks to hold down the sheet at angles, and the willow branch was the perfect height to create a hideaway. I stepped closer to get a better look, but she jammed a hand in my face before I got far.

"Empty the provision bag," Noni ordered. "Let's see what we got."

I did like she said and emptied the bag. Without Daddy giving me instruction, it was like this Noni girl had some sort of power over me. Her hair was lit up under the starlight, a few tiny strands broken off on top, waving free and rhythmic in the night breeze. I had the sudden urge to hear her sing. Her eyes drifted over the supplies approvingly until she inhaled quickly and slapped at my thigh.

"Ow! What'd you do that for?"

"Bug." She picked up the pork container and opened it. "You're welcome." Without asking, she took a pinch of meat, dipping it into the corner that I'd filled with sauce. "I'll take an even half of our food. Don't be taking extra 'cause you're a boy. We're splitsies on everything, got it?" She chewed quickly and swallowed. "Say, what's this?" Reaching behind my ear with her clean hand, she pulled her wrist back and waggled a coin.

I snatched Daddy's ball-marking quarter from her fingers. "Very funny."

"Thanks. Told you I did magic." She winked. "Got more where that came from. Where's your kit?"

Confused, I pointed to my art box, only to see Noni's scowl from the day before.

"No, your outdoors stuff. Matches, fishing line, stuff like

that. How're we gonna make a fire to cook stuff? Come to think on it, what're we gonna eat after we run outta that pig if we can't fish?"

"Use your magic if you're so good. My daddy taught me to butcher a whole hog better than anyone in Hilltop, and I can fish, too. Just didn't bring a pig or a pole."

She was right, of course. I should've brought stuff like the things she'd mentioned. Daddy would have. He probably didn't say anything because he thought it was common sense. Not to me, though. I'd brought paintbrushes, a lucky quarter, a golf book, and clean underwear.

"You didn't bring anything useful? What kind of kid are you, anyway?" She saw my face and softened. "Now, I didn't mean anything, don't be a lemon wedge. You are who you are. Call it lucky that I am who I am. We'll be fine." She stuck a hand in her pocket and came out with a small red pocketknife. "At least I've got this. My daddy gave it to me. Not much on it except a blade, a toothpick, and tweezers. The blade's dull, but it's something."

I took it and pulled out the tweezers, holding them up in a shaft of moonlight. "I'm a lucky boy, all right. This'll keep us good and safe from splinters."

"Was that a joke?" She lifted one side of her upper lip, sneering like a mean Elvis. "Not a very good one. Leave the jokes to me, crazy. That knife's better than nothing. Can't gut a fish with a paintbrush."

"And you can't catch a fish with a dull two-inch knife and a toothpick."

"Maybe I could." She eyed the urn. "What's that?"

I tapped the urn, hoping for a few words, but Daddy didn't say anything. He'd stopped snoring, too. "This is my daddy. I got to scatter his ashes. We're going to Georgia."

She took another pinch of pulled pork. "Fair enough. That who you've been talking to?"

"Maybe."

"He talk back to you?"

I stared at her, considering. Worst that could happen, she'd pick her prickly self up and leave and I'd be out somebody who seemed more pork-eating porcupine than girl. "Would you believe me if I said that my dead daddy's stuck and he won't get any peace until he's scattered on a golf course?"

Her big eyes got bigger. She dipped her finger in the sauce and licked it clean, then plucked a rib from the container and shut it tight. She looked down at the cover of Daddy's Augusta National book. "A golf course. That's a little loony, isn't it?" After a time, she nodded, her lips flicking around, then settling into a straight line. "I accept the terms of partnership."

"You believe me?"

Noni shrugged and gnawed at the rib. "Some things are true whether other people believe you or not." She let her head fall back until she was looking at the stars through a thick cobweb of willow branches. "My daddy used to say that people meet up with their life on the road they take to run away from it. But I'm not real sure what that means, even though I've thought on it now and then." Without moving her head, she reached out and flicked my knee. "So what are you running from?"

I touched the golf ball in my throat. "Don't know. What are you running from?" My eyes drifted to her arm bruise. "Are your parents mean or something?"

"I don't have parents anymore. But no, they weren't mean." She tossed the clean rib bone into a bush, her eyes fixed on the place it disappeared. "Mama died when I was a baby, and I lost Daddy on the day I turned eleven."

"So he died and you just ran off forever?" I was impressed.

She shrugged. "There wasn't anything left for me, so I started following the tracks. Now I'm wandering. That's my story. Part of it, anyway." She picked up a twig and started using it as a toothpick. "How much money we got?"

I dug through the bag and started counting. It didn't take long at all. I counted again, thinking I must have missed some bills, but nope. "Forty-one dollars and twenty-three cents." With the safety net of his blindness, I felt fine shooting a dirty look at Daddy. "Must have been a real slow night at Pastor Frank's."

"We'll make it work." Noni didn't sound worried. Maybe she was better at making things work for herself than I was.

"How long have you been on your own?" I asked, tucking the money into the bottom of the pack. "You don't look much older than eight." She was about the same size as me, just with a bigger mouth.

She kicked her shoe against mine. "Neither do you. I haven't been wandering long." She drummed the twig along her teeth. "And I'm eleven, not eight."

"I'll be twelve on Saturday."

She did her fancy one-eyebrow raise again, adding a *click-click* with her mouth, like she was telling a horse to get going. "You don't say. Looks like we're the same age, at least for a few more days. Well, happy early birthday to you. We're going to Augusta, right? That's what you said in the kitchen when you were talking to yourself."

"Yep. And I wasn't talking to myself."

"That's right, you were talking to ashes, which makes much more sense." She traced one of the Marlboro patches on the backpack. "Never been to Georgia. Have to get us a bag of Georgia peaches. We've got forty dollars, you said? Okay, here's where you get glad that we're in this together. I'm good with organizing things."

And by that, the willow winked, *she means taking over.*

"We'll take a bus close as we can," she said, "and then camp to save money for food. Where's the nearest bus station where no one'll know you?" She looked excited, like it was her daddy and her mission, not mine.

"Seven miles. Town called Heart."

Noni rubbed her hands together. "Okay, listen up, crazy. We better get the earliest ride out of town. We might as well sleep for a couple hours first." She patted the ground. "I'll wake us up at four or so." She disappeared into the sheet tent. "You sleep outside." She didn't have a watch, but for some reason I didn't doubt that at four o'clock I'd be shaken awake.

Noni's head popped out again. "Hey, Benjamin Putter? Did you bring a lot of paint and paper?"

"Enough. Why? And how'd you know my name?"

"Heard your mama call you Benjamin and saw your last name on the sign by the back door. And I thought maybe I'd try painting something later on, that's why. Now leave me alone. I'm trying to sleep. Gotta big day tomorrow—first day's when they look the hardest, so we got to make a good break from the Heart station. Could be tricky. Don't want to get caught." She yawned loudly. "Us needing to save your dead daddy's everlasting soul and all."

Instead of rolling into a heap like she appeared to be doing, I stepped over to the stream where a little moonlight held. Got out my paint box, crouched by the stream, and dipped a brush in. The first painting was simple.

May Talbot always loved the way skipped stones on the water let off circles that ended up touching one another and overlapping. I'd spent hours learning to get the watercolors to do that, starting with the biggest circles, keeping the outside faint, and going inside each one until I got to the smallest. I added a lily pad. I'd told May that I loved painting them. I told her I liked to picture frogs and dragonflies resting there, because sometimes they probably got tired and the lily pads helped them be right where they wanted to be without sinking. May hadn't laughed when I'd said that. She could have, but she didn't.

When the painting was finished, I put a rock on the corner of the paper so it wouldn't blow away and cleaned the brushes in the current, not seeing the color leak out but knowing it was leaving just the same.

A rustling came from the sheet. "I hear you moving around out there like some kind of garbage-eating raccoon. Can't sleep if I think someone's gonna steal that extra pork. What are you doing?"

I don't know. "Cleaning my brushes."

"Oh." Noni poked her head out and rubbed her eyes. "Know something? I do believe that you, Benjamin Putter, are the most interesting person I've ever met."

"Me?"

"Yep, you. Goodnight, Benjamin Putter."

"You can call me Ben."

"I like using full names."

"Then what's yours?"

"Just Noni to you."

"Fine. 'Night, Noni."

I put my box away and curled up under a curve in the willow's trunk, using my backpack for a pillow and sticking Daddy's urn in the crook of my elbow. Tomorrow I'd be leaving my smallest of small towns in Alabama for the first time in my life, with my father's cremation urn and a girl who was most likely trouble. Daddy used to call me a box turtle. Said I was more comfortable tucked in a shell than out in the world. He also used to say that a person who does magic tricks is suspect because you can't trust anyone who keeps an animal in their hat. But maybe his view on things and on me would change with his death. Maybe mine would, too.

It seemed only a minute later that I woke up with my arm hugging Daddy and my head hugging dirt. Getting my bearings, I looked around for my backpack. Took me another minute until I saw it. Noni was beside the stream, sifting quietly through my bag down where the break in tree cover let the moon give her a little light. She pulled out the cash bills, and without glancing around, stuck them in her back pocket. Then she stood up, left the bag, and walked out of sight.

I Can Be Bobby Jones

Teamwork, Daddy used to say. Golf is a solitary game that requires teamwork: The body, the mind, and the spirit all have to work together to produce an outcome. Those three things must touch each other and change each other and bleed together until they become focused on the same thing. It takes the Holy Trinity on your side, he'd say, then duck a swat from Mama. She hated when he blended golf and God together. She'd blush and say, *Bogart, with that talk, you're going straight to*—and he'd scoop her up before she'd finish and kiss the last word away, and they'd twirl together for a minute and be their own trinity, just Mama and Daddy and whatever made them love each other.

I thought about that while I watched the person I'd stupidly trusted steal my money and leave me behind as the moon got its last moments in before dawn took over.

I could still hear Noni's feet shuffling through the brush,

but that was soon drowned out by my own heartbeat, beating out its shocked *see that, did you see that*, pounding out its angry, *big-eyed thief, she's a big-eyed thief*, or maybe just banging out repeated rounds of *leavin' you again, someone's leavin' you again*. It's hard to tell what a fierce heartbeat is saying, even for me.

"Come on, Daddy." I scooped him up and scooted down to the creek.

She's only stealing what you already stole, said the backpack. "Not helpful," I told it, sticking Daddy inside and slipping it over my arms.

Noni wasn't too far away, and soon I saw her, paused at the other side of the creek, her head tilted up while she looked at the moon and chewed on a long piece of the wheatgrass that grew near the water. I couldn't help but watch her. She looked like a girl stuck in a painting, thinking about secrets that you'd never find out. After a while, a determined expression settled on her face where an unreadable one had been a minute before, and she walked off, straight through the trees and brush.

I was too thrown off to yell. Instead, I crossed the stream at another low spot, followed her to the back of the Hilbert property, and watched her skip straight to a clothesline hung with a variety of pants, shirts, and dresses.

After studying the possibilities, she chose a long-sleeved light blue dress with pockets that I'd seen Ginny

Hilbert wear at school, yanked it down, then scooted into the Hilbert's henhouse. She came out shortly after, dress on, her old clothes under one arm and her pockets bulging. With her free hand, she found a good-size rock and stuck a number of bills on their back porch using the rock's weight to hold them down. On her way back into the woods, she picked up a small metal bucket and hissed as she passed by the bush I crouched behind, laughing when I jumped.

"Glad you're awake, scaredy-cat," she said. "It'll save us time. Change into a different shirt—yours is all tore up." She turned her back on me and waved a little circle in the air. "Go on. Switch clothes."

I looked down at my chest. "It got ripped on the fence." I changed into another shirt, adding the ruined one to the Hilberts' burn pile. "You can turn around now."

She faced me and nodded. "Tuck it in when we get to the station. People'll think you're a runaway or something. Don't argue. We should look at least halfway nice for the bus ride. I'm wearing a dress, and I never wear dresses. Take off that backpack so I can put my old clothes in there."

"You stole my money." I pointed to the long-sleeved, button-down shirt in her hands. "You probably stole that, too."

"This shirt was my daddy's, if you need to know." She pointed to the lumps in her pockets. "And I didn't steal the money, I wanted some eggs. Haven't had any since . . . Well, it's been a while. I saw those chickens pecking around their yard last night when I went exploring a little. I was coming back for you."

"Sounds like a lie," Daddy said.

I wasn't sure I believed her either. "How come you took all my money with you?"

"*Our* money, Benjamin Putter. You and me are in this together." She tapped the backpack and unzipped it, pushing her clothes inside. "Along with your daddy in there. Now, I'm happy to help you, but I had a serious hankering for eggs."

"How are we supposed to cook them?"

She swung the bucket an inch from my nose. "This maybe. Haven't figured it out yet for sure, but they'll keep."

Daddy let something out like a growl. "Get that money back, Ben."

"Gimme my money back," I told her.

She pulled it from a pocket and handed it over. "Our money. Don't be greedy. Which way to Heart?"

I pointed north. "We hop on a road up there a ways and then follow it straight east."

"Well, let's get going. Say, what do you want for a name?"

"What?"

"You know, in case we have to say who we are."

I thought. "Bobby Jones."

Daddy laughed. "Gimme a quote, son!"

Without thinking, I recited his favorite. "Golf is the closest game to the game we call life. You get bad breaks from good shots; you get good breaks from bad shots, but you have to play the ball where it lies." Inwardly, I gave myself a kick. Try as I might to ignore them, all of Daddy's fact speeches and golfer quotes had been planted into me against my will and had settled in like golf-happy brain ticks, burrowing into my mind so deep that I'd never get them out.

Noni looked at me a little funny. "Good to know, crazy. I'll be Betsy Jones."

We walked north on a dirt road, and I watched Hilltop fade behind us as we cut across a tobacco field to a crossroad. Daddy was mumbling about something, so I hung back a good ways to listen to him while Noni walked ahead. It was still dark out, but the sky was getting a little lighter. We had maybe a two hour walk to Heart.

"Something's tricky about that one, Ben. Can't trust a runaway."

It *was* strange that she seemed so eager to hop onto my trip. And Daddy was right. There was something about her that made me think she'd be leaving me sooner rather than later. Hopefully not with the money. "I'm a runaway, too."

"But you've got a purpose. You're on a road trip with your old man. Just the two of us, spending quality time together." His invisible hand reached out to smack me on the back. "You and me, going to Augusta National Golf Club, can you believe it?" Ashy hands rubbed together with glee inside his urn. "And the Masters. I'm getting teary-eyed just thinking about it. We'll be right there with Hobart Crane for a whole tournament. He's my favorite."

Unless there was a bus straight to Augusta, the chances of us watching Hobart Crane play the whole tournament weren't good. But I didn't want to bother him with that detail just yet. "I know, Daddy."

"Hobart grew up in a small town, just like me and you. Poor boy playing at the Masters. There's a dream to shoot for, right? I doubt that girl even knows the name 'Hobart Crane.'"

Noni was far ahead now, slapping her sides like she was keeping rhythm to something. "Maybe she has a purpose, too." I thought about how she'd looked back at the creek, her head tilted up at the moon. I thought about how she was trusting me for some reason. "Let's just get to Heart."

I'd only been to Heart once. Daddy's brother, Uncle Luke, had traveled from Georgia to visit about two months back. He'd called on the telephone to talk to Daddy now and then, but I'd never met my uncle until the day when we'd all gone out to meet his bus at the station. That was right after Daddy found out he was real sick for the second time. Luke was a golfer, too, and had made it three years on the professional tour, but never qualified for the Masters before his back got hurt and his career ended. He'd taken a job at a public course in Georgia as consolation.

He and Daddy spent seven whole days cooking barbecue for customers, hitting balls behind the café, drinking too much, quoting old players like they were disciples, and trading facts about their favorite current player. Hobart Crane was a humble, hardworking man who persevered through tragedy, Luke'd said, clinking beer bottles out by the smoker. A man's man, who didn't give up on life even when he had a darn good reason to, Daddy'd said, clinking back.

Cheers to Hobart, cheers to his poor, long-since-passed-away wife and his poor newly-passed-away daughter, and cheers to the Big Five. Cheers to Bobby Jones, Walter Hagen, Byron Nelson, Sam Snead, and Ben Hogan. I didn't hear my name come up when they were drinking to things. That's around the time I started noticing that something was stuck in my throat, though I didn't realize that it was a golf ball until after Daddy died.

"Hey, Daddy? How come you haven't said anything about Uncle Luke? He's in Georgia. Maybe he could help." The last day Uncle Luke was with us, he and Daddy had a terrible fight. Woke me up in the middle of the night with the yelling and pounding and breaking of things. The next morning Mama drove Uncle Luke to the bus station, and I hadn't heard his name mentioned since. But it didn't make much sense to hold a grudge in purgatory.

"He's right in Augusta. You know that. And we're not getting help from him. You hear me? You stay away from Luke."

"Yes, sir." I knew that voice. That was his shut-down voice. It had an edge and a warning in it not to push him. I wondered where he'd gotten that voice from and if I'd inherit that from him along with his looks.

"Hey, don't you get quiet on me, son," Daddy said. "I know that tone in your voice. That's your 'I'm giving up on you' voice. You've got more fight in you than that, don't you? Don't go getting upset when people talk hard to you, your father included. You curl up like a flower at night the second you get told something you don't want to hear, boy."

He's right, said a crow flying overhead. *That's just what you do.*

"Why don't you tell me something about yourself," Daddy said. "It takes an awful lot out of me to talk."

I stopped walking. The golf ball in my throat got real heavy. Who has a father who says something like "Tell me about yourself," like they were strangers instead of part of each other? Then again, I couldn't recall my daddy ever asking me to tell him anything other than what he'd already taught me.

"Okay."

My childhood was flooded with names of golfer people I didn't give a flip about, so I figured I'd do him a favor and skip over names. I didn't think he'd want to hear about nice Miss Stone and mean Mr. Underwood and pretty Erin Courtney. I didn't tell him how my best friend was May

Talbot, or at least she had been, or how there was an unofficial Negro lunch table at our school, or how May had spoken little since she started coming to Hilltop Primary and even less since Mr. Talbot's barbecue business burned to the ground around the time Bobby Jones died last December. I didn't tell him that I'd been mourning someone important, too, or how part of me knew it was my fault that I'd lost her.

I didn't think he'd noticed that I never hung around with Bill Sweeney or Davey Burr or John Conner anymore, since they were all at the private school now. Their parents didn't want them mixing with me anymore. I stopped by to play when I saw them all over at Davey's house one day, but Bill shook his head and pointed at me to go home. I might have colored germs on me from staying at the integrated school, he'd said.

And I knew for a fact Daddy wouldn't want to know the names I'd been called for talking to myself and drawing pictures of trees outside school windows.

So I told him about how some boy had brought a salamander to school and put it right on a teacher's head, and the teacher didn't even notice because she had so much hairspray on. I told him how the halls and classrooms were less crowded this year, how the girls' bathroom toilet overflowed one day and flooded the hallway, and how the principal, Mr. Bottom, had come in one day to find his office covered in toilet paper.

He chuckled a few times and didn't once interrupt to tell me how the legendary golfer Bobby Jones had said that some people think they're concentrating when they're really worrying or how golf was the greatest game in the history of the world or how you can't hit too slow or too fast on the putting green or how a man's patience with a dead pig meant more than his patience with boring conversation.

He just listened. When he did talk, his voice sounded farther away. Weary. He asked me how far we were from Augusta and told me he'd better rest up. Then Daddy didn't speak again and my only close company was the lump in my throat. I had the strangest feeling that I'd imagined him talking in the first place. Or maybe listening to me talk was exhausting to him. Maybe that's why he didn't do it much when he was alive.

"Hey, crazy!" Noni waved from fifty yards ahead. The dirt had changed to pavement somewhere along the way, and we'd reached Heart. She grinned and pointed to the BUS DEPOT sign far down the street. "You ever been to Georgia?"

I shook my head and jogged a little to catch up to her. I'd never been anywhere outside of Hilltop, other than Heart and Mobile.

"Well, Bobby Jones," she said, slapping an arm around my back, "I haven't either. But I bet it's pretty enough to scatter ashes on."

Painting Tickets

A clock read six o'clock in the morning when Noni and I walked inside. The big indoor room held benches and a ticket booth and smelled like a combination of cleaning supplies and body odor. Posters for destination cities plastered the walls. We found the water fountain, a rusty piece of metal nailed to the wall that dribbled liquid even when nobody was there to drink it. Only after taking a sip did I notice the ghost letters above it, barely visible under a layer of paint. The entire wall was covered in the same white as the rest of the station, but you could see what else used to be there.

The word COLORED was hidden for the most part, but I could still see it. I bent to take one more sip of water, then moved to let Noni have some. While she drank, I noticed a cleaner-looking fountain attached to the opposite end of the station.

A uniformed maintenance worker shuffled over to the

side door of the ticket office. I heard a low murmur of tired voices. A few people were scattered around the benches, reading or staring sleepily at the air in front of them.

"Hey," I said to Noni. "You never said where you're from. Is there a chance anybody here might recognize you?"

She nudged me toward the wall map, and I caught her studying her reflection in the clear plastic covering it. She tugged at her long ponytail. "No. I'm a nobody now."

Blue, green, and red lines spread from the town of Heart like veins in the body of America. "We could go to Chicago or New York if we wanted," I said in wonder. I studied the map again. "Okay, Birmingham, Montgomery, Atlanta, or Chattanooga. Those are all in the right direction, for the most part."

"Atlanta," Daddy said, sounding confident. "Watch the station until you see an older lady, then go up to the ticket taker and tell him she's your grandma. Tell him you were just having a visit with Granny, and now you're buying a ticket home to your parents."

It sounded a little far-fetched to me. "Daddy says we should buy a ticket to Atlanta. He said to attach ourselves to an old person and the ticket person will sell us the tickets, no questions."

Noni eyed the urn in my arms with a look of approval I hadn't earned from her yet. "Smart man, that dead daddy of yours. I'll just tell the ticket taker that our granny lets me buy the tickets because I get a kick out of it. But we don't have enough money to get to Atlanta."

I studied the fare rate. "Says thirty-five dollars per person. Half that for kids. We've got plenty."

"Not after I left some for the eggs and clothes."

"How much did you leave?"

She shrugged. "Most of the clothes hanging on that line didn't look so good. I figured they needed extra."

The Hilberts had eight kids and could use all the extras they could get. "You're right about that, but you had no right to—"

"We're five dollars short. Don't worry, though. Just follow my lead." She walked toward a little white-haired woman who'd come through the front station door.

The lady fingered a cross necklace hanging around her neck and looked repeatedly at the station clock. She had no bags, other than a light brown purse.

"Follow me," Noni murmured. "And let me do the talking." She walked right up to the woman, gripping my shirt and yanking me along. She gave the woman a big smile. "Hello, ma'am. Who're you waiting for?"

"My Jimmy," she answered. "He'll be here on the eight o'clock from Branson, Missouri. Ya'll are welcome to keep me company." She patted the bench beside her.

"Thanks. We're going back to my parents in Atlanta. We've been visiting my grandmother. You sure look like her."

"Oh?" The woman patted her hair. "What's her name? I know just about everyone in the area."

"Mrs. Jones," Noni answered. "You wouldn't know her. She lives alone in a shack way back in the woods. Likes to live off the land. Doesn't trust the government. Eats a lot of squirrel." She rapped a hand on my shoulder. "This is my brother. He doesn't talk."

Doesn't talk? I opened my mouth to correct her, but she pinched my shoulder so hard that I forgot what I was going to say.

"At all. Not a word," Noni continued, her big eyes making it clear that there were more pinches where the first one came from.

The woman eyed me with sympathy. "Is that right?"

Noni nodded. "Sure is. Hasn't said a word since he got run down by a wildcat in the woods. Right near Granny's place, matter of fact. We found him curled up with slashes on his back the size of a ruler. It was one of God's honest miracles that he's alive."

The woman swallowed a look of horror and patted my knee. "Aren't you sweet?" she said, reaching a shaky hand out to pinch my cheek.

She smelled kinda funny, but looked nice enough. Part of me hated to admit it, but Noni's quick thinking might have helped us out. We had ourselves a ticket granny.

"'Scuse me, ma'am. I just have to go buy our tickets. I'll

be right back," Noni said, leaving me to squirm.

At the ticket counter Noni studied the departure times, and I saw her frown and talk to the ticket seller. She handed over all of our cash and then pointed to the old woman and me and waved at us. I nudged the woman's side and waved back at Noni.

"Yes, dear. That's your *sister*." The woman smiled and waved at Noni, who had turned back and was making clawing motions in the air and then shaking her head in apparent sorrow.

I'm silent. I'm not dumb, I wanted to tell Granny, but couldn't for obvious reasons. I stood a little and saw the ticket seller raise a hand to her mouth and shake her head a few times. Then she nodded, and Noni came back with a big grin.

"Six hour trip with stops, leaves at ten o'clock." She saw the question in my eye and said, "Get out your paint box, brother. That nice ticket seller said she'd spot us the five dollars if you'll make her one of your famous paintings." She smiled at the old woman. "My nonspeaking brother sells his paintings for charity, and all the money goes to research how to cure people from wanting to give up talking and only listen." She shuddered a little at the thought.

Good Lord, Daddy was right. This girl was full of tricks. I swallowed a Daddy word and gave Noni my best "what should I paint" expression. She ran over to the ticket office, peered inside, and jogged back. Then she glanced over at the ticket seller, and her eyes grew soft, her lips pursing out like she was thinking real hard. More than a minute passed before I poked her and she turned back to me.

"Mountains," she said. "That woman needs a picture of mountains."

I raised my eyebrows. *How do you know?*

She winked. "Magic. Magical, mystical, mysterious powers." Laughing at my expression, she kicked my shoe. "She's got about five photos pasted to the wall in there, all of them with mountains in them."

Inwardly, I sighed with relief. Mountains were one of my specialties. While I painted and Noni looked at Daddy's Augusta book, our adopted granny spread the word to other bus waiters about the sweet little silent boy and his special pictures. There were two colored women sitting on the next bench over, but I noticed that Ticket Granny didn't talk to them.

I sank into the landscape on my paper and lost myself for a moment. When I finally did look over, the old woman was holding Daddy on her lap. I'd taken him out when I got my paint box, and she'd gone and picked him up.

I must have inhaled pretty loud, because she looked over at me and smiled. "This is real pretty, dear. Is it for your painting supplies?"

Noni looked up from the book. "What's going on? You need more paint supplies?"

Mrs. Jones started to play with the top, and I lunged over and snatched the urn out of her hands just as she was about to try twisting the lid open. I almost shouted at her, but managed to let out a closemouthed moan, checking the clasp and hugging Daddy to me.

She gave me one of those dirty looks that grandma types sometimes will, like you passed gas real loud in church.

Noni reached over and smacked me. "Bobby Jones, you stop being rude." She clucked her tongue. "I'm so sorry, ma'am," she said, sweet as Mrs. Grady's walnut bars. "That's just got Granny's cookie mix in it, and my parents will cook our gooses if it doesn't get back in one piece. My mama still loves her mama's baking, you see. Says she can't make cookies as good as Granny's for nothing."

Well, the old lady ate that up. She nodded at the urn. "I can understand that. I certainly can. My Jimmy comes to visit four times a year and says that his wife's cooking has got nothing on mine." The smug look on her face shifted to concern. "Why're you grabbing your throat like that?" she asked me, scooting away. "You sick, honey? Need a lozenge? I got a lozenge. Oh!" She stood. "There's my Jimmy."

She dug in her purse, and I accepted a cherry-flavored cough drop. We said goodbye to Ticket Granny and Noni carried my painting to the ticket seller, who took one glance and looked like she'd just walked in her home door after a long, long trip. She met my eye and waved, then put her waving hand on her heart as Noni plopped back down beside me with two tickets.

"Can't believe that worked," I whispered, covering my face with one hand. "By the way, that was a good story about our Grandma Jones you told. I liked the squirrel part."

Noni leaned over and retied a loose shoelace. "That wasn't a story. My grandma, rest her soul, was backwoods and superstitious as anything. She had three life rules for avoiding bad luck. My daddy believed them, too. He even made me memorize them so I could recite them when we visited her." Noni sat up, cleared her throat, and shook a finger at me. "It's bad luck to trust the government," she said in a high-pitched, shaky granny voice. "It's bad luck to ignore a child in need. And it's bad luck to turn down a meal made with squirrel."

"Oh." I wasn't sure what else to say. Nobody'd ever offered me squirrel meat. "The only time my daddy got superstitious was on the golf course. He had lucky tees and ball markers, and he said it was bad luck to get into an argument before starting a round of golf. But I think he said that just so my mama wouldn't fuss about him skipping church."

While we waited for the bus, a few more people, mostly old ladies and old men, chatted with me after overhearing that I didn't talk at all. They filled in my silence with whatever they expected to hear and seemed pleased with my responses. I wondered how they learned to do that and why the words my mind filled Daddy's silences in with weren't so nice.

When our bus arrived, Noni told the driver in a loud voice how her brother didn't talk and not to be offended that I didn't say hello or thanks. Both of us took seats about three-quarters of the way back, ready to go home to our fake parents if anyone asked.

I let Noni have the aisle seat. We sat across from a very pregnant woman who kept rubbing her belly the way I rubbed at my throat, and I wondered if her baby was moving around in there, the same way my lump moved. She caught me staring at her belly and gave me a small smile. She was the only colored woman on the bus. Was it hard to be the only colored person on a bus, the way it was hard for May to go to my school? I didn't know, and I wasn't about to ask.

As we pulled away from the station, raindrops splattered on the window beside me but stopped within a few minutes. Whatever clouds had set them free weren't quite ready to let a storm pour down yet. I wondered what they were waiting for.

A Matter of Trust

I stared out the window as the bus drove along, taking me away from my first and only home and toward Daddy's final one. Flashes of planted fields, corn and soybeans, thick-trunked brown oaks, swaying branches feathered in new leaves, hanging gray moss, fading red roadside restaurants in need of fresh paint and new customers, old towns, white-chipped porch swings and rocking chairs, kids running-playing-pushing-staring, burn piles smoking, gas stations. We moved by it all fast, the window painting changing every time I blinked.

"Where'd you come from?" I whispered to Noni, not sure how long I'd have to pretend to be a non-talker.

"Doesn't matter," she said, pumping the skirt of her dress up and down. "Man, it's hot."

"But why were you in Hilltop? There's nothing there."

"There's good pork. I followed the tracks behind my house and ended up there. Good enough? You ask too many questions." Her mouth went wide in a yawn. "There are rules, you know."

"Rules for what? Being a . . ." *Being a runaway? Being an orphan?*

"I'm a wanderer and lucky to be one," she said firmly. "But there are rules. I'm not generally a fan of rules, but wandering rules are more like guidelines for living by." She reached down into her sock and pulled out a scrap of paper. "Here. I wrote 'em down so I wouldn't forget."

"Where'd you learn them?"

"None of your business."

"Maybe you just made them up." When her glowering began to make me uncomfortable, I swallowed hard. "What are these guidelines?"

She squinted at the paper. "Number one, always keep your focus on the next step ahead. Number two, don't ever be telling anybody the whole truth. Little truths are okay if you find someone to trust."

"And you trust me?"

Her eyes drifted up to the bus's ceiling. "Yep, I trust you."

"Why?"

She looked at the backpack. "Because I miss my daddy, too. Why do you trust me?"

I didn't trust her yet. I couldn't. There were too many blanks and whys surrounding her. Why was she so willing to come with me? Was she running from someone? How could I trust her when she'd given away a good chunk of our traveling money and then had taken over at the bus station? Sure, I felt bad that she had no parents left, and sure, it was nice to have someone to share a seat with, but she was a bossy thing, and there was no getting around that. I had the feeling I'd have to stand up for myself at some point or things wouldn't change.

Ignoring the seatback in front of me, which was pleading for me to tell a white lie, I looked Noni straight in the face. "I don't think I do trust you. Sorry," I added for cushion.

Her low-pitched laugh was followed by a snort and a nod of approval. "That's fair. You don't have as much faith as I do. But I think you're wrong. You're trusting me right now, and I appreciate that, even if you can't admit it." She kept shifting around, trying to get comfortable. "Know why you're trusting me? It's better than being alone. Same for me. And I've lost two parents, not just one, so you probably feel sorry for me, which is fine." Her head nodded a little as she yawned again, fighting sleep. "Sympathy can come in handy."

She smoothed out the paper scrap, which had crumpled in her fist. "Back to my guidelines—number three, don't talk to people you shouldn't be talking to, or your wandering time will be up for sure. That's all I could remember to write down. Now, stop talking my ears off and let me get some rest. Wandering's more tiring than it sounds." Wiggling her legs up to the seat, she wrapped both arms around herself and turned away, tucking her head into her body like a baby bird.

My paint box poked my leg through the backpack's fabric, so I took out my sketchbook and flipped to the third-to-last page. Most of the face was blank from the eyes down, but I'd drawn light outlines that could be erased and changed later on. Miss Stone told me that mistakes in art were okay. They were lessons in disguise, she told me. Clues to help you go about things a better way next time. From memory I drew a nose, then erased it, then tried again. Better. Ears and jawline came next, then the top lip line.

Daddy wasn't speaking, not even when I reached in the backpack and shook him around a little, so I stretched my arms high, then low, then leaned against the window and used the backpack as a pillow. When I closed my eyes, I drifted in a soft dream fog before recognizing our front porch. The fog parted, and I saw that it was a late-summer afternoon in August. Mama and a younger version of me were waiting for the day to cool and for Daddy to get home from the golf course, and I was floating above the scene.

An ache filled me when I realized what would happen to the Ben Putter crouched over a bunch of papers. I tried to yell a warning to myself, but I'd floated too high for the little boy to hear and my words were coming out as silence anyway.

Can't change something that's already happened, the golf ball in my neck sang out in a mocking sort of voice. I slapped it quiet.

Then I watched the younger me, knowing exactly what would happen.

A Gift for Daddy

I was eight years old, just days away from getting the pounding of my life from twelve-year-old Willy Walter, the beating given because I'd won the second grade art prize for my drawing *Pregnant Pig in Yard* over his sister's drawing *Portrait of My Brother Willy*.

All day through, with only one break for lemonade and a cold ham sandwich, I had sketched and planned a project for Daddy. I figured that maybe he didn't like me drawing and painting things like flowers and trees and Mrs. Grady snoozing and drooling on her porch, but he couldn't help but like a comic strip. Daddy always chuckled at the Sunday funny papers, and I knew that a special comic was just the thing to make him smile.

I'd thought long and hard before making up and drawing a five-page Abbott Meyers comic strip, based on the golfer character from the good-night stories he told me on rare, golden occasions. I drew forty-five frames of comics, and even Mama thought I was working too hard. The outlines were in navy blue ink, and I was so proud that I snuck into Mama's room and nabbed the set of colored pencils she'd already bought me for the upcoming school year so I could fill up the empty white space.

In my dream, I felt the same excitement I had that day when he pulled into the driveway, leaving a trail of disappearing dirt smoke. Running to the car, I pointed to my superhero and his weapon.

"Huh," said Daddy, glancing at the first frame. He reached into the trunk and pulled out his clubs. "Who's that supposed to be?"

"Abbott Meyers, Daddy. I made him a real superhero and wrote you a comic. See, it's called *Abbott Meyers Swings for Freedom Against the Hateful Wart Droid Assassins*. Look what he's got—it's a golf club that doubles as a Tommy gun. See? And the golf ball is a delayed-action tear gas bomb."

Daddy snatched a paper from me and studied it as we walked to the porch. I leaped up the three stairs and watched. Waiting.

He wrinkled his nose. "You've got the grip all wrong. Good Lord, Ben, weren't you paying attention last week, or was I wrong to think eight was old enough for the golf course?"

He grabbed the other sheets and studied them briefly. "Nope, not one good club grip in here." He waved the pages in the breeze like they were nothing at all. "Tell you what, I'll grab us some lemonade. You come on around back and hit a few into the net with me. We can have us some man talk and I'll give you a few tips on that grip. That sound fun?" He reached down, handed my gift back, and walked into the house, humming a tune.

I dropped the pages.

Mama leaned over me on the porch and made a neat pile of the papers. I waited until she went inside, too. Then I tore my gift to pieces and shoved the mess into the rain pipe.

I woke up as the Atlanta-bound bus was driving through a small town. Just as I blinked awake, the driver let out a word that not even Daddy used to say, hit the brakes, smacked into something in the road, and went spinning out of control. Even as my head banged against the seat in front of me, I could see out my window to a lake that said *We've got fish!* and a wall with painted yellow bricks that shouted *Hello!* and a café sign that said *Come on in for a spell!* and that's exactly what we did, blasting right through the front windows like we were extra hungry for pie.

Breaking a Heart

A pig caused the accident. I wouldn't have believed it if I didn't see a boy sitting on the side of the road, crying and looking at the mangled mess while the driver ran out there, I guess to make sure it was really a pig he'd hit and not a piggy-looking person. I joined the line of wobbly people and stepped out of the bus with my backpack on, into shattered tables and chairs, broken glass, and several exploded ketchup bottles that made the scene look worse than it was.

A woman stood behind the café's counter, her face full of grit and worry as she reached across the service slab and rubbed the back of a colored customer who was holding a newspaper in one hand and a forkful of pie in the other, his wrinkled face dotted with lemon crème and Cool Whip. A lit cigarette rested in an ashtray beside him, and a heavy-set white man in overalls was tapping his own cigarette in there, blinking at us like he couldn't believe what had just happened. Three more counter stools and a few tables held mostly older folks. Except for the counter, coloreds and whites were sitting at separate tables like in our school cafeteria, but all of them looked pretty much the same, holding shaking coffee cups and staring. They'd probably come in for the day's gossip. Now they'd gotten it.

I looked through the disarray for Noni, who'd scooted off the bus fast while I checked the backpack to make sure nothing had fallen out when we crashed.

The driver made sure we all were accounted for, holding a shaky paper and checking us off his list before asking for a telephone and reporting our location. Which was just north of Montgomery, but nowhere near Atlanta. We weren't even in Georgia yet.

Voices hummed and moaned while we all got our bearings. Everyone seemed to be breathing and fine, though the pregnant woman was tucked into a pile of broken chairs like a curled-up possum, crying quietly and talking to her belly, while another woman tried to comfort her.

"Hey, Bobby Jones," Noni said, pushing around a turned-over table and coming to my side. She squeezed my hand, her fingers doing the talking to say, *are you okay, I'm okay, are you okay, good, I'm glad we're okay*. She raised her eyebrows at the backpack, and I nodded to let her know that Daddy was fine. Patting her pocket bulges, she grinned. "The eggs made it, too."

The driver bellowed for everyone to listen up. "Ya'll just take a break and settle in. They can send another bus, but it won't be until six o'clock or so." He held up both hands. "I know, I know, that's five or six hours from now. I'm sorry. Ya'll eat a meal on the bus company if this fine woman can find a way to serve you."

The woman glared at him. "Got pie and grilled cheese. That's it."

"You got pig," someone joked, pointing to the road.

An even deeper stare met the joker's eyes and put them back to normal. Mama'd used that same look on Daddy a few times.

"That was Darry's pig," the café owner said. "My boy raised it since it was weaned to take to the state fair in a month. Pillow, he called it. Boy took more care with that barrow than, than . . . ." At that, she dropped her cloth and started crying.

"What's a barrow?" Noni whispered.

I raised my hand over my mouth. "Castrated hog. Meant for the market."

Noni went over to her. "Were you going to sell Pillow after the fair?"

The owner shook her head and took a handkerchief from her back pocket with a jittery hand. "No. We'd make more money by using the meat here. He already weighed over two hundred and fifty pounds. We would've gotten more than two hundred pounds of pork off him, but now it'll just rot on the side of the road. Bill Davis does all the butchering around here, and he's in Shreveport until Friday. We don't have time to drive Pillow somewhere else. I wouldn't even know who to call." She blew her nose, then gestured around the broken café. "Lord, look at this mess."

Without making eye contact with me, Noni put an arm on my shoulder. "My brother doesn't talk, but he can butcher a pig with a whole lot of love. Our Daddy taught him. Can we help you?"

The woman looked surprised. Her eyes swept over me, pausing at my hands and arms—my body's butchering tools. Tapping fingers along both hips, she seemed to exchange silent words with a man holding a broom by the front door. "Okay," she said. "That'd be a help, thank you. Barrett," she said to the broom man, "ya'll get Darry and go around back. We'll use all of him," she said to me. "Sausage parts too."

I don't know why I agreed to do it. Something about the way that little boy was crying on the side of the road, like he'd lost something more special than anybody but him could really know.

The café owner rummaged around a closet in the kitchen and handed me a pair of coveralls that I suspected belonged to Darry. I stepped outside and slipped them on over my clothes, then zipped them up while three men hauled the barrow off the road and around the building, its body so big that it would have stood over waist high next to me. Behind the café was a long field and a dirt pen attached to a small barn. A cow chewed its cud along the field's fence line, staring with kind, dull eyes.

Darry's father placed a set of knives and tools on an overturned barrel in the middle of the dirt pen. Three tarps were spread on the ground inside the pen, and the hog was dragged and positioned on top of one. A long cutting board was placed on the second tarp, and the third tarp was topped with large white buckets, ready to be filled with whatever I deemed worthy of keeping.

Pillow was a big mess, and the side where the bus had smacked into the hog's body left a few spots that would be too torn up for plate cuts. I needed to cut him open completely and clean him out before dividing the meat up for the café's menu. I gestured for a water hose and sprayed the body down, increasing the water's pressure with my thumb and trying not to look at Darry. His father had encouraged him to help, but the boy refused.

"It's okay, son," Darry's father told him, squeezing his son's shoulder. "You don't have to watch. I need to go check on the rest of the bus folks."

But Darry stayed, watching me from an overturned bucket.

I knelt on the tarps, making cuts to open the cavity. I scraped out intestines and organs, piling them into the buckets to be made into sausage, thinking how my life back in Hilltop had literally stopped me in my tracks, shouting at me clear as if it had a voice, letting me know that it wasn't about to let me run away.

The only time I'd ever helped butcher a full pig was when I was nine. Daddy brought home a live one instead of ordering a blood-drained whole hog. He made me watch while he scratched the pig's ears. He waited until it was good and happy and grunting away, and then he slipped the sharpest, thinnest knife we owned underneath the pig's neck and winced as he sliced across, smooth as running a dinner blade through warm butter.

The pig collapsed, and Daddy said it hadn't felt anything more than a horsefly bite. He said Grandpa Clay had shown him the very same slaughtering technique, and even though Daddy'd been twenty at the time, it'd still been hard to watch. He made me help gut the animal and take out all of its parts. I vomited and cried the whole time. Daddy patted my back and told me I was doing good and said he was sorry, but never once said I could stop.

Grandpa Clay thought slaughtering a pig by hand, up close and personal, was the only way a true barbecue man could show respect for his trade. Even the most delicious things can have an ugly side, he'd said. Nothing in life is as perfect as it seems, and when you take ownership for the messy parts, it makes you a better person because it gives you a clearer picture of the world. After it was done, Daddy had given me a new apron and said that I was officially a barbecue man.

Snap out of Memory Land and get back to work, Barbecue Man, a mosquito said, sucking my blood. *And try not to cry this time.*

"You either," I murmured, slapping it.

Noni showed up and set the backpack down, a piece of newspaper sticking out of her dress pocket and the corners of her mouth white with pie cream as she sat on the ground beside Darry. She had two plates in her hand and held one under his nose. "Pie?" When he made a point of ignoring her, she nodded. "I don't blame you." She set down the extra plate, cut a bite from her piece, and popped it in her mouth, chewing with a satisfied, interested look on her face, like she was eating Cracker Jacks at a baseball game.

"Pretty gross over there, huh?" she said to Darry, her mouth full of chocolate pudding and meringue. Then she saw me glancing her way. "Pretty gross!" she repeated. "The pig, not the pie. Pie's great," she said to Darry. "Did your mama make it?"

I stopped what I was doing long enough to see Darry give her another death stare.

She squirmed and blushed, stuffing pie in her face, which was probably the only way she knew to keep quiet.

"What's going on, Ben?" Daddy asked. "Where are we?

This little gypsy girl and some other folks were talking about a bus crash and how we're gonna have to wait a bunch of hours?"

The backpack with Daddy's urn was near me, propped against a wooden pen post. Noni saw me looking toward the pack and watched my face. She left her spot, came over, and pulled the urn into the daylight.

"We got to get on the road, son, so quit whatever you're— "

She tapped Daddy's urn. "Shh. I don't know if you're real or if you can hear me, but if you're jabbering in there, you quit it," she whispered. "Your boy's cutting up a pig, so stop distracting him or he might slip and cut off a finger. And the pig's owner already looks like he's about to vomit. A cut-off finger'll make him lose his lunch for sure." She winked at me and gave me a thumbs-up, returning to her seat.

Darry wasn't vomiting, but he was fighting tears, I could tell. His lips twitched and jerked up and down and sideways, even while the rest of him stayed still as a statue. Just before it was time to start with the big cuts, I closed the body cavity, and with all the hosing I'd done, the pig looked as close to okay as it ever would again. I let my hands graze that pig's skin, and I gave its ears a good scratch, even though Pillow wasn't alive to feel it. I motioned to the body and stepped back.

Darry looked stubborn for a minute and then stood

and came over and put a hand on the hog's head. His face crumpled, and then he leaned over and let his tears sink into his pig. He whispered words too low to hear. Then he rose, wiped snot from his face, and nodded.

"I hate you," he told me. "I hate you."

Then he sat back on the bucket and watched me finish taking his hard work to pieces. I knew it wasn't losing any prize that hurt most. It was other stuff that had him crying.

After I'd hosed myself down and taken off the bloodied coveralls, I found Noni back inside the café, where the bus driver was telling an angry crowd that, due to an unexpected shortage in availability, new transportation would be delayed until eight o'clock that evening. I glanced at the wall clock and Darry, who was sitting under it, slumped over a table with his nose bumping up against a ketchup bottle.

Noni put her arm around me and steered me toward the door. "Come on, Brother Bobby. Let's walk. I can't sit in here for another handful of hours."

When I looked back, Darry felt me staring and raised his head. He didn't look angry anymore. He just looked sad. I waved goodbye and turned, knowing he wouldn't wave back.

Hobo Song

We took our cheese sandwiches and wandered across the road from the café, sitting on a bench that overlooked a set of train tracks and the lake.

"How many pieces of pie did you eat?" I asked her. "You still got some on your face." I looked down at her rolled up sleeves, then at her bruise. I hadn't really noticed how strange it was. It circled the entire elbow like a perfectly straight armband, the edges of it looking like they'd been drawn with a ruler. I couldn't figure out what could have done something like that. It didn't seem to bother her, though.

Noni grinned. "Five. Had to try each kind. I wasn't about to miss out on pie. Wanderers never know when good stuff'll stop being available. Best to stock up when we can." She burped, wiped at her mouth, and took a bite of cheese sandwich.

I finished my sandwich, took out my sketch pad, and

started drawing in pencil. Darry came easy with his sharp features and overalls. The pig was more difficult, but I'd seen its face and knew its heft. The lines were soft at first, and I pressed harder when the shapes became clear.

Noni picked up a rock and threw it, then searched the ground and found a bigger one, hurling it nearly to the lake. "Nice one, Noni," she congratulated herself. "Say, Benjamin Putter, do you believe in signs? Like if you saw a sign that seemed like it might be from a dead person you loved, would you believe it? Like maybe a sign that something wasn't your fault and you shouldn't keep thinking it was?"

I let out a Daddy snort. "I think you're talking to the wrong person." I patted the backpack. "I've gone beyond signs with my daddy."

"That's right, he's talking to you. That's lucky."

"You hoping your daddy will leave you a sign?"

"Something like that." She picked up another stone and threw it toward the water. "I went away for a while after the funeral, and when I got back to my house, I knew that I'd never be able to talk with my daddy again. I knew that. The only other thing that was clear to me was that I needed to try to find him anyway." She dug in her pocket. "So I wrote down these wandering rules and started walking. I think he needs me to find him, somehow. I just need to find the right sign. I know that sounds crazy," she added, studying her shoes.

Her shoes looked like the extras you had to wear at gym class if you forgot to bring sneakers. They were nothing like May's shoes, which always looked like something she could wear straight to church. She usually kept a handkerchief with her to keep the dust off, which seemed pointless in a town full of dirt roads. But Noni's shoes were the opposite. Worn and smudged with stains from wherever it was she'd been walking before she met me.

"It doesn't sound that crazy."

She looked over my shoulder at the sketch of Darry with his arm around a pig that had a huge prize ribbon around its neck. I'd written WINNER in tiny letters on the ribbon.

"That picture doesn't belong to you," Noni said. "Stay here." She tore the sketch from my pad and went sprinting back to the café, throwing in a few one-handed cartwheels along the way.

What a show-off, said the bench beneath me. *Pretty good, though. She's no stay-in-her-shell turtle boy, that's for certain. In fact, if she were your sister, I bet your daddy would be more proud of—*

"Hush," I told it.

Within a few minutes, heavy footsteps and heaving breaths were followed by a slap on my back. Noni sank back into the bench. Her toes started tapping against the ground. "Darry likes it." She held up a small black rectangle. "He even found us a lighter when I asked for matches. I asked if there was any free pie left, but he started getting all grouchy again and I got the feeling he just wanted me to leave."

"Imagine that."

She flipped the lighter in the air. "We can build a fire for the eggs tonight. Got a spoon, too, for getting them out of the hot water. First tickets, now supplies. I'm thinking you packed the right things after all. You did good, Benjamin Putter."

"You mean Bobby Jones."

She scratched her elbow, the one with the bruise, and looked back toward the café. "Bobby Jones didn't have anything to do with that drawing. Say, I think I saw these tracks on the map back at the Heart station. They lead right to Atlanta, I'm pretty sure. Or close, anyway."

She was lying and we both knew it. "How close do they get to Augusta?" I asked her.

Noni picked up a pebble and rolled it between her finger and thumb. "The tracks are going east, the same way we want to go. What more do you need?"

"You heard the driver. A new bus is coming."

"Not until tonight."

Daddy cleared his throat. "I'm with the girl on this, Ben. Find a way to get going. We'll never get to the Masters at this rate."

"You sure pick your times to start talking," I said to Daddy.

"I've been talking since I met you. Don't be a turkey,"

Noni said. "There's something nudging at me about these tracks. It's a sign, maybe. I think we should follow them. Why wait around until eight o'clock at night for a bus that might run into another pig?"

"Because a bus is faster than walking."

"So's a train." She pointed far, far down the line, where a tiny dot had appeared. A train, heading our way. Heading east. Noni stood and started singing a low song.

My pencil stopped. I couldn't help but watch her and listen.

> *Gone wandering, Lord, got my wandering card,*
> *Wandering, wonder why life's so hard,*
> *Found my time on the rail, found a dry way to sail,*
> *Gone wandering, Lord, to my home*
> *Been trying to find my home,*
> *And I'll die on the rail, in my home.*

It was magic. The way she sang was magic. I'd never heard someone sing like that, with longing and hope and pain all blended up until you couldn't quite tell what you were hearing. Just that the words mattered.

The last note rang out low and mournful, and she looked lost when she met my eyes again. "It's an old hobo song. My daddy used to sing it while we watched trains go by behind our house. There's more, but that's all I can remember." She turned, and I saw her eyes squinting, like she was trying to make something come into focus.

"My grandma's café used to feed the railroad hobos," I said, "back when they'd come into Hilltop to work the fields. She told stories about how they'd appear and disappear when she was a girl, coming and going without any warning. She said some days she'd been tempted to leap on a passing train herself, just to see where they all went when they left town on the tracks."

I remembered how Daddy had hopped onto Grandma Clay's stories, calling the hobos Luckies. Saying they had all the freedom in the world. Nothing tying them down.

The train was getting closer, changing from a dot to a thin black line.

Noni nudged me with her elbow. "Let's hop that train, Benjamin Putter. We've got to get to Georgia."

"We've got to get to Georgia," Daddy agreed.

"Couple of best friends, aren't you," I mumbled.

"What?" both he and Noni asked.

That's right, the train tracks agreed with me. *They're just using you, the both of them. And did you notice how your daddy only talks when he wants something from you?*

You're being used, all right, the bench said. *But I guess you'll take attention any way you can get it, 'cause deep down you know he thinks you're worth—*

"Nothing," I said to all of them.

The train was still a ways down the track, but now I could make out mounds of black in each of the open freight cars. Coal. Smoke puffed out of the front like our smoker at home and it could have been a moving barbecue pit. The golf ball in my throat twisted in place until I reached up and rubbed on it. *Go away*, I said silently. *Make me*, it said back.

"Noni, you really want us to just jump on a coal train?"

"Yep."

The train was close now, probably less than a minute before the engine car would come charging past us. Coal pieces were piled in each one, some cars looking less filled than others, like those'd gotten less from a bad pour off the filler. Either that or the coal on those cars had done a better job of settling in for the ride. There must have been tons and tons of it with the number of cars on that train. "Where's all that coal going?" I asked, half to myself.

"One way to find out," Daddy answered.

"We can't," I told him. "We shouldn't."

He sighed, and the disappointment hit me right in the gut, just like it always did. One sigh was all it took. I wondered if Daddy knew how much power was in his sighs, even his dead ones.

"Look." Noni's eyes flashed back and forth over the train as the engine car passed us. "There. We just run alongside and haul ourselves onto a ladder. There's enough space to hunker down and ride between cars on the platform, or climb on top and sit there. It'll be an adventure." She yanked me up.

I shook my head. "No, we'll just wait. We already paid for the bus."

But she stepped toward the train anyway. "We're getting on this train, Benjamin Putter."

"I'm starting to like her. Let's get on the train, Ben," said Daddy.

"You don't even know for sure where it's going. No," I said to both of them. "We'll wait for the next bus."

"Listen to me, Benjamin Putter," Noni said, ripping the backpack from my arms.

"Hey! Give that back!" I lunged toward her, but she spun and I lost my balance and fell, pieces of track gravel digging into my palms, breaking my fall.

Her hair whipped back with the force of the passing cars, a few pieces clinging to her face. "No!" she shouted. "My daddy watched all kinds of trains, but none made him sing the way a passing coal train would. This is a sign. I have to—"

She turned while I got to my feet again, and the rest of her words faded with the sound of the train shrieking past. Looking back over her shoulder at me, she started jogging alongside the train. "You have to trust me!" she called out. "It's better for both of us this way."

I caught up and tried to snatch the backpack, but I was afraid I'd knock her the wrong way and she'd get run over. "Give him back!"

She took the bag off her shoulder, swinging it like she was ready to throw.

I ran after her. "Hey, stop! The bag'll fall and get run over! The rest of your precious pork is in there, not to mention my daddy's ASHES!"

She lowered her arm, even as she kept jogging, and I thought I had her. The train was starting to speed up as the front of it left town and she'd miss her chance. But instead of giving it back to me, she put both backpack straps on and ran faster. She looked back, her voice slipping in and out of the air around me. "You . . . not about me . . . about helping him . . ."

I didn't know what she was talking about. All I knew was that she wanted to take my daddy on a train ride to God knows where. And then I'd be left behind, watching him go off somewhere without me, like all those times he'd spent playing golf. Like a ball and grass and a set of metal rods were better than me. Like golf was so great, he could barely tear himself away to come home.

"Noni, please stop!"

She turned again and smiled a strange, sad, hopeful smile, then caught a train rung. Hauling herself up the ladder, she heaved the pack over the side of the car. The bag bounced once, twice, then lodged itself in a corner. Without pausing, she scooted back down the rungs and let go, tumbling to the side of the tracks while I slowed to a shocked stop. Ten cars passed me before my head fully processed that Noni'd actually let go of the pack.

Daddy was gone.

So was my paint box.

So was the rest of our pork.

I had the strangest feeling that most all of me was gone along with those things, and the part of me left standing on the side of the tracks was nothing more than an empty plate full of gnawed-on bones.

Then Noni scrambled over, grabbed my hand, and looked me in the eye. "Sorry I had to do that. Get running."

I'd never been a fast runner, and it'd take a miracle to catch up and not get killed trying to climb on. "We'll never make it."

She yanked me. "That doesn't mean you don't try anyway. This trip is gonna get old real quick if I have to keep telling you what to do. Now, *run*."

Metal scraped against the train tracks, chugging and shrieking and creaking and rushing to haul its load far away. Daddy was leaving me again along with it, that was certain, but this time was different. This time I had the chance to run after him.

I took it.

Coal Dust

Pumping my legs after Noni, I watched her hand reach for a metal side ladder rung and miss every time another full car passed us. Three times she did that before catching hold and swinging up to another rung, then climbing over to the narrow platform that jutted out at the end of each car. She turned to extend her hand again, this time to me. She was yelling something.

"What?"

"Close your eyes! Just *run!*"

I did. Once again it was like Noni had woven a spell, her magic making me do things that Benjamin Putter knew were wrong and were completely outside the laws of life besides. Things like *don't open your backpack for strangers*, and *don't let people make out like you don't speak*, and *don't run beside a moving train with your eyes shut*. But somehow, it worked. With my eyes closed and my legs pumping, I became some kind of superhero—The Incredible Flying Ben "Bobby Jones" Putter. I became someone my Daddy would be proud to clink a glass to.

By the time I grazed Noni's fingers with my own, opened my eyes, and grabbed the side ladder, my legs were moving so fast that I practically flew through the air and landed on the bottom rung. Reaching out one foot and getting a tight hold on the end of the train car, I swung around and squeezed in beside her on the platform. We crouched there and caught our breath, laughing in shock and relief, two runaways from Alabama on a train that went steadily about its business, not knowing or caring we were there.

Blurred tracks flew by in the open space between cars. A bar of thick metal and a heavy latch connected us to the next box of coal. Noni crossed over the bar and latch, and I followed, hugging the next car's end ladder like it was my mama. When she started up the ladder, I followed again.

We piled onto a sea of black stones and let the wind cool us for a brief moment. I'd never seen Alabama from a coal train, and it looked different from the landscape I'd passed in the bus. It felt different, too, watching growing fields of corn on one side and budding tobacco and farmhouses on the other, me sitting beside a girl and not talking, just looking. The colors were everywhere and *every*where and *everywhere*. I opened my eyes wider, trying to take in the whole picture at once.

Bluewhitelightskygreenbrowndarkfieldyellowpurpleblue-pinkflowergreenbrowngold.

It was a wonder like I'd never seen, and if I hadn't been hunting my dead daddy's ashes, and if my paint box wasn't in the backpack alongside him, I believe I would've liked to take out my watercolors and make an abstract painting of the view for May Talbot and see what kind of story words she picked for it.

Sounds nice, said the view. *But you* are *hunting your dead daddy's ashes.*

"Right," I said. "Let's go."

Over the coal piles, down the end ladder to the small platform, across connecting bars and latches, up the next car's ladder. Repeat and repeat and repeat. Though I looked ahead for Daddy, I couldn't make him out in the line of black boxes in front of us.

"What if he fell?"

"He didn't."

She might have been lying, but it can get tiring on your heart to go around thinking maybe people were always lying to you. *I'll be back by supper*, Daddy would say before staying out after hitting balls, playing guitar with friends instead of coming home to me and Mama. *Your daddy'll be home to take you fishing, don't you worry*, Mama would say before shaking her head and gritting her teeth. *More painting time*, she'd say, like it was what I wanted to hear. *You know your daddy loves you anyway*. That last one wasn't a lie, because maybe she thought that was something she knew. But love isn't a fact, it's a feeling, and the feeling that my daddy loved me was like catching fog. It was there, but I couldn't get a solid hold on it. I think maybe it was that extra word that made it all seem slippery. It was the *anyway* that made it feel like a lie.

"Okay," I told Noni.

We went up and down eighteen coal cars before we found Daddy. Noni and I were both filthy-exhausted by then, covered in coal dust from head to toe. It was well worth the time and effort when I saw the backpack tucked into the corner where Noni'd tossed it. The sight of the urn nearly made me cry, and my neck lump moved a little, rotating a slow dance of relief.

"Benjamin?" Daddy coughed himself awake from whatever blank space he'd been in. "Where the heck am I now?"

"You're on a coal train, Daddy. Heading east."

"You jumped the train?"

"Yep."

There was a pause while my father considered me. "Good boy," he said.

With a smile that stretched right through the lump in my throat and into the pool of lumps surrounding me, I felt my insides get filled up until I swelled with that *good boy*. That *good boy* was like a long drink of cool water. That *good boy* made me wonder if I couldn't keep my daddy around if only I could keep finding pigs to butcher and trains to jump on. Maybe I could become who Daddy needed me to be and maybe he could do the same for me and maybe he wouldn't have to go anywhere because he would realize that he'd belonged with me all along.

"He okay?" Noni asked.

I nodded. "Noni? About you taking my daddy . . ."

"Look, I'm sorry," she said. "I didn't know what else to do. But we're a team, okay? I'm going to help you, and you'll help me. So far I've been carrying more than my load of the helping part, but you'll get there." She put her hand on my shoulder and leaned close. "I've got faith in you, Benjamin Putter."

"I butchered a whole hog," I reminded her. "And I just drew a picture that got us a lighter and a spoon."

"Which you wouldn't have had to do if you hadn't picked the wrong bus. But I won't hold a grudge."

"Wrong bus? If you'd brought any money from wherever you came wandering from, maybe you could have taken your own bus."

She frowned. "But I like having company."

That caught me off guard. I searched her face, but she didn't seem to be joking. "You've got a funny way of showing it. Don't take the urn again. Okay?"

"Fine." A remnant of the stink eye she'd had when I met her flared up, along with her nostrils. "And don't *you* go trying to stick your nose too much in my business."

Has to get the last word, doesn't she? the coal beneath me pointed out.

Don't let her, suggested a Marlboro patch.

"Fine," I told her. "And next time you decide one of us can't talk, pick yourself."

She nodded. "I just might do that."

I wasn't expecting her to agree. "Oh. Well, okay."

The sun was starting to head toward setting. It was maybe five o'clock. With the train's movement, the Alabama heat felt cooler and it was downright pleasant, other than a line of dark clouds following behind us at a distance. There wasn't a thing in the world to do but dig out a little sitting spot for all of us and eat the last of the pork and wash it down with the last of the water from my bottle.

Noni and I threw pieces of coal off the train, trying to hit things, and had a gentle Hell's snowball fight with the smaller scraps. She took off her shoelaces and tied knots, showing me a bowline, a clove hitch, a fisherman's knot, and a few others. I told her about Daddy's favorite golfers, the Big Five, letting Daddy interrupt to test me on quotes, and decided my next fake name would be Walter Hagen, Bobby Jones's biggest rival of the day.

She said she'd be Wendy Hagen and told me that if you pressed coal hard enough it turned to diamonds. She made coins disappear from her hands and wouldn't show me how to do it and then plucked the coins from hidden spots. I swear her hands were empty, sleeves pushed back, when she plunged her hand deep down in the coal and came up with a nickel. I begged to know the secret, but she only winked and said if she told me everything, it wouldn't be magic.

Eventually we quieted down and just stared at the landscape. We passed through a town and Noni waved at a confused driver who was stopped at the safety gates, waiting for the train to go by so he could cross the tracks. Behind him, I saw a general store and a short line of buildings and a large sign that said:

WELCOME, YA'LL, TO GRINK

YOU'LL MISS US IF YOU BLINK

Population ~~324~~ ~~187~~ 99

Pulling the road atlas from Daddy's backpack, I opened it to the Alabama page and searched east of where we'd crashed. Nothing.

"Try Georgia," Noni said, flipping through the atlas.

It took less than a minute to find the smallest of dots. "There it is." I traced the space between Grink and Augusta. "We've got a ways to go," I said, shifting around to get comfortable.

We spoke in quieter voices then, and I told Noni about Miss Stone, my art teacher who'd left my school one month ago because the school decided there wasn't enough money for art or music now that they'd lost so many students to the white-only school. Her job had gotten butchered away, like the school was a pig and art class was hacked off and thrown in the no-good pile. I told her how Miss Stone was the nicest person I knew. Noni told me that my mama was the nicest lady she'd ever known because she'd fed her for free and had given her an extra-big piece of pie and hadn't asked questions.

I hoped Mama was doing all right without me and that she wasn't too worried. I hoped she'd agree that I was doing the right thing for Daddy.

The world was soaked in the prettiest kind of light, and as the sun got lower in the sky, I told Noni how Daddy'd died of lung cancer. "What happened to your dad?" I asked her.

She picked up a piece of coal and rubbed it between her hands. "I'm not ready to talk about it. Okay?"

It was okay, but it wasn't what I wanted to hear and I felt stupid for being so open with someone who refused to tell me as much as I'd told her. She'd said back in Hilltop that she'd be my partner. My friend. But I got the idea that Noni, though we were traveling together, didn't want or need a friend. Not a close one, anyway.

Did you think this girl was gonna turn into a replacement for May Talbot? asked an extra-big piece of coal. *Nobody can replace May.*

I threw the coal piece hard, banishing it for speaking the truth, watching it fly into a field and wondering if it was too late for me to fix things between me and May.

"Don't be mad at me for not being able to tell you the whole truth." Noni reached her right hand around her front, letting her fingers circle her bruised elbow. "I know you've got questions, but I've got to follow my wandering rules." She met my stare, her chin shaking a little, maybe from the cars rattling along the rails. "They're all I've got to guide me, okay? That and finding the right sign. Those things are all I've got. Maybe I can tell you more later. Just not now."

"All right."

We'd been on the train maybe an hour past Grink. Sunset oranges and reds and pinks weren't too far off, and the wind from the train's movement began giving me the shivers.

"How long do we have before dark?" Noni asked with a yawn. "I'm a little tuckered."

"I don't know. About an hour, based on the sky. Maybe two," I said, pleased that I knew something she didn't seem to.

I wondered if Noni and I would be sleeping on the train. Then I started thinking about nights I'd gone to bed late, after waiting up for Daddy. I thought about how I'd shuffle my legs under the sheets, rotating them in and out, in and out, to keep the cloth cool during the summertime night heat.

I thought about hearing Daddy come in and how I'd always wondered whether I should jump out of bed to go see him.

I thought of what a strange feeling it always was, to be right in my house and not know where I belonged: in bed asleep or saying goodnight to my father. I never knew what to do and nearly always ended up sitting on the edge of my bed, waiting. I wondered if that's what Daddy felt like now, stuck in purgatory. Like a boy at the edge of his bed.

And then I thought that Dr. Bartelle at church was probably right. I thought too much and did too little. But I could change. This trip could change me if I let it. It was as I was absentmindedly shuffling my legs in the coal, moving instead of thinking, that I accidentally kicked my father off the train.

Georgia Peaches

I didn't see where he landed. All I saw was his gray-silver urn fading away, disappearing like brush paint fading into a creek. All I heard was the train and my voice screaming one word, not slow and beautiful and perfect like Daddy had said *Augusta*, but fast and panicked and messy.

Noni jerked out of some spell beside me, her head darting back and forth. "'Wait?' Wait for what? What's wrong?"

The coal was too busy forcing me to a standing position to answer. I scrambled up and it shifted under me, saying *Jump now, jump now, jump now*. My fingers pointed over the side. "The urn," I managed to whisper. "Noni, how fast are we going?"

Her expression was partly shadowed, but I saw the moment when Noni's horror turned to resolve. Instead of telling me I was crazy, she spread her arms wide and closed her eyes. Then she blinked them open and peered over the side. "Too fast for comfort. Make sure not to hit a tree and jump far enough to clear the tracks."

Swallowing, I scanned the landscape and saw lights in the distance, spread far apart. We were in farm country of some sort. I didn't even know for absolute sure what state we were in. I'd be jumping into nowhere-land. "Fear of jumping," I whispered.

"What?"

"Sam Snead said 'A player should correct one fault at a time. Concentrate on the one fault you want to overcome.' Right now fear of jumping is the fault I want to work on." I didn't tell her that Sam Snead also said "Of all the hazards, fear is the worst." "He won eighty-two professional golf championships and—"

"Face your fears, crazy—that's a direct Noni quote. They might not go away, but at least they'll know you're up for a fight."

Threading my arms through the backpack, I crouched on the edge, counted to three, and was shocked when Noni jerked me backward.

"Geez, crazy, climb down the ladder first! You'll be closer to the ground." She tilted her head toward the space between two cars.

"Oh. Right."

She raised an eyebrow, impressed or pitying, I couldn't tell. "I like your enthusiasm, though. Leaping without thinking. Shows loyalty."

I scrambled down the ladder to the platform at the edge of the car and jumped.

Slamming into the ground, I knew how a golf ball felt when it got smacked off the tee with a driver club, hit for maximum distance. My feet managed to hit first, but quickly crumpled beneath me, leaving my side to blast into the earth and slide across what felt like extra-hard grass. The impact was terrible, but somehow my body knew to tuck and roll, just like I was doing a fire drill in class, not jumping off a moving train. Curling up like an armadillo, I let myself roll over and over again until I came to a halt.

Just as I was ready to attempt standing, I heard Noni moan about thirty feet away.

I hobbled over to her and helped her up. "Come on."

It took about ten minutes of walking before we caught sight of the urn. Daddy was sitting under a tree, one in a long row stretching out from the tracks, sprawled on his side like he was taking a quiet evening nap.

Fighting the rush of hurt that made my right side feel like it'd been placed on a smoker grate, I ran to the urn and swept it up in my arms. "Daddy? You okay? You still in there?"

Snoring. Sweet, heart-relieving snoring. My dead father had slept through falling off a train. "Noni, where are we?"

There was a tired smile in her sigh. "Benjamin Putter," she said, "I do believe that we've jumped into a peach orchard."

I leaned against the small tree trunk and looked up at the branches and leaves. They were darkened by the coming twilight, but I could make out little balls hanging here and there. She was right. Peach trees lined up like a welcoming parade. Peach trees to my left and right and in front of me. Peach trees as far as I could see.

Abbott Meyers, one of them said with a wink. *Your daddy just fell into Abbott Meyers territory.*

"Abbott Meyers," I agreed.

"Who?" Noni asked, stretching her arms up, then touching her toes. "That one of your daddy's Big Five?"

"No, just some made-up boy who played golf and caddied. My daddy told me bedtime stories about him a few times. How he'd climb a tree and stay on the course after caddying if a full moon was due, so he could play golf for free all night long. Stuff like that. There was always a peach in there somewhere, because he said Abbott lived in Augusta, Georgia, and Georgia's supposed to be full of peaches. They were just stories, though. Abbott Meyers is a nobody."

I was lying to her a little. Abbott Meyers wasn't a nobody to me. Daddy wasn't one for saying any kind of goodnight, either because he was out back, smoking cigarettes and smacking balls into his backyard net every night, or he was out with his buddies, telling tales to the men at Pastor Frank's. So when he chose to come into my room and ask if I wanted a story . . . well, those evenings were maybe the best, most easy I'd ever felt with him. I soaked up every word and stockpiled Abbott Meyers stories in my head the way our neighbor Mrs. Grady stored air tanks and canned ham in her basement bomb shelter.

"Sounds nice. My daddy was too tired from work most days to read me books, but he always let me stay up late with him while he watched too-loud television."

I shook away memories and rummaged through the backpack, coming up with the road atlas. I looked down at the slumbering ashes and was glad Daddy wasn't up to see the sun set on the Wednesday before the Masters began.

Time was running out.

"We need to find a road and figure out where we are," I said. "We'll walk through the night."

"Not a chance." Noni cracked her back. "Wandering's no good if you do it in the dark. Let's find someplace to sleep."

At the rate we were going, we'd miss the entire first day of the Masters tournament. And if we couldn't make it there by the second day, there was a chance that Hobart Crane wouldn't make the cut for weekend play and Daddy would miss being near his favorite player on the tour. "No. We need to find a road." I put Daddy in the backpack and started to pick it up.

She stuck a finger right on my nose and shoved the backpack to the ground with her free hand. "Listen, my daddy went to Georgia six times for work, and every time I asked him to bring me back a Georgia peach. He always came back empty-handed, saying the peaches weren't ripe yet." She held both arms out wide. "And now I'm in Georgia, surrounded by peaches. We *have* to stay. Just one night."

Her voice was talking to me, but her eyes were on the orchard, scanning over the trees like she knew she was meant to be among them. "It means we're on the right path. I'm going to find him, Benjamin Putter."

"Not in a peach orchard."

Noni sighed. "I didn't say I'd find him here. I said this was a *sign*. Us landing in a peach farm is a sign for you, Benjamin Putter, with those peach stories your daddy told. And it's a sign for me, too. Not *the* sign I'm looking for, but one that we're on the right track." Reaching a hand out, she slapped the backpack. "Some of us aren't lucky enough to have talking urns to guide us, so we got to go with instinct. I swear, you are the most faithless runaway I've ever met."

She looked so sure of herself. I wanted some of her confidence. Her faith. I wanted to know that Daddy would end up all right, that Mama and I would end up getting by, and that May and I would end up being friends again, but those things were all floating around like fireflies that didn't want to get jarred up and stared at and used to keep away the dark.

There was no road in sight. There was little chance that we'd make it to the first day of the Masters by walking through the night. I knew that. And my stubborn partner wanted to stay. The wanting was pouring off her in waves so strong it was like she was making the peach branches sway, not the wind.

"Okay, you win. But we rise first thing. *First thing*, got it? We'll flag down a car for a ride if we have to."

She slapped me on the arm. "You bet! I'll make dinner as a thank-you." With a grin, she dug through the center of the backpack, coming up with four intact eggs. "I nestled 'em good. Eggs like to be nestled." She pointed west, beyond the line of peach trees, toward a thin line of tall trees that probably meant a creek. "Let's head thataway to find a place to settle in. Hey, Benjamin Putter, do you know how to build a fire?" Noni asked, pulling out the lighter.

"Do you know how to run your mouth?" I asked her back.

She narrowed her big eyes. "You're still not funny. But that was better. I assume that's a yes." She scratched at her sock, where she'd been keeping her wandering rules. Her fingers lingered there, like she wanted to get them out and read over them again to settle herself. "I only asked because I wanted you to feel useful. I know how to build a fire, too. I don't *need* your help. I guess I'll take it, though, things going faster with two people." She smoothed her dress, then scratched all over. "This coal dust has me all itchy." Moving her lips up and down so quick that I couldn't be sure if it was a grimace or a grin, she nodded at me and started walking. "I never really had a friend before," she said, not turning around. "You're all right."

I was all right. I didn't know what to say to that, but as I watched her stride forward, I could feel a smile on my face that stayed for a moment before it melted back into questions.

Do you really think you can trust a person like that? called the creek. *If she doesn't need your help, what's she doing with you? Is she helping you, or using you?*

"Don't know," I murmured, following her without any answers.

A Reminder of Secrets

The wind had picked up a little since we'd jumped off the train, and by the time we found a sheltered spot to build a fire, the highest branches were waving back and forth. We were filthy with coal dust, so after rinsing in the creek, I dug pants number two and shirt number three out of the backpack, Noni changed back into her jeans and T-shirt, and then we spread out to search for wood.

Daddy'd given me a campfire lesson once, in preparation for a camping trip we were supposed to take the next week. He'd hung up the GONE FISHING sign at the café the night before we were gonna leave, and I'd been so excited. But it turned out that our trip had slipped his mind. He'd gone fishing with his buddies. So I'd never actually built a fire other than the barbecue kind, but I remembered every word he'd told me.

Even if it'd fallen to the ground somehow, any green

wood was useless. Fires like solidly dead things and won't stay burning if you try to give them something freshly dead or branches that are still fighting for life. Fires don't like rocks, either, so I gathered creek stones to make a circle barrier to keep our fire from spreading where it wasn't wanted. I wondered if that made the rocks feel better, knowing that even if they couldn't hold water back, they could stand up to fire. *Water beats rock, rock beats fire, fire beats wood, wood beats . . .* I looked up at the trees, old and quiet, leaves shuffling like a lullaby. "I don't know that you're looking to beat anybody," I told the trees, finding my way back to Noni.

It took some coaxing and a few Daddy words before the fire burst to life, but soon enough, water boiled in the bucket, which hung from a neat little rig made from two broken-off forked limbs with a straight, thick stick between them. With the two of us holding each side so it wouldn't collapse, it worked pretty good.

The sun was nearly gone and it was maybe seven o'clock at night. The reds and oranges and purples were faded and faint at the edge of the horizon, like they were trying their best to show color in the midst of a murkiness that'd taken over most of the sky.

Noni'd put her long-sleeved shirt over her T-shirt, but the sleeves were pushed up and that bruise on her elbow was showing, black and blue and deep purple. It was a dark and ugly mark, but I couldn't help seeing how, in a way, it was beautiful, too. It was a bunch of colors all at once, blended together like a sunset. A watercolored bruise. "Hey, Noni. Where were you when you got that?"

She blinked. Too many times. "Doesn't matter."

"What's it from?"

She placed her hand over the bruise, blocking it from view. "It's a reminder, okay? Nobody did it to me, if that's what you're asking. I was the only one there when it happened. It doesn't hurt at all."

"A reminder of what?"

"What do you care? To not take stuff that doesn't belong to you. That good enough for you? Now quit asking questions." She looked up at the treetops, which were starting to shift faster in the growing wind.

"Fine. Sorry."

If there was any part of me left that thought Noni might fill in for May, being told for the second time to stop asking questions settled things. Unless she'd spotted a butterfly or was busy hogging the green paint, May let me ask any question I wanted and I let her do the same. I'd listen, and then she'd listen. I'd help with her drawings, and she'd write words on my sketches, telling me what story she thought they told. Our friendship felt like an even trade. We fit together that way. But Noni was like a tricky springtime: nice and bright and calm one minute, smacking you with rain the next.

She picked up a stone and threw it high in the air, weaving her hand underneath before catching it, rolling her fist around and then opening her fingers to reveal nothing. She'd made that rock disappear. "I'd sure like to see my daddy's face one more time. Or hear his voice. You're really lucky, you know," she said, pointing to the urn.

Psst! said one of the boiling eggs. *Maybe Noni could come live with us. Maybe she's only being tough because she's all alone in the world.*

Yes! said another one. *She'll soften up. She could fill the empty space. Some of it, anyway.*

Don't listen to them, said the bucket. *She's keeping secrets.*

"Tell me about your daddy," Noni ordered. "We've got another few minutes on the eggs."

Daddy was still snoring, making it safe to talk about him a little. "He loved golf and barbecue," I told her. "He was busy with those things a lot. Most all of the time."

"Tell me what he was like."

I wasn't sure what to say. Noni had been a decent, if a little secretive, partner, but I didn't know her well enough to tell her the less-nice things about my daddy. I looked up at the darkening sky. "He was kind of like the stars," I finally said. "If he was paying you attention, it was like someone had lit up the sky only for you. Made people feel good about life just by talking to them. All of the café's customers thought he was their best friend, and they all called him Bo, just like

Mama did. Mama said she'd never seen a man able to charm people so much just by being around."

It always made me feel a strange combination of jealousy and guilt, the way those customers took to Daddy. I would work the café, wiping tables and taking out plates, half fascinated by their ease with my father and half wishing they'd go away, so he'd try to charm me instead. My eyes blinked open when a drop of water hopped out of the bucket and burned my hand. "Tell me about yours."

Tapping the spoon to get ground dirt off it, she stirred the eggs a little before locking eyes with the fire. "He was always good to me. He got me a school tutor so I could travel with him. Sometimes we'd go on camping trips together, just him and me." She got herself one egg and handed me the spoon.

I managed to scoop out an egg, letting it nearly burn my skin before trading hands to cool it down. "Sounds nice."

"Put that bucket water in the water bottle when it's not so hot," she told me. "Hey, wait," she said, just as I was peeling my first egg. "Don't eat that until I get back." She jogged toward the orchard, dancing as she went. Her silhouette jumped and did rough, wild Noni twirls against the trees. "Just wait," Noni called behind her. "I'm bringing you a surprise."

I scooped out the other three eggs and set them aside to cool. Noni hustled over a few minutes later, her shirt half pulled up and full of something. She dropped the shirt, and a big load of thumping balls hit the ground and scattered, making a sound like when Daddy would dump a bucket of range balls behind the house.

The sky was almost too dark, but those small peaches were still too young; anyone could see that. "You can't eat those. They aren't ready yet." We served fresh peach cobbler at Putter's Pork Heaven, but it wasn't usually on the menu until late May or June and didn't last much past July. Then it was apple cobbler, so that we were using fresh stuff. We kept jarred fruit, too, but it wasn't ever as good. That fruit kept the taste of being trapped, like its heart died the second it got sealed up in glass. But I'd take jarred over unripe any day. "Just throw those away," I told her.

Her face fell, and she took a hesitant bite of one, spitting it out and throwing the remaining peach toward the stream. "Georgia peaches are terrible. No wonder my daddy never brought me any." She picked one up off the ground, started to throw it, then held it out. "Sure you don't want to try?"

"Nope. They'll be fine in another month or so, but not now. I'm not gonna get sick before we get to the Masters."

Her second throw thudded off a tree trunk. "So that tournament is this week, for sure?" She smiled at the fire. "I knew it. That's why you have that golf course book. You really want to scatter your daddy on Augusta National Golf Club during the Masters, don't you?" A flush crept up her cheeks.

"What do you care? You said you don't know anything about golf."

The flush deepened. "This has nothing to do with golf. Or you." Her toes wiggled around like they'd caught fire, and she tapped her front teeth over her bottom lip a few times. "I looked at that Augusta book at the bus station and on the train while you were busy staring at whatever you were staring at. One of the pages said that *miracles* have happened there during that tournament. I could use a miracle. A miracle, Benjamin Putter, is the reason I'm here. And I'm not leaving you until I get one." She sat back and nodded to herself. "It's settled, then. I'll find the right sign there. I know it. I'm gonna find him at the Masters."

For some reason, her sureness annoyed me. "That's my daddy's spot. You can't just decide it's yours, too."

"Sure I can. And out of the two of us, you're the nice one. I'm sure you know how to share."

I felt my nose scrunch up. "The book meant golf-related miracles, not the other kind."

"I'm not picky." She lifted the Augusta book, grabbed two eggs cooling on a rock, and stood. "I'm going to eat my dinner and figure out the best spot for the right sign. You can eat dinner with your daddy. Maybe he's got something important to tell you. Or maybe you have something important to tell him. Either way, you should talk to him while you can," Noni suggested. "Because tomorrow morning we're getting ourselves to Augusta and then *poof*!" She flung her head in a circle. "He'll be free."

"He's ashes, not a genie." I picked up a fallen peach and tossed it into the fire, wondering where she'd go after she found the right sign. "And I don't have anything important to say. Besides," I said, hearing a low hum, "he's snoring."

She waved away my words with her egg-holding hand like they were bothersome gnats. "You never know when people will be gone forever. Or gone forever for the second time, in your case. Most people would give anything for a chance like yours." She stood, then brought the urn to me. "I'll give you two some privacy. I'm going to take a walk around the peaches, try to figure out our next steps." With that, she strode off with choppy strides, whistling her hobo song.

The wind blew harder, the tops of large creek oaks changing their dance from delicate to wild. Noni was right. If I didn't try to talk to Daddy, I'd regret it later. There were probably only so many times in life that a dead person came back for you to save them from an eternity in purgatory.

There was only one big thing that I could think of to ask him. To ask *of* him.

I just wasn't sure I wanted to hear his answer.

The Biggest Sucker in Alabama

Thunder rumbled from somewhere in the distance, the night's darkness hiding clouds that were there even if they didn't make noise or do anything but grow thicker in silence. My side ached, and every one of my muscles felt ready for rest, but the sky seemed wide awake, stealthy and alert. Crouching above, ready to spring something on me. It was that same unfinished storm, following me from Hilltop and waiting for the right moment to strike.

I piled more wood on the fire, wishing it would tell me how to ask Daddy to stay, but all it did was crackle and pop, murmuring something about me already having the words. If I did, they'd gone somewhere to hide from the coming storm, because I wasn't even sure how to start, other than clearing my throat.

"Hey, Daddy?" I tapped the urn's side until I heard sputtering waking-up noises followed by a yawn. "Can we talk for a minute?"

"Sure, okay. Go ahead and talk."

"Do you remember that day we played two rounds of golf together?"

"Golf?" I saw him brighten, sitting up with a grin. "You bet I remember that day. I shot a 70 on the first round, then double-bogeyed two holes on the second and still landed a 74. That was a heckuva time."

"I remember that day, too." I dug out the photograph. "You were happy. You were happy to be with me, at least until I started having trouble with my golf grip."

"That's right, you were holding your clubs wrong again. Nothing that practice can't weed out as you get older, though. Gotta work on your stance, too. Yep, that was a fine day, son. Wish we'd gotten to do that more."

"You mean you wish we'd gotten to spend more time together?"

"Why, sure. Sure."

I swallowed hard, my hand reaching up to rest on my neck lump. My entire body felt heavy with something, like I was nothing but a big barrel, filling up fast and running out of room. I had to try before it was too late. I pulled him into my lap. "Then maybe you don't have to go so soon."

"What?"

"You could stay, Daddy. I won't tell anyone about you, but you could stick around for another month or a year or—"

"Ben, I have to go." He sounded annoyed or confused or both.

"No, you don't." I stood up. "You don't need me to scatter you this week, or this year, even. I'll take you back to Hilltop with me. You can stay with me forever. We'll be fine. We'll hop another train, going the opposite way." I looked in the direction of the train tracks. "We'll find a—"

"I don't think you understand, son. That's not the way it works. If you don't get me scattered in the right place soon, that's it for me. I'll sink back into the waiting place forever. We've got one chance, and we don't have much time."

"Oh." Feeling like I might fall over, I sat back down, leaned over, and set him by the fire, the heat's nearness making something flare up inside me. "I understand. You have enough time to see the Masters tournament, but not a week more. Not even a day more."

"Now, Ben." His voice was dangerously soft. Warning me that I better back off. Sit down. Be a quiet little Putter. "I didn't raise you to take that tone with me."

I was surprised to hear an angry laugh tapping at me to get out and even more surprised when I let it hit the air. "No, sir, you didn't. You didn't raise me much at all. That was Mama's job."

Did you hear that? the fire flames said, rising up in a blast of fierce wind, trying to get closer to us.

I did, I did, said the wind. *Who-eee, that boy's asking for it.*

Well, he's gonna get it, the flames crowed back.

"Boy, you better watch it," Daddy growled.

"Or what?" I stood again, and another huge gust blew Daddy's hat off my head. "You'll fetch a switch and teach me a lesson? You weren't even daddy enough to whip me now and then for being a disappointment. You didn't bother. I guess I wasn't worth it." Good Lord, did that just come out of my mouth? I waited for the shame to soak through me, but it didn't. It felt good to finally say my thoughts out loud.

He stood up in his urn to match my height. "You're talking crazy. Is that the kind of father you wanted me to be? You wanted a whipping?"

"I wanted *something*," I said, a mean blood running through me. "I wanted something more than a stupid, made-up story about a stupid, made-up kid golfer once a year."

"Oh yeah?" Daddy was pacing now, his eyes getting fiery. "What did you want?"

"I wanted . . . I wanted . . ." I stopped talking, suddenly not sure what it was that I wanted.

"Well, what about what I wanted?" Daddy's urn hadn't moved an inch, but I felt him step closer, saw him stare into my eyes with intensity, with a harsh pain that I'd never seen while he was alive. "You have *no* idea what I gave up, what kind of responsibility got shoved on me without my permission. You don't get to choose in life, Benjamin. You got stuck with me as a father and I—"

"Got stuck with a boy like me," I finished for him.

"Hey!" One of his urn-bound pointer fingers was right in my face. "Don't you put words in my mouth. You don't know everything you think you know." He was breathing too fast, and a coughing fit sprang from his ashy throat. "I wasn't talking about you," he said between hacking. "I was talking about . . ." He trailed off and breathed heavy, the way he did after getting burned bad at the smoker. "Look. I wish I had more time. But you have to let me go."

I didn't care what he wanted. He couldn't leave me if I didn't let him. "You stay. You *stay*, Daddy," I ordered.

"*Let me go*, son."

I think deep down I knew that a talking urn couldn't replace my father any more than Noni could replace May Talbot. There were too many differences, and the world wasn't a painting where I could just add in the parts I wanted most to see. But I didn't care about that, and I didn't want to go to a golf course, and I didn't want to scatter my father's ashes, and I didn't want to be forced to say the goodbye I'd missed out on a month back.

"No," I said, low and firm. "If you can show up in the kitchen as a bunch of talking ashes, you can choose to stay. So choose to stay."

"Listen to me, Benjamin. When I was a boy—" He said something else, his voice shaking, breaking, so choked that I couldn't make out the words. "I *have* to go," Daddy said, sounding clearer. "We talked about this, son, and you told me you'd get me to Augusta. You promised. You need to keep that promise."

"Keep my promise?" The whirling gusts weren't choosing a direction, so my voice carried all over and nowhere. I could barely hear myself. "You're telling *me* to keep my promise?" I said louder. "All the promises you broke, and now I'm the one who's supposed to keep my promise?"

"Ben, just calm down."

But I couldn't calm down. I saw myself sitting on the front porch, waiting for Daddy to get home. I saw me and Mama eating dinner, the third place setting empty for the fourth time in a week. Saw myself sitting half-up in bed, stomach muscles cramped from going up and down each time the house creaked, thinking he was home and might poke his head into the room. Not even to say goodnight. Just to see that I was there.

I saw all those things, and pain twisted my insides, then left me hollow, then filled me with the color red, and all that red started to heat up, becoming a hot, hot furnace, a blazing barbecue pit of lonely that had been stoked for years.

"You *left me*," I yelled into the night, but a battling wind blew my words right back at me. "I would have gone anywhere with you, but you always left me behind!" I kicked dirt dust into his side. "Do you hear me, Daddy? Are you listening now? I hated you for that!"

"Ben." His voice cracked. "You didn't let me finish. I was going to tell you that there's a reason I'm not—"

"You could have taken me with you!" My mind raced all over the past. "I hid my drawing stuff in the couch and under my pillow, and I tried to have a golf grip you'd like, and, and . . . and I made you a comic strip! And I cut up pigs and I got arm burns!"

"Hey, nobody ever said—"

"And I *can* play sports, and I hit a triple on the dirt field once and I shot an 80 one day at the golf course once when you brought me with you, but you went off to play with your buddies."

"Hey, those *buddies* and I have been through more than you'll ever know, and—wait a minute. Hold on, did you say 80? Who-eee, Ben, that's incredible!"

"I threw out my score card," I said, my voice coming out hoarse, all the loudness yelled out of it. I looked into the fire, seeing May and Daddy and school and the Talbots' barbecue place and our café. I looked into the fire and everything was burning.

"You threw out the score card? Why on earth would you do that?"

My heart couldn't say it, but my body was in charge and the words poured out, they poured out like river water, like rinsing water, like the tears I couldn't cry because I'd been too busy trying not to turn into even less to him and blowing away. "I knew you'd be proud of me for it," I said. "And I wanted you to . . ." My heart was somewhere on the ground, and the golf ball lump sank with it, down to my belly, then back up to my throat. "I wanted to be enough for you without it."

"Ben." Daddy opened his urn mouth to say more, then didn't. After a long pause, he let out a big Daddy sigh. "I'm sorry."

He was sorry. My anger fizzled out at those words, like a firework dying in the sky. And the smoke left behind wasn't anything you could light up for another round. That was it. Show was over. My daddy was sorry that he couldn't love me enough. He was sorry that he couldn't love me the way that he loved golf. And here I was, mixing around with a mouthy runaway and risking my life jumping on and off trains to get him to a golf course.

Well, if that didn't make me the biggest sucker in Alabama, I don't know what did.

"I'm sorry, too, Daddy," I whispered. "I'm sorry about what I have to do."

We Both Lost

Daddy's urn and its shadow looked smaller in the firelight. He didn't say another word, not even to ask what it was that I had to do. He was done talking to me. Maybe he'd given up on me for good. Those thoughts made my next words feel stronger and flow easier. Made me know I was making the right decision—the only decision that made any sense.

"I'm not letting you leave me again," I told him. "I'll be doing the leaving this time. We're going back to Hilltop, and I'll leave you right on your shelf." I turned away. "Let's see you get to Augusta yourself."

"Hey." A tight grip squeezed my arm. "What are you talking about, Benjamin Putter?" Noni pulled me around to face her, then grabbed her bruised elbow, holding it like it hurt. "We're all going to Augusta."

"We're not," I said. "Trip's off." I pointed to Daddy. "I know it and he knows it. He's not even fighting back." I leaned down to the urn. "Round's over, Daddy. We both lost." I put on the backpack, scooped up the urn with one hand, picked up my fallen hat with the other, and started walking toward the farmhouse light in the distance.

"No!" Noni hurried ahead of me, then turned, blocking my path. "Where are you going?"

I pointed to the farmhouse. "I'm going to knock on that door, ask to call my mama to come get me tomorrow, and see if I can't spend the night inside. I don't feel like camping."

Noni's lips fell open and her heart leaped to her eyes, broken-looking. Then she narrowed those same sad eyes and shook her head. "We're going to Augusta, Benjamin Putter. And we're going to that tournament. Both of us."

I pushed her aside and kept going, ignoring the way she caught up and kept pace beside me. "It's over," I said calmly. "You're not in charge of me, got it? You think you can use me, the way he tried to. You still haven't told me anything about who you really are or why you're running. And you know what? I don't care. You can get to Augusta yourself, too."

"No." Banging against my shoulder, she stuck her face right in mine. "I don't know what story you plan on telling those farmhouse people, but you better beat me there if you want whoever's inside to believe you over me. Got it, crazy?" With that, she pulled Daddy from my arms and sprinted through the orchard.

Well, look at that, she did it again, a tree told me. *That's twice she's taken your daddy.*

And she stole the money that first night, one of its peaches added.

Oh, that's right! That makes three times that girl has taken off with your goods. Either she's a master thief, or you're just a—

"Oh, shut up," I said.

You shut up, the tree said back. *And run, boy. Run.*

I sprinted through the peach trees, branches hitting me as I skipped rows, weaving in and out, trying to find the best space to move. *Faster, faster,* a big branch said, whipping me like it thought smacking with words and wood could change what I was. Make me something both more and less human than Benjamin Putter.

"I'm done trying!" I yelled. "I'm going home!"

Go, go, the next ones said, like they hadn't heard me at all, hadn't heard me say right out loud that I was done trying, even though it was clearer than clear to me. My running was so wild that I fell twice. I looked up from the ground after the second fall, and Noni was nowhere in sight. As I cut around the side of another tree, a cluster of young peaches collided with my left eye and I slipped again. A glance up revealed Noni's silhouette leaping up porch steps and banging on a door.

She won, said the nearest peach trunk.

I agreed, and stayed down, catching my breath and wondering what exactly I'd lost. After a minute, maybe two or three, I rose and walked until I came to a row that lined up with the farmhouse light ahead. Furious thunder blasted far behind and above me, and I saw the booming sounds claw at the sky, get a grip on the wind, and get blown straight to me, where they echoed in my ears along with my heartbeat.

To the pounding beat of my blood pumping in a peach orchard, I scraped together a quick story. Then I forced myself to run the last hundred yards to reclaim what remained of my father: bone dust, ash, and a voice that I had finally spoken my mind to. He wasn't going to change, and even if he did, it was too late for us. Because talking to me or not, my daddy was dead.

And it was time to go home.

ROUND 2

HOLE 1

It's Me, Walter Hagen

Just before knocking on the door, I forced worry and brotherly concern into my expression, which was a big accomplishment considering my current feelings toward the girl who'd kidnapped my father. The farmhouse door opened to a woman in a bathrobe, and for a moment I forgot what I'd planned to say. Green foam rollers covered her head, and her tiny frame was smothered in a fluffy pale blue robe. I couldn't help thinking of Mama, who'd put her hair up like that the night before Daddy's memorial. Except instead of smelling like Mama's gardenia perfume, this woman smelled like butter and cooking spices. I shook off the memory and scent and plunged into my story, hoping I sounded sane but sufficiently desperate.

"Hello, ma'am, I'm Walter, and my sister Wendy just ran in here like some kind of maniac, didn't she?"

"Why, yes. In fact—"

"Anyway," I cut her off before I could forget my lines,

"our daddy died and she ran away with his urn and I went after her and then she jumped off the train like a darn lunatic and I had to jump off to save her and then she came running here and I came running too and you can't trust a thing she says and we need to get home!" I finished out of breath, proud of what I felt was a solid performance.

"Oh, sweetheart." With dry, gentle hands, the woman pulled me into a short front hall. "You come on in. I'm Joy Marino. Your sister was just telling me about you poor things." She stepped aside, revealing a lip-chewing Noni, who stopped her gnawing and rushed toward me.

I flinched, thinking she was about to smack me, but soon felt her arms squeezing me in a firm . . . hug?

"Oh, Walter," she wailed in a worried voice, "I told you to stay at the campsite and I'd come back for you."

"What?" I hated to admit it, but her pretend concern was a little stronger than mine.

Her chin lifted off my shoulder. "Mrs. Marino, ma'am, he was sucking his thumb and crying so badly, I didn't think he'd pull it together enough to follow me."

I pushed her away. "What do you think you're doing?" I spotted Daddy's urn, sitting on the hall table next to a clay peach full of plastic flowers. "See?" I said to Mrs. Marino. "She took it!"

Noni stepped back, and the two of them stood there, looking at me like I'd wet my pants and they felt real bad for me. They clucked together like two gossipy hens, and it hit me.

"You told her I'm crazy, didn't you?"

Noni shook her head mournfully and reached out to hold Mrs. Marino's hand. "I told you," she whispered loudly. "Mama says he's not quite right. He's so full of anger."

"You got that right." It took all I had not to find a whole pie in Mrs. Marino's kitchen and cram it in Noni's mouth to shut her up.

Knowing that another attempted hug would most likely get her a knee to the stomach, the traitor kept her distance but locked eyes with me. "I told her the truth, Walter. That you stole Daddy's urn and ran away. I could not *believe* it when you hopped on that train, but I had to protect you from yourself."

"Oh, come here, Walter." Mrs. Marino nodded, stepping closer to place a hand on my head. "And then you jumped off the train?"

"He did, and I had to follow," Noni said. "It hurt so much, but it was worth it because he's my brother and I'll take care of him no matter how crazy he is." She smiled sweetly at my slightly bared teeth.

"Is that where you got that bruise, honey? From falling?"

Noni looked at her elbow. "What?"

"That ugly bruise, dear. You got it from the train?"

"Oh." She looked at me. "Yeah."

Mrs. Marino moved her hand from my head to my cheek. "You poor boy. You must be very sad and hurt and lonely."

I had opened my mouth, but her assessment left me speechless.

Noni's big eyes were still aimed right at me. "I also told Mrs. Marino how heartbroken Mama would be if she knew you'd taken off with Daddy, and it's a good thing that she's over in Oklahoma visiting poor sick, dying Grandma at the Home this week, instead of at our house in Grink. And I told her how our older brother Willy will come pick us up tomorrow."

"Willy?" I asked.

"He's probably Peter's age," Noni said to Mrs. Marino, then dared to step closer so she could squeeze my hand. "Mrs. Marino was telling me about her son, who surprised her by applying to an engineering college far away. He got a full scholarship."

The woman nodded, her eyes turning misty. "We miss him terribly, and it was quite the shock. Mr. Marino and I never went to college. We always thought Peter would become the sixth generation on this farm, not want to put up skyscrapers. It's harder to be proud of something you don't understand, but we can't help being happy for him. He's a good boy."

"They bought Peter a *used truck* for graduation, thinking he'd use it around the farm," Noni said to me, squeezing again. "He didn't need it, so it's just been *sitting out by their barn.*"

Mrs. Marino smiled. "It was just a junker and probably couldn't hit forty miles an hour, but my husband sure was excited to give it to him. He told Peter we'd keep it for a year in case he changed his mind and wanted to come back to us and be a peach farmer like his daddy. I think a piece of him thinks if he leaves it in the same place, Peter will come back to us. I tell you what, though, that thing's an eyesore if you ask me."

"Mrs. Marino told me the truck still has a full tank and the keys are still right on the seat. Isn't that *so sweet?*" Noni said, then mouthed the word *Augusta*.

"No," I told her.

Noni frowned. "It's very sweet, if you just keep your mouth shut and *think about it*. Think about it *for me* if you can't for yourself."

I'd already told Daddy that we weren't going to Augusta, and now Noni wanted us to go there anyway, all so she could look for a sign that she would probably never find? I wasn't biting on that bait. If she wanted to steal a truck, that was her own business.

But I also didn't feel like charging out the door and finding a road so I could start walking back to Hilltop. And the thought of calling Mama and explaining everything and begging for a ride home suddenly wasn't too appealing. Truth was, I didn't feel like thinking about anything that night. I'd let Noni's story stick for now.

Mrs. Marino turned to Noni and glanced between the two of us. "Hmm. Well, you two must be worn out. Walter, your sister's about to call your brother." Mrs. Marino was speaking slowly, like she thought maybe I'd hit my head. "Why don't you come in the kitchen and have some peach cobbler made with last year's preserves. Mine's the best in three counties. Then we'll get you tucked into the guest room. Phone's in the family room, honey," she said to Noni, pointing. "Mr. Marino's in there, watching television. He'll tell you our address and some easy directions from Grink. Now, I have half a mind to call your mama, but I imagine that she's full up on troubles, what with your father and your grandmother." A bittersweet smile came to her face, and the thin lines beside her eyes bloomed and multiplied. "You know, I ran away from home once when I was sixteen. Mother wouldn't let me get a summer job as a lifeguard over at Chisolm Lake, and I was *so* mad."

"Did you run away to get the job?" Noni asked.

"No, dear. I made it about half a mile down the road and spent the night with my girlfriend Susie. And oh, did I get an earful the next day. Hope your brother's not too hard on you."

"Thank you, ma'am. I'll call him right now."

Within minutes, Noni was sitting next to me at the

kitchen table, shoving cobbler in her face while I rubbed my neck lump. "This is great, ma'am. I'm so sorry for the inconvenience. Can I use your bathroom?"

"Down the hall on the left." When Noni was gone, Mrs. Marino patted my hand. "It's good that your sister brought you both here."

I didn't say anything. It didn't matter what Mrs. Marino thought. I listened to her chat, holding a noiseless Daddy in my lap, suddenly feeling awfully sad and hurt and lonely, just like she'd said. And more tired than I'd ever been in my life.

I'm not all certain what happened after that, but there was the kitchen, warm with creamed-corn-amber-yellow walls, and a hanging painting of the farmhouse, and a hanging painting of peaches, and counters lined with jarred peaches, and Noni skipping into the room, her swinging arms knocking peaches right off the wall. There was gasping from her and Mrs. Marino, and an apology, and a turned-over frame on the floor with a crack down the middle of its back, and the painted farmhouse saying, *Look what she did*, and the broken frame crying, *What happened?* and a cutting board with a roller on the counter saying, *Shh, it'll be okay*, and there was a wet towel and a whistle from a kettle that sounded like a lonely train and a mug full of something steaming and thick, like the walls were a cow that had been milked and what came out was hot melted butter and honey.

There were long minutes spent at a table filled with

Daddy's silence, and there was me not asking if he was still there because the world had gone distant and I'd gone silent too and I was hurting and because you can't be seen talking to yourself in a stranger's house. There was some dusky talk that faded away. There were towels and a washcloth placed on a closed toilet lid, the door closing, and me washing up. There was a bed and me being pushed into it and told to stay.

There was a woman standing over me and me reaching for her rollers, saying *Mama*.

There was the woman hushing and murmuring words that didn't come out like words, but I knew they meant everything would be okay, maybe because this woman had magic just like Noni and could do spells, like the sleeping spell she was doing on me.

Could Be, Hope Not

When the curtains parted the next morning, I woke slowly in a soft bed filled with soft sheets, and for a moment I wondered if maybe Mama'd gotten mad, sold all of Daddy's golf equipment, and had gone overboard with the Sears catalog, ordering me a whole new bedroom and maybe a houseful of hats for herself.

There was a sweetroll scent to the air that made blinking awake comfortable until I realized a lady who was not my mama was staring at me expectantly, like I was an abandoned chicken she'd found and nursed back to health, and now she wanted me to get up and lay an egg or two.

"Good morning, Walter," said Mrs. Marino, the butter and cinnamon wafting off her like it had the night before. "You get up and we'll get you some breakfast. You look like you could use a good meal." She tapped the top of the backpack on the floor beside me. "I washed a few of your clothes.

Hope you don't mind. Wanted to play mother, I suppose, what with Peter gone."

First I'd adopted a bus station granny with urn-grabby hands, and now I'd gotten myself a peach farm mama who smelled like she was made out of French toast. I sat up, trying to recall exactly how I'd gotten those new family members and why none of them could replace the one who'd left me. "Hmm?" I said, sitting up.

"I was worried your sister's dress would stain, but I know a few tricks."

Speaking of tricky, said the curtains. *Where is that little liar?*

You better set her straight today, the bedside lamp advised.

Or kick her to the road, suggested the blanket.

"Thank you. Where's . . . Wendy?"

"She's eating. We thought we'd let you sleep in for a bit."

My head jerked around, searching for a clock and finding none. "What time is it?"

"It's a little past ten. You were up real late, so I thought I'd let you rest."

A cold splash of guilt swept over me, and I jumped out of bed, bumping a startled Mrs. Marino back toward the door. A little past ten o'clock on the first day of the Masters! My golf ball lump pressed hard against its prison, hissing that we'd missed it, we'd missed the opening, the first shot, Daddy's heroes traveling the holes. How in the world would we get to Augusta? And where exactly were we?

"Where's my daddy?" I asked Mrs. Marino, who stood there looking tongue-tied. "Where is he?" I demanded, looking around the room.

Psst, said the tall boy in a photograph. *Doesn't matter. You gave up, remember?*

"Oh." Then I did remember. I remembered the fight and the fact that I no longer had a mission.

Mrs. Marino pointed to the edge of my bed, where the urn was lying on its side. "You slept with it. Are you okay, dear?" Her hand went to her chest as she eyed the hallway. "Should I get your sister?"

I pulled myself together and rubbed at my face. Act how Noni was acting last night, I told myself. Nice and sweet. "Oh gosh, ma'am, I'm so sorry. I had the worst nightmare. I don't believe I was quite awake just then." I shivered my shoulders a little, still fake fearful from the fake nightmare. "Thank you for taking us in, Mrs. Marino. I don't know what I was thinking, running off like that."

You were trying to bring your daddy everlasting peace, the photograph reminded me.

But then you gave up, the ring on Mrs. Marino's hand said. *Not very nice.*

The hand left Mrs. Marino's chest and moved to my head. "That's all right, dear. You've had a shock. Your brother will be here soon. You get dressed and come eat, okay?"

"I will, ma'am."

She closed the door behind her, leaving the room quiet.

"Daddy?" I whispered. "Are you still there?"

Nothing.

I picked him up. "Daddy, are you in there?" I asked louder. "Please answer me." He wasn't snoring, so he was either ignoring me, or he was taking a break from me in purgatory and would be back, begging for me to change my mind, or . . . Well, I didn't want to think about the alternative. And I also didn't want to think about Noni, who'd told me to have a talk with Daddy in the first place. Hmph. I had a few words for her, too.

Down the hallway, I stepped past framed photographs of families in front of peach baskets, families staged in front of peach trees, kids with peach juice running down their faces. Happy faces. Good memories caught in time that had the magic to erase bad ones. I stopped and looked closer. As I stepped forward, they went back in time, clothes and trees in color, then black-and-white, then faded black-and-white, then almost yellowy. The last photograph, the one right next to the kitchen, was the oldest. The people were posed in front of the peach trees, standing beside a wooden wagon.

Other than the oldish look to the clothes on the man, woman, and three boys, you could tell it was years and years ago, because nobody smiled. Now everyone makes you smile, so you can look later and see how good life was.

The man in the oldest photograph was stubborn-looking.

Defiant. I wondered if his daddy had been a peach farmer, too. Maybe that man's daddy was a banker or a clock fixer and said to his son, *Why can't you just be a banker or a clock fixer? Wanting to grow peaches is a waste of time. You should get inside more, be more of a thinker.*

A hand touched my shoulder. "There you are, dear. Now, come and sit. Get your fill."

While I ignored Noni's light under-the-table kicks and ate pancakes in silence, Mrs. Marino chattered about this and that, but my ears were too full of my chewing to really hear much. Noni's Coca-Cola shirt and jeans had been washed, and her hair was neatly braided. It almost felt like we were really brother and sister, eating breakfast and getting ready for school.

"You two keep each other company until your brother Willy gets here. I'll be back in an hour to check on ya'll, okay? Mr. Marino's fixing a fence on the back nine acres if you need him. Walkie-talkie on the table'll reach him if ya'll need an adult before I get back," she said, leaving the room.

The minute she left, I kicked Noni a good one. "You're the worst partner in the world."

She had the nerve to look offended. "I am not. You're just not seeing the big picture."

"Oh, and the big picture is that now our fake brother is going to pick us up? Why'd you have to choose the name Willy, anyway?" Willy Walter was the biggest bully in Hilltop, and just hearing his first name made the ghosts of the bruises he'd given me ache and whimper.

"It was the only *W* I could think of. You're Walter. I'm Wendy. I figured we'd all be *W* names."

"You're a liar." I kicked her again.

"*Ow.* Is that right, *Walter Hagen*? Or did you want to be *Bobby Jones* again? I'm not going to kick you back, but that was unnecessary."

I kicked her a third time. "Do you mind telling me what on earth you're doing?" I asked. "Who did you call last night?"

She scooted her chair back, careful to keep her legs out of kicking distance. Leaning forward, she forked another bite of pancake and took her time chewing and swallowing. "I called the barbecue place where my daddy and I used to get take-out chicken. He hates using phones, so I always called. We ate there a lot, and I had the number memorized. Confused the heck out of them, especially when I started giving directions. Listen, as soon as the missus is off the property, I'll check around for supplies and we'll get going. It's late, but I figured extra sleep might put you in a better mood." She stood and peeked out of the window curtains. "I wish one of us had driven before, but we can figure out that truck. Can't be that hard. It's our best option by far."

"First you want to hop a train and now you want to steal a truck?"

Noni stuck her tongue out. "It sounds mean when you

say it like that. You heard Mrs. Marino—she said it was an eyesore. We'd be doing her a favor by taking it to Augusta. And driving on country roads can't be too dangerous." A hint of worry crossed her expression. "I don't think. If we don't go fast. Right?" Her shoulders finally fell. "Maybe it won't even start."

I shook my head and sipped on a glass of orange juice. "I can drive." The defeated look flew off her face, replaced with a slap of shock and glee and . . . Was that a little jealousy? My goodness, it was. I had Mama to thank for that. The few driving lessons I'd gotten were from her, not Daddy. She said that a country boy should learn that kind of thing early, and it was always good to have an extra driver in case of an emergency, so I'd taken the truck down the road and back a few times. I only hit Mrs. Grady's postbox twice. Barely dinged it.

"I *can* drive," I repeated carefully, "but country roads are bound to turn into bigger roads near Augusta. And, anyway, my trip's over. I need to find my way back to Hilltop."

She shook her head. "You need to change your plans, that's what you need to do. Because what *I* need is for you to drive me to find my sign. Don't be selfish just because you've already gotten your second chance." She raised her chin and leaned to the right, looking out the kitchen window again. "Maybe I'll check that chicken house outside for eggs."

"What? Why do you like eggs so much?"

She shrugged. "Eggs remind me of my daddy, I guess. He once ate seventeen boiled eggs in a contest. Couldn't get enough of them. And I'm glad you're on board with the truck idea. We'll be in Augusta in no time at all." She pushed aside her plate and looked across the table at me. She looked a long time, until she was sure that I saw her. "Benjamin Putter, I'm asking for your help."

"Tell me again, why's it got to be Augusta for you?" I asked, annoyed that her admiration for my driving talent had gotten watered down so quickly. "That was *my* daddy's dream. Why would your father leave you a sign there? Don't you have a place of your own to look?"

Her arms went limp. The bruise on her elbow seemed even darker than the day before. There wasn't any purple in it now, and it looked more like a band of darkest storm clouds, the same that were billowing outside the window. "I told you. I have faith that I'll find my miracle there."

"You think you'll find a miracle at Augusta just because you saw a couple of pictures of the place and read a few words about it? Noni, you shouldn't be looking for faith in a book full of golf course photographs. It's not like it's a Bible." Though that's exactly how Daddy talked about it. "You can find a better place to look."

She shook her head. "I'll find him at Augusta. There are some things that go beyond understanding. I *feel* it, Benjamin Putter. I just feel it, and . . . I'm afraid I'm running out of time." She stared at her lap. "If I don't find the right sign there soon, I never will."

The glow of hope and confidence I'd seen shining off her in the peach orchard had faded. It was up to me whether or not she'd lose it altogether. Daddy'd said that things were impossible right up until they weren't. I wanted to believe him. And something in me wanted to help her. Even if my own journey was done.

"Please, Benjamin Putter. I thought you were my friend."

Goshdarn it. For the first time she truly did remind me of May Talbot, sitting far across the school cafeteria, staring at me and saying those same words with her eyes. Telling me something I already knew—that not standing up, walking over, and asking to sit beside her made me the same as every white person who thought that colored students should have their own table. Not standing up made me the same as everybody who thought May was different. Who thought she was less and that she deserved to be kept apart.

"I'll get Daddy and the backpack," I said. "I'll drive you there, and then you're on your own. Don't take too much provision stuff, Noni. We're about to borrow their son's truck and—"

She was over the table before I knew it, her arms around me. "You won't regret this. You might even change your mind about your daddy between now and then. And I won't take too much stuff, but I can think of one small way we can pay them back." She raised her eyebrows and made a wiggly painting motion in the air with her fingers. "Better make it fast, though." She glanced at the small clock in her room. "That Hobart Crane fellow your daddy likes so much is already playing golf. Think you can finish in fifteen minutes?"

"No."

"Well, try. You ever finish up that drawing with the good eyes?"

"I got a little more done, but no."

"Finish it sometime. That one is gonna be good, I can tell," she said.

I got out my paint box and opened it up at the kitchen table. Noni and I were leaving soon, and I felt her taking charge again, but I'd be the one driving, and that was something. And maybe I'd caught a little of her magic, because I knew what the Marinos needed me to paint for them.

I took out one of the two small canvas frames I had in my box. It was only five inches by five inches, but it'd work good. It was meant for oil paint, I think, but Mama must not have known the difference. I'd come home from a day of school that'd been empty other than getting my pencil stuck in Erin Courtney's hair, and it'd been the best surprise ever to see four small canvases stretched over wooden frames, sitting on my bed like it was Christmas. When I made the first painting and handed it to Mama as a thanks for being the best mama ever, she'd blushed and said, *Aren't those a trick? Where'd those fancy things come from?*

I took one of the jars from the Marinos' counter and studied the picture on the label for a moment, mixing colors until I thought I had the right ones. Then I got a mug of water for rinsing and started out by staring at the back of my eyelids.

Even if it was just for a second, Miss Stone had told me to always start a painting or drawing by visualizing what I wanted to do and how I'd get there. I'd learned that unless I was just experimenting, I needed to be confident in my strokes. If something went wrong and I got off course, I'd make adjustments, adding a little red or yellow or white, fixing mistakes as I went along, focusing on the finished picture. Always keeping that image in my mind until I got there, or got as close as possible without starting over. With my time limit, I didn't have the option of starting over.

Take a good look, then close your eyes, Ben.

Pinks, yellows, reds.

Now find your grip. Feel it.

Browns, a hint of green leaf.

Keep your eyes closed and see the hole. See the distance between where the ball is and where it needs to be.

Lighter shades in the place where the light hit the fruit.

Now feel yourself swing. Feel how easy it should be. It should be easy, feel right, not forced. See the ball going there, right there, right where it belongs.

A dark gray for the small shadow around the base.

Send the ball home.

I opened my eyes, touched the paintbrush's handle against the lump in my throat, and started painting. Stroke by stroke, seeing it all play out like it had in my head.

The colors layered on one another, thicker than I normally would do, making the painting textured, making it look like all I had to do was reach out, just reach out and the fruit would be mine. All I had to do was take what I wanted. But I couldn't, of course. It was stuck to paper. Forever out of reach.

The painted peach was still drying on the kitchen table when I packed up and walked out the door to take Peter Marino's graduation gift for a drive to Augusta, Georgia. I'd drop Noni off and turn around. Only one thing held me back from feeling right about that. I still had to get rid of the golf ball stuck in my throat. I knew it wouldn't leave me if I went back to Hilltop. Was it possible that the ball in my throat wanted to get to Augusta as much as Daddy did?

Maybe Noni was right. Maybe I should think about giving Daddy and me one more chance.

It might be too late, the porch floor creaked beneath me.

That's right, he's been awfully quiet, said the steps.

He might already be gone forever, said the ground between me and the rusted truck.

"Could be," I said back. "Hope not."

HOLE 3

Empty Roads

Big Fiver Byron Nelson said that one way to break up any kind of tension is good deep breathing. He was wrong. I breathed in the lingering scent of Mrs. Marino's pancake breakfast clinging to my clothes and tried to be patient, but the truck wasn't cooperating. I'd managed to get a promising whirring sound out of it twice, but the engine cut out every time I tried to move my right foot from the brakes to the gas. The truck's pedals were too far away to stay seated, so I was half standing in the driver's seat, my eyes shifting from the clutch to the orchard, praying that Mr. Marino didn't finish mending his fence too soon.

"Just start the darn thing!" Noni said, her feet dangling off the passenger seat, swaying next to a half loaf of bread, a container of peanut butter, a jar of pickles, and two lengths of camping rope she'd found in a closet. She had a lapful of eggs, too. "I thought you knew how to drive!" She turned and looked back at the driveway. "The missus might get back early, so hurry it up!"

"I'm trying," I said, teeth clenched while I pushed in the clutch, started the engine, then gave it a little gas. I wished Daddy was talking so I could get advice on the right way to let off the clutch. "And you might be a little nicer."

She shrugged. "I might, but then I'd be somebody else and not me, in which case you wouldn't be about to borrow a truck so you can drive me and your daddy to Augusta National Golf Club. And *you* might be nicer to *me* for not letting you get stubborn and ruin your dead talking daddy's dream. Now you've got a chance to do the right thing. You would have felt guilty the rest of your life, and nothing's uglier to feel than guilt."

May Talbot's face flashed in the windshield for a second before I blinked her away.

Noni gave herself a little harrumph of approval. "And I'm not mean, I just know how to speak my mind. You should try it sometime."

The engine died again. I'd give it a few seconds before trying another time. "It's hard to get a word in with you, unless you're stuffing your face with pie or cobbler. And I did try speaking my mind and now my dead talking daddy won't talk anymore."

"Oh." Her voice lost some of its sharpness. "Sorry. I'm sure he's just taking a break."

"Maybe." I picked up the urn and gave it a good shake, hoping he'd shout at me to stop. He didn't. This was the longest he'd gone without talking since he'd spooked me back in the kitchen. Letting my anger loose to his shiny urn face had freed up space inside me, but him going silent afterward made me sick to my stomach. Like I'd blown the best chance I'd ever gotten to make him proud of me. To make him *see* me.

I put my grit and worry into turning the key again. The entire truck sputtered like it had before, then sighed with relief along with me as it roared to life.

Woo-hoo, thank you! it shouted. *Been waiting for this, let's drive!*

I gave the dashboard a pat, looked in the rearview mirror, and backed up, trying not to hit the barn. "Get the map out, Noni. Let's figure out where we're going."

"How're we gonna do that?" she asked.

Shifting into first gear, nervous sweat sinking down my side, I rolled us down the Marinos' long driveway and paused. The sun was just under halfway up the sky to my left. East. I turned toward it, ignoring the arm Noni'd flung out to steady my own.

"Geez, take it easy," she said. "Don't fly off the road."

So she was nervous about driving, too. That made me feel a little better. I shifted into second gear. "Look at the road atlas and flip to the Georgia map. You gave the Marinos' address to that barbecue place, didn't you? What town are we in?"

"Feather."

"Then find Feather."

She brought her legs up on the seat with her, holding the map close, her finger going up, then down, shifting left to right. Finally, after what seemed like forever, she laughed. "There we are! We're about halfway through Georgia, halfway down. Looks like that train was going a little south. Sorry about that. Keep heading east and north a little, stay off the big roads, and we've got maybe this much left." She held out her hand, showing me the distance between her widespread index finger and thumb. "Two hundred miles, maybe."

"I hope we can get two hundred miles on one tank of gas."

We drove past peach farm after peach farm, all of them with trees lined up nicely in a row, standing in the places they should be, doing their jobs right. I wondered if any of those trees ever wanted to run away and go join a pecan grove instead, or if they all felt like the peach orchard fit them perfect.

The roads weren't completely smooth, but after the stop signs became few and far between, I got comfortable enough to put the truck into third gear and was content to stay there. There was something magical about driving down a road, just me and a mysterious girl who, try as I might, I couldn't stay mad at. I grinned and tilted my head Noni's way. "Told you I could drive."

"Indeed you can, Benjamin Putter. But there's still plenty of time for a wreck, so pay attention." She twisted open the pickle jar. "Pickle?" She stuck a spear next to my face. "I'll hold it for you."

"No, thanks."

I wished Daddy could have seen me driving when he was alive. The golf ball in my throat grew heavy at the thought of him, the whole him, sitting beside me, maybe giving a lesson, correcting my grip on the steering wheel the same way he did with golf clubs.

I shifted my stance. It was uncomfortable driving like that, but it looked like we'd maybe make it to Augusta if the car didn't die on us. I wouldn't go too fast, not wanting to break the engine or get pulled over. We'd be okay. In the back of my mind, I wondered what I would do once I got there. Should I stay with Noni? If we made it onto the grounds, should I scatter Daddy even if his voice didn't show up again, telling me to do it? Or should I do like I said back at the orchard and take him back to Hilltop?

"Pass me Daddy, will you?"

Noni tucked Daddy beside me, anchoring him with the pickle and peanut butter jars. I glanced at the black line declaring the gas tank to be full, hoping it wouldn't sink down too fast.

Aw, don't worry, the gas gauge said. *I'll stop when I stop, nothing you can do to change it.*

When we realized that empty roads made for somewhat relaxing driving, we played with the radio and soon were singing along, shouting out made-up lyrics to the songs we didn't know, Noni and me trading high and low notes, mixing voices together in a way that sounded like something between two crows fighting, two sheep laughing, and two pieces of sunshine slamming into the windshield, like if we sang loud enough we could blast away the clouds filling the sky.

Daddy was a terrible singer. He used to serenade Mama at the café, screeching loud in an off-key voice every time he brought a load of meat in from the pit, embarrassing her until she'd sing a few lines for him, give him a kiss, and tell him to get on back.

After a time, the radio stations all turned to static or adults talking about things we didn't care about, and we let silence take over. It took me a while to get up the courage to say my next words. I tried to keep my voice real casual. "Hey, Noni, tell me something about you."

She shuffled around, trying to get comfortable. "I already said I'm not ready to tell you the whole truth yet. I don't know why you can't keep your nose out of my business."

And I don't know why her business had to hop onto your business, the steering wheel harrumphed. *She's an Augusta thief, that's what she is.*

"Noni, take the wheel for a second, will you?" With a white-knuckled grip, she held both her breath and the wheel while I shifted my position. "Thanks. Well, how about some little truths? You've already told me a couple. A few more couldn't hurt."

"I don't know." Keeping her eyes on her lap, she reached

in her pocket, touching but not removing something. I thought it was her wandering rules, but when I glanced over quickly, I saw a folded piece of newspaper sticking out—the one I'd seen in her pocket at Darry's café.

Her hand pushed, shoving it out of sight. "Fine. Little truths, that's it. Noni's a nickname. I like pork with a lotta sauce. And I can read lips. That's how I knew what you said to May back at your house."

"How'd you learn that?"

"Seemed interesting, so I tried. It's not as hard as you might think."

"Okay." I looked over at her, hoping for more.

"I always wanted a brother or a sister."

"Me too."

"My daddy and I talked all the time, every day, but it's not the same as having someone close to your age around." She tucked her knees up and wrapped her arms around, like she wasn't sure if little truths were allowed after all. "I lived near a train track—told you that already. There was something about that railroad yard in Hilltop that made me ache the minute I saw it. Same thing when we hopped the coal train. And, well . . ." She squirmed against her door and squinted at the sun. "There's something else. Something bad I did."

This is it, I thought. *She'll tell me about that bruise.* "It's okay. You can tell me."

"I took something from my father on the day that he left me forever. His favorite thing in the world. Something that he loved most."

"What did you take?"

A corner of her lip disappeared into her mouth, and she chewed. Her fingers lifted in the air, and she closed her eyes, reaching. The hand dropped with a dull thud against her thigh. "I don't want to say. But I was mad at him for taking me with him everywhere and not letting me go to regular school, so I took it." She sighed. "He said school wouldn't suit me anyway, because I had a fiery personality and a dragon's temper. He said I could try to make friends anywhere, even traveling, I just needed to be more friendly. Who knows what that means, though."

"What? You've got a temper?" A smack on the arm was my answer. "Sorry. Thought maybe I'd gotten good at jokes." I turned my head from the road to see Noni resting her head on curled up knees.

Fingers digging through her sock, she found the scrap of paper with her wandering rules on it, studying them. "I can still see myself taking it," she said. "And then I lost it and couldn't get it back. I tried, but just got stuck. I called for help, but he didn't hear me. Then the thing I took from him was gone." The paper disappeared into her sock. "And then he was gone, too."

She put her legs back down. "Part of me thinks if I get it back somehow, he'll be okay, wherever he is. And then maybe

I can find a home without him." She unscrewed the pickle jar again and took out a big spear, the juice dripping all over her shirt while she crunched through it. "Stupid, I know."

"It's not stupid."

She took the backpack and put it against her door, leaning against it. Her left arm lay limply by her side. "I'm gonna rest my eyes. Do some thinking."

I looked at her elbow bruise again. It almost looked alive, like it would talk if a person took enough time to really listen. A *reminder*, she'd said, *to follow the rules*. The bruise was like a solid cuff, chaining her to something I couldn't wrap my head around. If someone had been beating on her or grabbing her, which had crossed my mind, the mark left behind wouldn't be so even. For the life of me, I couldn't imagine what thing or situation would cause something like it, or why it didn't seem to be getting better, while the smoker burn on my arm from earlier that week had hardened already, shelled over with new skin.

While Noni slept, I drove on, staying on country roads and driving a steady thirty, thirty-five miles an hour. Any faster and the engine started sounding funny. I stopped to pee on the side of the road one time, and Noni tapped me once to do the same. Soon enough, it was an hour or two before twilight. We'd already missed tournament play for the day. I figured if we got to Augusta that evening, we'd have plenty of time to stick with our plan of trying to sneak over the fence somehow. And getting into town at night would work to our advantage, people in general not reacting well to almost-twelve-year-old drivers.

I rolled my window down and let the last two days blow into me as I steered the truck, Augusta calling us closer. Dark, mean clouds filled the rearview mirror. We were surrounded by them now, like they were boxing me into a smaller and smaller space until I'd have no place to run away from the fact that Daddy was gone and I had to go back. No place to run from facing whatever waited for me in Hilltop.

Noni's father had told her that people meet up with their life on the road they take to run away from it. Was my life hidden ahead somewhere, or was my life chasing after me, begging me to wait and give it a second chance, clawing at me the way last night's thunder had clawed at the wind?

I murmured the questions out loud, hoping something in the truck or the road or the scenery would answer me. But all those things were as quiet as the road was empty. We'd barely passed a single person, and I found myself wondering if a road could feel lonely.

"Daddy?"

He didn't answer. The hum of the truck became louder in his silence. The vibrations almost hurt my ears.

The gas tank was getting low. Real low. Almost empty, and it was starting to grow dark. I fumbled for the map, tucked into Noni's arm, and checked the place names covering the Georgia page against the last town we'd passed through. We'd driven a little too far east, trying to stay on country roads. We'd turned north at some point, staying along the Savannah River, which separated Georgia from South Carolina, and to my surprise we were no more than fifteen or twenty miles south of the black circle marked AUGUSTA. I felt a surge of warm, golden relief shoot through me, and I let out a bark of laughter.

When I looked up, it was too late, and my startled laugh became a horrified yell that woke Noni, who screamed and pointed.

"Look out!" she yelled. "Turn the wheel, crazy!"

It was too late to tell her to put her seat belt on.

It was too late to realize that mine wasn't on either.

It was too late all around, but I slammed on the brakes anyway, wrenching the wheel to the right so we'd miss the front cab of the truck that had snuck out from a tiny side road without me noticing. The driver didn't see me either and was pulling out with a long, rickety platform hooked up behind him filled up and stacked five cages high with—

"Chickens!" Noni yelled. She wrenched the wheel far to the right, aiming us into the side ditch and right toward a huge oak, looming over us with Spanish moss that I had a feeling wouldn't do cow plop to cushion the blow of a crash.

I hip-shoved her off me and turned the wheel back left a few inches. "Better chickens than us!"

I swear, life slowed in that moment, and those chickens all turned together, staring us down like they were preparing for battle. Ten feet from impact, it occurred to me what was happening. The most famous chicken in Hilltop, Mrs. Clucksy, had some kind of psychic connection with chickens in Georgia, and she'd sent out a call for revenge. She might have gotten her precious cash egg stolen, but I was about to pay the price for messing with her.

Good Lord, I could almost hear her cackling into her beer nuts.

In those seconds before we slammed together and became one big mess, vengeance-based bravery abandoned Mrs. Clucksy's soldiers. The wild panic of those chickens, the helpless flapping of their wings as they put all their effort into trying to escape from the flimsy, thin metal bars that held them back—it was like a mirror rushing closer and closer until I was forced to look deep inside. And those chickens must have felt the same way, because the group of them, all as one, called out just before I crashed into them, and our thoughts were a perfect match.

Please stop! followed by

I'm not ready! followed by

I hope you choke on your next whiskey shot, Clucksy! followed by

Goshdarnit, this is gonna hurt.

Chickenland

A tidal wave of water rushed into my face, and I blinked enough to see Noni's big eyeballs and mouth shouting things I couldn't hear. Dizzy, head throbbing, and half-drowned, I let myself be pulled from the truck and walked to the side of the road. I moved my head in the white and brown feather blizzard snowing down on me, then collapsed on the ground.

Frenzied, flapping wings and a heavy brown feather pillow smashed into my face. I shoved it aside and curled up as a pointy thing, or maybe two pointy things, poked and pecked at my belly. Wrenching myself to one side, I managed to jerk clear enough of the whirlwind to see that the world had transformed into Chickenland, openmouthed squawks and irate fowl filling every inch of my vision.

I didn't need Noni around to read their lips. They were mad at me, and in addition to serving as Mrs. Clucksy's henchmen seeking revenge for the stolen egg, they also seemed to know that Mama was bargaining with the bank so we could add barbecued chicken to Pork Heaven's menu.

Squawk, *Thief!*

Squawk, *Butcher!*

Squawk, *Barbecue THIS!*

Chicken cages lay scattered across the road, some open and empty, the full ones holding hens looking plenty upset that they'd missed their chance to peck at my thieving, smoker-stoking hands. The truck we'd hit was parked sideways in the middle of the main road, and a hairy faced man was chasing a chicken beside it, trying to keep two others under his arm while yelling obscenities.

Frantic tire marks were visible in the packed dirt road he'd left. A set of black, burned-rubber tracks veered off the concrete road, turning into smashed-grass tracks and ending at the Marinos' truck, which had a smashed bumper on the left side.

Noni's hand felt my forehead and her lips were doing something. Moving. Talking while an arm lifted our water bottle over my head like she was about to douse me again.

"What happened?" I asked, shoving the bottle aside.

Her eyebrows sprang apart, and Noni hugged me hard. "You're okay. We clipped the edge of the chicken platform and you got knocked around."

"Daddy," I said, and there was the urn in my face.

"He's fine. Now get up."

"You okay, son? This girl here told me you were both fine." Hairy Face stepped near me and studied my eyes, a stray feather stuck to the side of his angry mouth. "You nearly killed all of us."

"Don't exaggerate," Noni told him, batting a charging hen to the side. "There's one dead chicken in all this mess, and you're probably on your way to sell them to a grocery store anyway. And you're the one who pulled out without looking," she snapped.

"Louise was my best egg layer, young lady. And if you're gonna bring up rules of driving, you both look a little young to have a license. Where are your parents? Whose truck is that?"

"What?" I asked, and sat up, pain spots clamoring for attention all over my body. Pain, but not the broken bones kind. I sat fully upright and touched my sore tongue, my fingers coming back a little red where I'd bitten it. "Did I faint or something?"

"No," Noni said. "I don't think so. You were mumbling and moaning to yourself, which isn't too out of the ordinary now that I think on it, but your eyes weren't shut more than a minute."

"Are you okay?" My arms and legs were full of aches and pains, but she seemed fine.

"Eggs got smashed, but that's about it." She ran over to the ditch where our truck had ended up and pulled out the backpack and map. "This gave me a good cushion. You were standing up in that weird position and—"

"You two better come along with me," the man said, putting a hand on Noni's elbow.

She jumped away like he'd been trying to slice through her arm. "No way."

"There's a local police station not ten minutes from here. You can call your parents from there." He looked at Peter's truck. "And I can give them the license plate of your little joyride if it doesn't belong to your folks."

"Wait!" I said. I got up, stumbled around, then fell and put a hand to my head. "I think we should listen to him, little sister. I don't think . . . I think . . . I think I should get to a doctor. I don't feel right." I screwed up my face. "I think I'm gonna puke." I turned away from him, managing to catch Noni's eye with a wink.

Immediately, the man's annoyance turned to concern. "I've got two boys that play football. Vomiting's a sign of concussion. You need to see a doctor. Here, I'll help you into my truck."

He held out a hand and Noni slapped it away. "Are you crazy! We're not getting in a truck with a *stranger*, especially one who uses foul language while chasing his chickens. Go drive to the police station and send an officer our way. We'll trust one of them, but you could be a complete loony case. You could want to kidnap us for ransom money."

"Or sell us for drug money," I said.

"Or sell us to a circus," Noni added.

"Or kill us," I chimed in.

"And then eat us," Noni nodded, reaching a protective arm around me. "Mama says there are all kinds of weirdos in the world."

"Well, for God's sake, I'm not one of them."

"Well," Noni said, pointedly looking at the feathers in his hair and the scared-chicken poop all over his shirt. "You're not doing a great job of proving it."

Looking conflicted while a trio of hens made their way into the ditch to peck for bugs, the man hurried to his truck. "Fine. I'll be back with an officer for you, and to pick up my chickens."

The moment he'd driven out of sight, we ran to Peter's truck. "That was quick thinking," I said.

"You, too." Noni climbed into the seat, then sighed and hopped out. She ran to the front of the truck cab, bent down, and I saw a wad of white go flying past. She hurried back and strapped in. "Didn't want another Louise on our conscience. Let's get out of here. Backtrack a little and then take a different side road."

After five minutes of trying, I couldn't get the engine to turn over. The one time it did, the truck died before I could get us out of the ditch.

"Maybe your daddy knows what to do," Noni said. "Ask him."

I tried, but Daddy still wouldn't speak. "Oh no." I tapped

the gas gauge. "Empty. That man'll be back any minute now. And we're only fifteen miles or so away from Augusta." I let my forehead drop against the wheel.

Noni pointed across a nearby field to where a forest started. "Let's go." She heaved the straps over her shoulders and looked at me. "Sure you're good to walk?"

I was sore all over, but there were still miles to go and the sky overhead was dark and hard to read. What day was it? Thursday. Close to Thursday night. The first day of the Masters was over already. "I think we better run."

Only after hiding ourselves among the trees did we realize that we'd left the food in the front seat. When Noni stepped to the edge of the woods to look, the man had arrived back at the Marinos' truck, along with a police car. They would check the glove box and find the registration and return it to the Marinos. There was nothing to do but sip on water. I didn't realize how exhausted I was from driving, but I felt my eyes wanting to close in spite of myself.

"We can rest for a while, Benjamin Putter, and then let's get walking." Without asking, she gathered stones for a ring, twigs and sticks, and lit a fire. Both of us sat watching it, hearing crickets, locusts, light wind rustling through branches. Critters scuffling and distant bird calls. Crackling wood. I got out the photograph of Mama and set it on a rock.

"You miss her?" Noni asked.

I didn't answer the question. "Maybe you could live with us."

"What?"

I picked up the photograph. "Mama always wanted a girl. They wanted more kids, but I guess they just couldn't have any. You could live with us."

She shook her head. "No." She opened her mouth to say more, then closed it again.

"Why not? What are you gonna do after you find your sign? Just disappear?"

She looked into the fire. "That's one of my specialties. I just remembered another wandering rule: Don't get too comfortable or think you belong. When it's time to leave, leave. I'll be fine. But that's real nice of you to say that, Benjamin Putter."

I felt the disappointment hit me low in the gut, clutching and clenching. Then again, maybe it was just hunger gnawing at me. It was hard to say. "Will you sing something?" I asked. "Maybe that song from before."

"Okay." Facing the flames, Noni let her voice out loose and lower than seemed possible for her little body, like she was channeling the person who'd taught her the song.

Hard times behind me, hard times ahead,
This train here don't stop 'til your dead.

Train is rolling, can't slow it down,
So ride those rails 'til you under the ground.
Saw a good man climb, saw a bad man fall,
Think they was the same man after all.
Gone wandering, Lord, got my wandering card,
Wandering, wonder why life's so hard,
Found my time on the rail, found a dry way to sail,
Gone wandering, Lord, to my home.
Been trying to find my home.
And I'll die on this rail, it's my home.

Her voice was even more haunting than the last time I'd heard it. "Your daddy taught you that song?" I glanced over and caught her grimacing at some memory.

"Yep. I think he liked those songs because they're mostly lonely. When my mother died, he must have felt that way, too."

"Where are you going to go after Augusta?"

She shot me a Noni glare. "Chicago, Atlanta, the ocean, the desert, the sky, the mountains. Pick one and quit asking. That's for me to worry about."

Between Daddy's silence and Noni's secrecy, I was starting to feel colors bubbling inside me again. It wasn't fair that screaming a few truths made Daddy go away. It wasn't fair that I'd done what Noni wanted by taking the truck and still she was holding back from telling me things. It wasn't fair that I didn't know how to fix things between me and May.

I felt myself march through a line, thin as a single paint-brush thread, and something inside me broke. "What kind of person tags along on someone else's trip so she can find a sign from her dead father? For all I know, you've got fos-ter parents chasing after you, and I'll end up in trouble." I pointed to her bruise. "Or maybe somebody hurt you, and you're running from them."

She picked up a rock and threw it against a tree, hard.

Then another one.

And another.

"Just tell me the truth," I said. "I'll believe you."

"I'll find the right sign," she snapped. "I have to. I don't want to talk to you anymore right now. I'm exhausted, okay? And I don't need anyone to believe me, got it? The only thing I need is for someone to believe *in* me. I thought that person was you." With that, she rolled over and didn't say another word.

Nice going, Putter, said the pile of camping rope. *Now the alive person isn't talking to you either.*

I didn't answer or throw it in the fire, like I was tempted to. The rope was right.

I was alone.

Night Sounds

I added sticks to the fire, seeing Noni's eyes flutter and shut. I knew we had to get going soon, but something in me wanted a reason not to move on. I'd give us one painting's worth of rest time. Maybe two, then we'd get going.

I got out my box and, after thinking for a little bit, I drew water. More water in watercolor for May Talbot, who, like Noni, didn't want to talk to me anymore. Who, like Noni, probably just wanted a person to believe in her. Who, like Noni, maybe thought that person was supposed to be me.

Capping the Savannah River in white here and there to show movement and adding streaks for that reason as well, I made green tree shapes on a brown shore and had my river turning a corner to I-don't-know-where. With a shaky hand, I touched my brush to gray and drew a small object, barely visible, right near the river bend. I imagined that the urn had been swept down the length of water and was about to disappear, having no way to stop.

In the barely there light of the fire, I watched that gray spot, waiting for it to do something to save itself. Maybe I'd draw a log sticking out to catch it. I touched the brush to gray again and pressed it on the object, letting it grow until it became something else. It became a boy.

Wait, the boy was saying. *Wait Daddy, please wait, see how I drove a truck for you, I drove it far, I've come so far, I'm a man of action now, don't you see me, just wait and you'll be able to see—*

A fire spark hit my cheek, and I struggled to make sense of everything. It was like the world was moving too slow and too fast, the journey to Augusta going too slow and too fast, so slow and so fast that I couldn't stop it, only watch, I couldn't ever stop it, I couldn't ever stop Daddy from dying, from leaving, I could only take a breath of air and get water instead.

It was Augusta that had started this. Augusta National Golf Club. Augusta had been pulling on me since Hilltop, teasing with obstacles while drawing me closer, letting me know exactly who was in charge of this journey.

Augusta had brought Noni and her strange bruise to Pork Heaven.

Augusta made that bus crash into a pig.

Augusta blew enough wind behind me as I ran that I caught up to a moving train.

Augusta yanked me into a peach orchard, then urged

me down the road in the used truck that belonged to a boy whose father was proud of him.

Augusta pushed me past the town of Feather only to be blocked by a truck pulling a load of chickens.

Augusta was pulling and shoving me toward it the whole time, poking gentle, then hard, tugging and pushing and dragging me toward the greatest golf course in the world, where Daddy wanted me to crack open his urn, see his ashes, and say the hardest goodbye I'd ever have to say.

I didn't know how to stop any of it.

Some things were impossible to fight. Some things you didn't have any control over. Some things just happened to you and it took everything you had to whisper to the world that you'd keep trying.

I added a black rock to the very, very end of the river scene and hoped the boy would catch it before he was rushed off the side of the painting into the real world, where he didn't belong.

I'd just set that painting aside to dry and started on another when Daddy's waking-up sounds broke me from the picture. I stifled the urge to hide my art supplies when he stretched out his throat with grumbles and low coughs. And then he spoke.

"Hey, Ben. Whatcha doing?"

His voice was hesitant and weak, but the relief I felt was so intense, it was almost painful.

Thank God! was my first thought.

You don't want to know what I'm doing, was the second.

"Ben? Are you there?" He didn't sound mad at all. Maybe he wanted to forget that I'd yelled at him.

"I'm here." I felt both wary and bold with him. I didn't want to drive him away again, but if screaming at him like I'd done in the orchard didn't do the trick, I figured not much would. "I'm . . . I'm painting, Daddy."

"Huh. What are you painting?"

"A sunset." I took a chance. "It's one of the things that works best with watercolors because everything melts together just like the sky does."

"Well, you always did like to make pictures. You're pretty good, if I recall."

I smiled to myself. "I've won a few prizes."

"That right? How come this is the first I'm hearing about it?"

"I never brought them home."

"Oh." He cleared his throat. "Why not?"

"You never seemed to care about stuff like that. So I stopped showing you."

"Oh," he said again. "Well, I'm not all that smart, Benjamin." His voice winked. "All God's work went into my good looks. I probably wouldn't have said the right thing, anyway."

Maybe I hadn't said the right things either. Maybe I should have said more. Tried harder. Mrs. Marino showed up in my brain. *It's harder to be proud of something you don't understand.*

I rubbed my neck. "Before my art teacher, Miss Stone, left, she gave me her phone number and said if I wanted extra lessons, she would help me. She said that there were schools for people who get really good at drawing and painting, and there were competitions I could enter. She said she'd write me recommendations. She's called, but I haven't called back." I paused and waited for him to snort or say I'd better keep up the barbecue business, or worse, say nothing, letting the silence fill with words anyway.

Instead, Daddy whistled. "You don't say. That's something. So you're that good, huh?"

The day Miss Stone had told me she'd never seen such talent as she saw in my watercolor paintings had been the best day of my life. The glow I'd felt was like ten of Daddy's "good boy"s. But I didn't want to hurt his feelings, him wanting me to get my glows from barbecue and golf. "I'm getting better. Each one still takes me time. You know, Bobby Jones had a quote that makes me think of painting."

Now he snorted. "You don't say. Well?"

"He said, 'It's nothing new or original to say that golf is played one stroke at a time. But it took me many years to realize it.' Drawing and painting is kind of the same way for me."

"Wise man, that Mr. Jones." I saw Daddy nod to himself.

"Lots of things are like that, you know, Ben. Being a father is like that."

"Oh." There was something changed in Daddy. Like he'd softened up in a way that I'd only ever heard in his voice when he was telling me those few Abbott Meyers stories. This talk we were having felt real, like it was the right time to ask a question that had been weighing on me since his death.

"Daddy, did you know you were gonna die?"

A heavy sigh was followed by a heavy cough. "I guess nobody knows for sure. The odds of me coming out of that operating room alive weren't good." Another sigh, a slightly shaking one, like his urn was close to overflowing with whatever he was feeling. "I told your mother to stay hopeful. It wasn't a lie. It was the right thing to say." He paused, and I saw his eyes squint together. I saw him reach out a finger and thumb, squeezing the bridge of his nose the way he did when he was apologizing to Mama. "Those were the last words I said to her before they knocked me out. I held her hand and told her to stay hopeful."

It was almost too much, hearing that. I felt nearly overflowing with something myself.

"Nobody lives forever, Ben. You know what Walter Hagen said. You're only—"

"—here for a short visit," I supplied. "Don't hurry, don't worry. And be sure to smell the flowers along the way."

"Smart boy. So, are we back in Hilltop yet?"

"Huh?" Wait. Daddy thought we were still going back to Hilltop. He thought I'd given up on him. He didn't know that I'd changed my mind.

And he still sat there and asked you about your painting, the fire said. *And he answered one of the questions you've been wanting to ask him. Without expecting anything in return.*

He sure did, said my throat lump. *Now, isn't that something?*

It *was* something. It was something powerful enough to sway me into a decision on whether or not I'd be turning around after getting Noni to Augusta.

"No. We're not in Hilltop," I told him. "We're one long walk away from Abbott Meyer's hometown. We missed the first day of the Masters, but I'm gonna do my best to get you in there and get you settled by tee time on Sunday."

Daddy sputtered and hooted and perked up like I'd poured a pot of extra strong coffee on his ashes. "Hot dog! I mean, hot *dog*! Do you mean it?" He whooped a few more times, and I saw the victory dance he'd done the summer he'd driven to Birmingham for a pitmaster contest at the state fair and won a prize for the king of contests, roasting a whole hog on a pit made of cinder blocks. He'd celebrated with a double round of golf at PJ Hewett Municipal the next day and came home glowing from a hole-in-one and his lowest score ever.

I couldn't help laughing, looking into the past and seeing

him twirl Mama around with one hand, picking me up in his free arm and swinging us all around in the kitchen. "Yep, Daddy, I mean it."

For the next few minutes, I listened to him talk excitedly about the beauty of the course, the sacred space it was, the talent it took to play the Masters, and his hopes for Hobart Crane. I let him talk. I'd heard it all before, but for maybe the first time, I really listened.

Then I let our talk fade out and listened to the night sounds, feeling a renewed sense of purpose. I would get Daddy to Augusta, and I would find a way onto that golf course, even if I had to battle all the pigs and peaches and chickens in Georgia to get there.

When the fire died out, I shook Noni awake and we started walking.

Cradle of Dreams

There's nothing like giving your father a piggyback ride to his dream destination to make you feel like your life has gotten a little mixed up. As we approached the outskirts of town, Friday morning air flowed through the open fingers of my free hand, thick and humid and heavy with coming rain. I waved against it, and the wind answered my hello with a gentle pressure that had me standing my whole self straighter to feel and breathe in how the world was different here on the edge of Augusta, Georgia.

We stuck along the riverside, where warm breezes perfumed with blossoms and earth and all sorts of other smells drifted around as we got closer to town. Gasoline and growing things. Concrete heating up with the day's sun and potatoes frying. I wanted to swallow those smells, catch them in a jar to sniff at later. I nearly made myself lightheaded, trying to suck Augusta inside me. I almost expected to see an eleven-year-old Abbott Meyers walking toward us, tipping his hat my way.

Instead, we came upon a thin man, sunburned and shaggy-looking, his stringy blond-brown hair and chin stubble in need of a haircut and shave. He crouched against a tree, watching over a set of five or six fishing lines. He stood at the sight of us, straightening a threadbare army jacket and pants.

He smiled a happy, helpful, innocent smile filled with yellowish teeth. "Nice backpack," he told me. "New to Augusta? Need some information and a map?" Holding up a finger for us to wait, he limped over to the tree and rummaged through a garbage bag next to it, coming up with a stack of pamphlets.

He wasn't the best-looking of welcoming committees, but seemed friendly enough. "Actually, yes," I told him. "A map would be great."

"Five dollars," the man declared, his smile straightening out as he changed from welcome crew to businessman.

"That's crazy," Noni said. "And we don't—"

"Crazy's crazy." He shrugged, waving the pamphlet. "And a boy in need of a map is a boy in need of a map," the man said. "Oh, fine, three dollars."

"I'm sorry," I told him. "We don't have any money."

The man plopped to the ground with a disappointed grunt, scattering the pamphlets with a casual fling of the arm. "Of course you don't. That would've been too lucky for me. Just take one," he said, eyeing our appearance, which after miles of walking wasn't much better than his. "You look a little rough, and we got to take care of our own, don't we? Besides," he said, laying a finger on one nostril and blowing out the contents of the other. "They're free at the visitor center. Got any food?"

I shook my head.

"Darn. Haven't eaten since Wednesday. The VFW does grub on Monday, Wednesday, and Fridays, and there's a church in town that does Sundays. Park Street, if you need it. Wednesday noon to Friday nights are always hard on the belly, though." He pounded on his absent belly and coughed like Daddy used to.

I picked up one of the fallen maps, wanting to move along but not wanting to be rude, especially not to a man who'd probably killed people during the war. "How's the fishing around here?"

He picked up the fallen pamphlets, wiping and stacking them neatly and placing them back in the bag. "I come here every week and I never catch a thing." With a swift hand movement, he took a short comb from his back pocket and tried running it through his long hair. Tangles soon had him grooming face hair instead. "Where ya headed?"

"Um . . . a golf course. Augusta National. Is it on the map?"

His eyes twinkled. "The big one, huh?"

"I guess so." He stepped over to me, and I was surprised to smell soap. Now that I got a closer look, he wasn't dirty after all. I was just seeing his clothes and hair. Well, and the teeth stains, but even Daddy had some of those.

"There." He jabbed a clean fingernail near the top of the map, where two wavy-edged ovals of light green bumped each other. "It jams right up against a whole 'nother golf club—Augusta Country Club, see? ACC's course and clubhouse and property aren't quite as nice as Augusta National's, but then again, not much is." He sniffed at me and backed away. "I do hate to be the one to tell you this, but I don't think you'd get into either place dressed like that. Fancy *gentlemen* over there, most of them never seen the backside of Vietnam. If you're thinking of getting in without a ticket, you'd best wait until nightfall. Three morons got kicked out earlier this week, and there was a big hoo-ha. Not that you're morons. Well, you might be, for all I know. Anyhow, both courses are all the way on the north side." He pointed upriver. "Follow the water a ways, and then you can walk through town. Begging's bad this time of year, though, I'll warn you that."

"Thanks, sir," Noni said. "Why do you keep fishing here if you don't catch anything?"

"Oh, something'll take to my worms one of these days." He winked. "I got to be here if I want to catch it, don't I?" He turned his attention back to the fishing lines. "Stay and talk, if you want."

Noni nudged me, her elbow saying, *Time to go.*

"Good luck with the fishing sir," I told him. "We've got to be moving on. Thanks for the map."

The river man raised his hand in answer, not looking up as we left him.

There was more to see in Augusta than in Hilltop. Sidewalks and cement roads and houses, buildings and businesses. Restaurants, offices. Even a fancy-looking arts and crafts store. More people, too, both white and colored, young and old. It was still early, but we saw folks walking to work, folks sipping coffee at diner windows, folks trimming bushes and mowing grass before it got too hot, kids walking to school together. Hilltop's neighborhoods were more separated, and though signs banning people from stores were gone now, I noticed that I'd never seen May in town. When I'd asked Daddy about that, he'd said the west side of town had other places for groceries and goods that were closer to the Talbots. It made sense that they'd go to those stores, he'd said.

Just as we passed a bank with a clock declaring the time to be 7:32 a.m., Noni barked with delight and pointed ahead. Up the street a block, gathering around a thick tree near a building's parking lot, was a group of people. Behind them, sitting there like Augusta had decided to throw us a bone, was a long table filled with food.

Half a block farther and I could see it was doughnuts,

fruit, jugs of juice and steaming coffee. A big, clear jar marked DONATIONS sat there as well. My step lightened as we approached the crowd, which we now saw was focused on a tall man in an ugly white suit, a blue shirt, and a black tie. He held a clipboard and had slicked-back hair, two things that reminded me of the physical education teacher at Hilltop Primary—the one who'd laughed when the boys called me things that I'd never repeat to my mother, let alone my father.

"Real casual," Noni whispered, patting the backpack that I'd taken over carrying. "Grab and go."

"'Grab and go'?" I whispered back. "Who *are* you, anyway? Some kind of professional thief? Didn't anyone ever give you a sense of right and wrong?"

"Says the boy who stole a money egg from a chicken. And yes, I was given a sense of right and wrong. That alone would be fine if I was just a soul floating around, but I was given a body, too, and that body was given a stomach, and that stomach wants one or three of those doughnuts. Wanderers have to eat, you know."

"I'm hungry too." It was fortunate that wandering guidelines worked in favor of empty stomachs. I wanted badly to catch my first glimpse of Augusta National, but the chances of us sneaking in during the day weren't good, considering the fact that ticket holders would already be lined up and we still hadn't seen the course and we'd need time for planning our approach once we saw what we were dealing with.

The second day of the Masters would have to be played without Daddy there.

He hadn't spoken since our talk the night before, and I was worried that he'd disappeared again. I'd figured on asking him the best way of getting on the course. I'd pictured us talking strategy together, like a captain and soldier, huddled together close. But it looked like Noni and I might be on our own.

"Okay, let's get some food. Be careful." It wouldn't do to draw the attention of some runaway-grabbing adult, so we'd need to be cautious or we'd never see the outside of the golf course, let alone the inside.

Just as we arrived at the table, the crowd broke up and people began mingling among one another with a low hum like a beehive, waiting for the queen to tell them to get to work.

Slick Hair came over right as Noni was lifting a doughnut, lightly tapping her hand with a chuckle. "Now, darlin', I know fighting for justice can strike hunger into a person's belly, but this food's for after." He patted her on the head, not noticing the stink face Noni set on him.

"After what?" she said.

A woman came around the table, dipping beneath the plastic sheet and coming up with a stack of signs—thin, pale wood lengths attached to white cardboard rectangles. She handed one to each of us. "Here you go, children. I don't believe you went to school with my Catherine and Lucille. What are your names?"

"Byron Nelson," I told her.

Noni raised a hand. "Bridget Nelson."

"Your mama let you out of school for this?" she asked us both. She passed the stack of signs to another woman, who distributed them among the crowd of men and women, all around Mama's age.

"I'm taking a break," I said. Following her eyes to Daddy's backpack with the bucket hanging off, I added, "We're going camping this weekend."

"I don't go to school," Noni said.

The lady nodded in a knowing way and straightened Slick Hair's tie. "We've taken our girls out, too. But where are your parents? Did you come alone to help the cause, bless your hearts? This'll be perfect—you see those news cameras over there?" A shadow passed her face, and she jerked around and grabbed Slick Hair's hand. "Honey, they're interviewing the Negroes over there! You better start."

He straightened his tie and marched across the parking lot.

"Now," the woman said to us, "you get right up in front and wave those signs, okay? They'll see how our children's education is being taken away." She looked up, distracted. "Listen, you tell your folks about the new school that's opening. Freedom Academy, we're calling it." She turned and her face lit up with excitement. "Here come the buses! Places, everyone!"

Noni shrugged and moved aside a stack of newspapers to reach for a plate of doughnuts while everyone was facing the other way, surging like a soft wave toward the building. She shoved a chocolate one in her mouth, passed me one, and put a string of grapes in the backpack.

"I guess we'll get more after whatever we're doing. I'm not above working for my food." She shouldered a sign and joined the group, which was approaching the steps of what I now recognized as a school. Slick Hair had gotten himself a bullhorn and was giving a speech about fighting against tyranny and injustice.

A dull aching started in my throat, the lump growing thicker as six school buses turned the corner and approached the parking lot. I stared down at the sign in my hand, turning it over to see the words and having a flashback to the first time I'd seen the insides of an animal, bloody and wrong and nothing like the way it looked from the outside.

I scanned the pile of newspapers, and two headlines caught my eye: FORCED BUSING LEADS MORE PARENTS TO WITHDRAW STUDENTS and EMPTY CLASSROOMS: DESEGREGATION ORDER PROVES LARGELY INEFFECTIVE. A photograph showed a classroom, empty of students except for a colored boy and a colored girl, seated next to each other in the second row from the front. A lone white boy sat in the front row, at the opposite end of the classroom. The children looked to be about my age. Another photograph showed people standing together, holding signs. It was just like Hilltop, when the bus that picked up high schoolers started picking up the older kids from our colored neighborhood. And when May and the other students came to my school.

The Augusta buses came to a halt, and I saw immediately how they were only half full. The newspaperman had turned away from a colored woman and was gesturing to an opening bus door. Children started exiting.

In Hilltop, there had been a big rally of white parents and a man with a bullhorn just like Slick Hair's. I could hear the sound of speeches all the way down the road, but by the time I got to Hilltop Primary, those parents were already marching down the street, taking their boys and girls to the newly formed Hilltop Christian Academy, set up in the old church building. I remember the look on the faces of two of my friends as their mamas hauled them off. When I'd waved, it was like I'd already gone invisible to them. Like I'd never been there at all. And some of them had left their signs behind on the ground. Signs like these.

I pictured May walking past these signs, the way she must have done in Hilltop.

"Noni!" Dropping the sign, I ran over to her, but she'd already dropped hers, her eyes panning over the other posters' words, a confusion, then a sickness coming to her face that let me know she felt exactly like me.

GO HOME, NEGROES!

CUT THE COLOREDS—WHITES HAVE RIGHTS

And the worst one of all, the one that had the most hate screaming from it, was a photograph of Martin Luther King and the words, NEGROES WON'T RULE THIS SCHOOL: YOUR KING IS DEAD.

I knew about Dr. Martin Luther King Jr. and how he got killed for trying to change things. I was in first grade, and Miss Stone told us the day after that it was an awful thing and it was okay to feel sad or angry or scared. I wondered if May had felt that way. I'd never asked.

"Here, honey," said Slick Hair's wife, putting the sign back in Noni's hand with a smile as the first bus drove away and the second one began unloading. "Can you believe all these Negro children? And to think, they were gonna bus my girls across Augusta to some horrible colored school, in the name of desegregation. It just sickens me to pieces."

Noni stared at Slick Hair's wife, stared at the signs, stared at a colored woman being interviewed. There were four or five other colored parents standing with her, and I found myself thinking of Mrs. Talbot and wondering whether she had stood like this outside Hilltop Primary on the day May started school. The crowd was quiet enough to hear the interviewer ask the woman why she wanted her child to go to school there and for us to hear the answer.

"As I understand it, this school has books that my son's school doesn't," she said. "They've got other things, too. Better things. I just want my son to have the same opportunities. Equal opportunities."

Equal.

A few years back, Mr. James Walter, one of our Pork Heaven customers, started talking about some business that had happened in Birmingham when I was just a baby. He said he didn't see why things had to change and that keeping things separate but equal was working just fine. Mama told him that it was easy to say that from where he sat and then said she was sorry, but we'd run out of lemon cake, which we hadn't. We kept being out of food that he wanted most, and eventually he took his appetite elsewhere.

I'd wondered about Mr. Walter's chair for months, staring at the spot in the café where he'd sat—a magic chair where it was easy to say things. I thought maybe Daddy and I could sit down and eat one day, and I'd sit in that chair. When I'd finally sucked down enough nerve to ask Mama about it, she'd said there was no magic chair. The thing that man was sitting in was his skin color. She said being white had made things easier for me, too.

The interviewer turned away from the mother and began talking once again to the camera. Noni had dropped her sign again, and Slick Hair's wife picked it up, confused. She reached it out again.

"I'm not your toilet seat," Noni told her, knocking the sign to the ground.

The woman blinked. "I beg your pardon?"

"Don't try to plop your ugly inside of me." She glared and then tore a few signs out of shocked adults' hands, throwing them to the ground before grabbing my hand. "Let's go." She was in a fury, her body coiled up, fists tight. She pulled me through the crowd, across the parking lot, and over the street from where the white parents had been having their meeting a moment before. She dropped under a tree, and I sat beside her.

Noni breathed slowly, her eyes staring at the crowd. "I'm not sorry for what I said to that lady," Noni said. "They're nothing but bullies. All of them. I'm glad I never went to school. Their kids are probably just like them. They probably helped make those signs."

The buses were almost empty and the television cameras would leave soon. The show would be over and those people would be coming over for refreshments, like they were at some kind of garden party.

"Bullies," I agreed, thinking about how Willy Walter had beaten me up on multiple occasions, for no good reason. How he'd stood over me after the big blows and shoved me down every time I'd tried to stand, until I'd been too exhausted to do anything but lie there on the ground and pray he'd go away.

There'd been one day in the cafeteria when his sister, Ann, had offered May Talbot a birthday cupcake during school lunch and then waited until she'd gotten close to smear it on her dress. The smear made me so angry, but I hadn't done a thing. I'd been afraid of what might happen if I got angry, so I just stared, feeling shaky, which was maybe as bad as laughing like some boys and girls had done.

I'd been a coward that day. Anger needs bravery to go with it. But bravery, the part where you try to put your anger and fear and frustration into doing something, into changing something, that was the hard part. Looking at the face of a girl stepping off that bus, her brown eyes as deep and her back as straight as May Talbot's, I was ashamed of myself. May was brave every single day. She had to be.

I wanted to be brave, too.

Maybe May needed a friend as much as I did. Maybe she was sad about Miss Stone leaving, too. Maybe I was less mean than the kids who whispered taunts at school, but I wasn't showing it. Maybe there was a part of me that still saw her skin color instead of just seeing May.

Daddy always said that golf was the game that most tested a man's character, because you had to call penalties on yourself. There were moments when no fellow golfer or official would be there to make sure you followed the rules. You had to admit mistakes and violations your own self, then try your best to play better.

"Noni?"

"Yeah?"

"How do you change a person's mind about something?"

She chewed at a piece of her dress. "I don't know."

I didn't know either. And maybe trying to change people's minds wasn't enough. You had to change their eyes and their heart, too.

The sky above issued a grumble like a hungry man's belly, and a thought struck me; maybe I couldn't make the world a fairer place that day, but I could think of one way to make a small change in the life of one man. And maybe that was a good start. I unstrung the bucket from my backpack and handed it to my fellow runaway.

"Noni," I said quietly. "On the count of three, I'm gonna get up and grab that big bowl of fruit. I want you to take this bucket and fill it with as many doughnuts as you can. Then run."

Noni's grimace turned into a curious grin. "Where are we running, Benjamin Putter?"

"We're going back to the river."

Doughnuts and Strategy

It was several minutes before the river man looked up from the fruit bowl. Half the grapes and apple slices had been eaten, the oranges handed back with the explanation that they didn't suit him much. He hadn't touched the doughnuts yet, but had them tucked between his legs. Noni and I sat beside him under the big oak, watching the fishing lines dangle in the water. "Thanks," he finally managed. "My name's Tom Barry."

"Sam Snead," I said.

Noni half grinned. "Sally."

Tom studied us both. "I know code names when I hear 'em. No harm, though. Where'd you find this grub?"

I explained and he nodded. "Same folks who give me dirty looks after fighting their war. So what do you want with a golf course?"

Tom reached for his first doughnut while I showed him Daddy's urn and explained what we were hoping to do. His lips twisted in thought after I'd finished. "A tough operation. Bad timing with the big tournament going on."

"He wants to see it," I said, then felt myself redden. "I mean, he wanted to be there, at least for a day, and then be scattered by the time they start playing on Sunday. We were thinking we'd sneak onto the property tonight."

"Maybe we could just ask someone for their tickets," Noni said.

Tom laughed. "There are charitable people out there, but not the kind who would give up their Masters tickets. And the people selling them aren't likely to even give you a discount, let alone a clean giveaway. No, sneaking in's the way to go."

Noni looked down at a strange bulge in her pocket. "Oh. Okay."

"Well," Tom said, coughing again, "I may not be much to look at, but I know a thing or two about sneaking around bunkers. You got any reconnaissance on this place? Something to tell us about the terrain we're dealing with?"

I pulled out the Augusta book. "There are photos of the holes in here. And a basic layout of the course."

Tom grabbed it, his face filling with something close to excitement and purpose. "Well, let's huddle up and talk strategy." He looked up at the sky and sniffed the air. "We'll have to factor in the rain. It's coming tonight."

A few hours later, Tom had eaten his fill and we had our plan. As he'd told us, ACC's golf course and property was smashed right up against Augusta National's, and it wouldn't have the same issues with guards and security. Our goal was to get onto ACC grounds and then hop the barrier fence between the two golf courses.

The second shot at hole eleven, all of hole twelve, and the first two shots of hole thirteen on Augusta National are known as Amen Corner, and that's the place Tom had suggested getting in. Daddy'd once told me that some reporter wanted a fancy name for that section of the course, so he'd named it after a jazz record.

I didn't care much about Amen Corner's history, but I liked the name; if you're gonna hop a fence and hunker down in a place you don't belong, it doesn't hurt if there's some kind of religious-sounding bent to it. There was the most tree cover there and multiple escape routes, or so Tom said, looking at Daddy's Augusta book. We could pop out the next morning real casual.

"Thanks for your help," I told him. "You can keep that bucket. I wish we could repay you." I turned to Noni. "We should have taken some of that donation money from the table, too."

Noni blushed and pulled out a fistful of bills. "I did." She held it toward him. "Wasn't sure the right time to give it to you. Here you go, sir. Take it all." She turned to me. "I thought maybe we could use it to buy tickets. But I don't want money from those people. Do you?"

I stared at her hand. Getting into the Masters was our

goal. But the protest we'd seen was fresh in my mind. May Talbot was there, too. That money was probably meant to buy more poster paper and markers, to make more of those signs.

"No," I said. "I don't want that money."

"I'll take it." Tom grinned and snatched the dollars from Noni's hand. "Thank you, miss. Probably not the cause they intended to fund, but don't mind if I do." He began straightening the bills, then suddenly jerked his head toward the water at the sound of faint, high-pitched metal tinkling. "Ho! Look at that!"

One of his fishing lines was tugged taut and his bobber sank, causing a tiny bell tied to the line to ring. "What do you know," he said, putting down the empty bucket and picking up his line to see a wiggling fish. "It's my lucky day. Hope some rubs off on you. Now, go on, like I said, and scout the premises before you make a move to get into ACC. And after you hop that fence between the two properties and get onto Augusta National, make sure you stay low and slow."

I nodded. "Like barbecue."

"Huh?"

"You gotta be patient. Cook it low and slow. That's what my daddy used to say."

"He was right. Now, go on and make him happy." Tom grunted. "And watch out that nobody's laid a trap for you."

Fisherman's Knot

We walked to Augusta National first, getting there at ten in the morning. I had to get a glimpse of it, and I thought maybe Daddy would perk up and start talking at the sight of his beloved golf heaven. But he didn't.

Tom Barry had been right about the Masters ticket scalpers that were lingering in the area. They were there to sell last minute tickets to people who didn't have them, but there wasn't an ounce of sympathy among them for two kids who didn't even have money to bargain with. Since none of the latecomers making their way to the entrance area seemed willing to give up their day at the Masters, the idea of getting in with legitimate passes was definitely out.

After walking along the perimeter of the neighboring golf club, ACC, we walked over to the river bottoms far north of Tom Barry to change into our decent clothes, having decided that just walking in might do the trick. The only problem was that, although security wasn't combing the grounds at Augusta National's less fancy neighbor, the ACC was still private property, and any person walking around would need a reason to be there.

When I suggested we both go in together to check it out, Noni shook her head.

"No good," she said. "What if something bad happens and we get caught?" She pointed to the urn. "This is the best chance we've got to scatter your daddy. You can't let him down. I'll go alone, to test the waters first."

She was right. If we got hauled into some office at ACC, there was no way we'd make it into Augusta National that night. "But what if you get caught? You wanted to get into Augusta National, too. If something happens, then you won't—"

"I know." She stared at the ground for a moment, then raised her head. "I want to do it for you."

I didn't know what to say. If Noni's daddy had thought she needed lessons in how to be a good friend, I hoped he was watching over her now. She'd proven him wrong. "Thank you."

Noni smiled, but I saw just a hint of worry in her eyes before she blinked it away. "I'm a good talker. I'll be fine."

"What if someone asks who you are?"

She shrugged. "I'll tell them that I'm John's niece, then hurry along like I belong there."

"Who's John?"

Rolling her eyes, Noni picked up a rock and tossed it toward the river. "It's a country club packed full of men. Chances are, they've got a dozen men named John. I'll walk to the clubhouse and around part of the course, pretending to look for Uncle John, to see if it's the kind of place that would let a girl do that sort of thing. If it is, we'll be fine." She eyed the backpack. "I'll leave that behind for now, but it might draw attention when we both go."

"We'll say our mama dropped us off so Uncle John can take us camping," I suggested. "Worked with that protest lady."

"Good. I'll be back."

She walked off, whistling her hobo song the way she'd done back at the orchard. The sound reminded me how much she wanted to find a sign from her daddy. There was a part of me that wondered if she'd just run off once we hopped the border fence and got inside Augusta National that night. I had the strangest feeling that she was waiting for the right moment to leave me.

I picked a yellow flower and plucked off the petals one by one.

She'll be back, she won't be back, she'll be back, she won't be . . . I let the flower fall before I could finish taking it to pieces.

I walked along the river with the backpack on, Daddy sticking out the top for air. A good-size stick presented itself, and I used it like a golf club, whacking small stones and twigs ahead of me and moving where they landed—making my own private riverside round of eighteen holes and wondering if I'd ever play a round of real golf again in my life. Improper grip or not, I wasn't a bad player.

"Ben? Did we make it?"

I let out a breath I didn't know I'd been holding. "We're in Augusta, Daddy." I filled him in on our meeting with Tom Barry and what Noni was doing. He wholeheartedly agreed and told me a few stories about miraculous shots that had been made on the twelfth green, where we'd be sneaking in.

After an hour or so of waiting for Noni, he ran out of golf facts, and the two of us just sat, listening to the birds and being together. I untied the camping ropes from the outside of the backpack and practiced the bowline knot, then tied a clove hitch around my leg the way Noni'd done around my finger with her shoelace back on the coal train.

I felt strangely comfortable with Daddy. And with our final goodbye approaching fast, I felt like talking while I could.

"Daddy?" I said, breaking the quiet.

"Yeah?"

"I liked those Abbott Meyers stories you told me. Back in the orchard, I said they were stupid. But I liked them. A lot." With the other length of rope, I moved on to the fisherman's knot, used to tie two ropes together so they'd become something longer.

"You liked Abbott Meyers?" He chuckled. "Yep, he was

just a poor boy who never quite made it to the PGA tour. Lots of talent, though. People think golf is only a rich man's sport, Ben, but Walter Hagen, Sam Snead, Ben Hogan? All poor boys who found a way in. I think Abbott took comfort in that while he snuck bites from the rich men's abandoned sandwiches after they were done eating."

I grinned. "I liked the one where he disguised himself, entered a tournament, and beat the pants off that man who never tipped him."

Daddy laughed. "I liked that one, too." He cleared his throat. "You know, Ben, I think golf made Abbott Meyers feel less lonely. I think golf was Abbott's only friend."

I didn't have any friends at all. I couldn't get a handle on Noni or where she'd be going after she found her sign. And May felt out of reach. I missed her. I didn't want to lose her. "Mr. Talbot came to the memorial service Mama had for you at the church," I said. "There were a few empty seats, but he stood at the back."

"Well, that's nice that he came."

"May came over the day after, all by herself. Mrs. Talbot called before and spoke to Mama for a while, and then May brought flowers. I saw from the kitchen. She hugged Mama longer than anybody else who stopped by, and Mama didn't pull away."

"Well. That's nice, too."

I wanted to ask if Daddy would have gone to Mr. Talbot's

memorial if things were reversed and what he'd think about Mama sending me to take flowers to Mrs. Talbot and me giving her a long hug, but I didn't. I thought about Mama's face when May hugged her. How her body had relaxed. Then I thought about Mama telling Mr. Walter we were out of lemon cake and wondered if maybe Mama and Daddy didn't see eye to eye on people keeping their heads down when it came to colored people.

Daddy didn't say anything else, so I kept talking.

"People are mean to May at school," I said, dropping the rope beside me. "Even some of the teachers."

I could have told him more. I could say how the teachers at school sometimes looked the other way while students said ugly words or dumped saved-up pencil shavings on the colored students. For years, I'd been telling May about the names I'd been called, but that was nothing compared to what the new students had gone through. At group recess one day, I'd seen a new second grader—a well-dressed, straight-walking girl who could have been May's little sister—get her shoes yanked off while she was on the swings. She screamed and screamed as the laces were taken out and scissored in half.

May had walked over and bent down and shushed the girl, her face angry. Fierce. I'd never seen that side of May.

The little girl's eyes got wide, and she'd backed away. May stepped toward her and said something else. Instead of crying more, the girl nodded, wiped her nose, and got quiet. And then May had pulled her into a hug and held her close, rubbing a hand over her hair and whispering something in her ear.

I'd been across the school yard under a tree. Just watching.

"That's too bad," Daddy said slowly. "That's a real shame. Makes you wonder if she'd be happier at her old school."

Picking up a fallen leaf, I tore it in half. "I thought it'd be nice to have her at my school. Why are people like that?"

Daddy let out a smoker's sigh, the kind that rattled. "You have to understand that this change—coloreds and whites mixing in schools—it's new here. I believe that all you children deserve to have equal learning. I do. But people need time to get used to change. If you force it on them, there's bound to be some resistance."

"Like the Talbots getting their barbecue place burned down. That's what you mean." I picked up another rock. Tossed it in the river. "Sometimes I think I should say something. To those kids or teachers. But I don't. I freeze up."

I saw him scratch his chin, trying to think of what to say. "Son, I know you've been friends with May for a while now. But you're both getting older. Life gets more complicated when you get older, and being friends with a colored girl isn't going to make your life any better. Or easier. And trust me, it's not going to make her life easier either. Best thing you can do for that girl is ignore her. Except for if she drops by with her daddy. Sure, you can still talk to her then. Don't want to be rude."

"I don't understand."

"Everybody wakes up with something hard, son. Something maybe they're afraid of facing. But people have to get up anyway. I'm sure you'll have enough to deal with, just growing up and being the man of the house for your mama. What goes on with the Talbots is their piece of hard. It's not yours. You just keep your focus at school and things will be all right."

I stared at the silver on the urn, seeing Daddy leaning over a club, eyes on the ball. "Putters keep their head down," I said. "You told me that. But you also used to tell me that Putters are men of action. Which is it, Daddy?"

He paused, and I thought he was getting angry. But when he spoke, he just sounded wary, like he was wrestling with something he couldn't see. "In general, I'm a man of action. Men are meant to be active. But you can't play golf in the rain, son, and this business about race and segregation and coloreds and whites is one heck of a thunderstorm. There are times in life when you've just got to duck and cover, keep your head down, and hope those ugly clouds pass by soon. There's nothing you can do to hurry along Mother Nature."

I knew about keeping my head down. I kept it down when people called me names. I kept it down when they called May names. And I'd kept my head down with my daddy. Something inside me was getting tired of staring at the ground. Grandpa Clay said that you had to take ownership over messy parts in life, to admit they were there in order to change the way you saw things—to give you a bigger picture of the world.

"But it's not Mother Nature, Daddy. It's people. So why can't you be a man of action with—"

He sucked in a breath, cutting me off. "Life is short, Ben. Sometimes it's just too short to fight other people's battles. It's too short for people to change."

I stared down at my fisherman's knot. It was nice and tight and would hold a good amount of weight without coming apart. "So you don't agree with colored people getting treated different . . . but it's not your place or my place to do anything. Is that what you mean?"

It took a minute for him to answer. "Yeah. I guess that's what I mean."

On the train, Noni'd said that the ropes had to be the same thickness for a fisherman's knot to work. If one was different, the knot wouldn't hold together. With the two pieces of rope in my hand, I thought of what Daddy'd just said.

"I think you're wrong," I told him. "I hope you are."

"What am I wrong about?" Daddy asked.

I tugged on the rope ends, feeling the knot hold. "I think people can change. And I think if people don't say anything when someone gets treated bad, they'll just keep getting treated bad."

Daddy looked at me—I felt his eyes through the urn's walls. "You're young. Sometimes life teaches you hard lessons. Life's hard parts can take away the beliefs you want to hold on to."

I closed my eyes and looked right at him. "Maybe the hard parts, even the ones that aren't yours, are teaching you that you should believe in something better."

Daddy paused. "Maybe you're right, Ben."

But I had a feeling that he wasn't talking about the same things I was. He wasn't talking about May having a hard time at school or Mr. Talbot not being allowed at Pastor Frank's. He was talking about whatever hard parts had been in the life he'd led.

I let my hand curve over the knot in my lap. For the first time, it occurred to me that whatever my daddy thought, whatever beliefs he had held on to or let go of, they were his own. And they weren't the same as mine. And that was okay.

I'd always wanted him to be proud of me. To be the son he wanted. To be close and for us to hold each other together. Was that even possible if we weren't the same kind of rope?

I wanted to think so.

The sound of Noni crashing through the brush distracted me before I could say anything else. She was skipping and whistling, looking like she'd just won a free pass to an egg and pie festival. With a wide grin and two cookies she'd swiped from a display that was just sitting right in the ACC's clubhouse, she told me that people had been nice. The two of us would be able to walk around the property, wait for a moment when nobody was watching, and quickly sneak over to the spot where we'd jump the fence to Augusta National when night fell.

"Just be polite like me," Noni said, "and we'll be fine. I was my usual charming self, and they didn't question a thing."

I didn't doubt it. If there was one thing I'd learned about my secretive partner, it was that despite her inability to stick with a mood for long, she could manage to turn on the charm with adults when need be. "How come you're never your charming self with me?" I asked.

"Still not funny." She wrinkled her nose and handed me a cookie. "Showing you my true self is a testament to our friendship. Consider yourself lucky."

"But you haven't shown me your true self. You've barely told me a thing."

She walked toward the road, not turning as she called back to me.

"Come on, Benjamin Putter. Let's go get a few more of these cookies and sneak over a fence."

Amen Corner

L ooking up at the sky, dark as Noni's bruise, I felt like I was seeing Hilltop's Willy Walter walk down the road, a wicked grin on his face as he considered whether to knock me down and kick me, or punch me in the face first. A long roll of thunder sounded as we stood within striking distance of the nine-foot obstacle to my daddy's salvation. Augusta National Golf Club was right there, less than fifty feet away. The pitter-patter gumdrop rain starting to fall didn't fool me for a second. The sky was just licking its lips, letting drool drop down while it got ready to pounce.

"You hungry, Ben?" Daddy said. "That was a pretty loud growl." Daddy sounded awake and excited.

"Very funny, Daddy. That's thunder, not my stomach. It's about to start raining hard as horse pee out here." I wasn't in the mood for humor. He was nice and dry there in his ashy state, tucked away with our clothes for tomorrow, but I'd be getting soaked through.

Sure enough, within minutes, the rain's pressure increased and there was no escaping it, even crouched among bushes. It was biting rain, the kind that feels like a million tiny bees are swarming, and batting them away wouldn't do a thing but make them angrier.

"Hey!" Noni shouted, wiping her face.

"What?" I could barely hear over the pounding bullets of water. The drops stabbed me all over the place, including the eyeballs when I was stupid enough to look up. I was grateful for the tree cover, but it wasn't doing a whole lot of good. The foliage muffled some of the violent storm, but the wind whipping through the world felt like leftovers from somebody's winter up north.

"Flashlight!" she yelled, banging against the pack on my back.

"No!" We'd decided not to risk using it unless it was an emergency, since someone could see the light, and I couldn't see how it would help with all the rain practically blinding us anyway. "Come on!" I screamed at Noni, approaching the barrier and looking for the best place to start climbing.

Just before I made contact with the fence, a crack of lightning came down on the tree next to me, and a huge branch shot right off and headed my way. Hurling myself down, I curled up and ducked, feeling it slam into the ground right beside me. A sharp side branch had torn into the backpack. I moved away from the fallen piece of tree and felt a tear.

It was maybe a hand's length long, and something soft was right inside it. Noni's dress for the next day was probably ruined, but we'd have to deal with that later.

Just as I looked up, another crack landed right on the fence itself, and sparks exploded like Fourth of July come early. A scream sounded through the mess. I jerked up, looking for Noni and seeing nothing but trees, leaves, trunks, bushes, ground, all of it getting thrashed by the worst storm I'd ever seen, let alone gotten stuck in.

"Noni! Where are you?" There was no answer that I could hear over the rain, and I plunged farther into the brush, calling her name. It felt like emergency time, so I stopped and managed to find the flashlight, my cold, panicked fingers slipping off the switch to turn it on. Daddy yelled something, I didn't know what. All I knew was that I had a face full of rain and a girl to find.

The flashlight finally turned on, and shining beams of light were mine to wave in the darkness as another bolt of lightning flashed and crashed. "Noni!"

I thought I saw her and ran forward, light bouncing off leaves and dirt, but when I plunged through the bushes, it was nothing. The same thing happened twice more. "Noni!"

A moan sounded close by.

There.

She was on her knees, head down, huddled under a lightning-struck branch the size of a man's leg. Her arms were over her head, her right hand tightly clutching her left elbow.

I rushed over and didn't say a word, just turned her over and grabbed her shoulders, pulling her close and hearing her whisper the words *I'm okay*. Then my arms slipped around her and hers did the same to me, and we clutched each other close and didn't let go.

"Somebody talk to me!" Daddy shouted from the pack. "The lightning didn't get you, did it?" he yelled anxiously. "Ben, listen to me! Just get out of here! Forget the Masters!"

"Any closer and I would've been ashes just like you," I yelled through the downpour, pulling away from Noni. "And we're not going anywhere."

The storm was a test, I knew it. Augusta was testing me, to see if I was worthy. It wasn't enough that Augusta was going to take my daddy from me now that we were actually talking—now the course was questioning me. Whether I was a good enough messenger.

It was Augusta who'd laid the trap for me.

I stood to face the fence. "That the best you can do?" I shouted to the golf course. "We're coming in, whether you like it or not!"

"Ben, don't—"

But I didn't let him finish. I had switched to full-on soldier mode. "Quiet, Daddy!" I ordered, wishing I had camouflage paint on. "I'm trying to save your soul. Come on, Noni."

Wiping a couple of leaves from my wet face, I spit on my hands and rubbed them together because it seemed like the right thing to do. Taking a deep breath, I ignored Augusta's attempts at intimidation and launched myself at the fence, climbing up with speed I didn't know was in me. I felt a shake beside me as Noni followed. She slipped at the top, her foot coming around to smack me in the face.

"Sorry!" she yelled.

Instead of saying it was okay, I grabbed the foot, and we both tumbled over in a repeat of the fall I'd taken back at Pastor Frank's chicken yard, except this time I had a girl's body to cushion me. "Sorry!" I shouted back at her.

"What's going on? Who's sorry for what?" Daddy was yelling so loud that he forced himself into a coughing fit.

"We're in," I told him. "Just sit tight."

"What else am I gonna do in here?" he called back.

The minute we were over the fence, within sight of the twelfth green and the tee box for the thirteenth hole, the storm grew to a furious climax, beating us mercilessly until we found cover. Even as the world raged around us, the smells, the smells, the *smells* of freshly soaked Augusta grass and azaleas were overpowering, almost choking me. Feeling smothered by the very shelter that protected us from the storm, I took off the backpack and set it beside a tree. I had to find air.

I found myself stumbling toward the open space. Toward

a golf green. Noni shouted something through the squall and ran after me. I bent on the edge of the twelfth green, my soaked hands reaching out to feel the perfect grass.

Noni bent beside me with the flashlight and started to yell something. Then she looked at my face and I looked at hers. We both had rain pouring down our cheeks like we were crying our eyes out. She plucked a piece of grass, a longer piece from just off the green. She handed it to me, lifting it near my lips. "So it's part of you!" she shouted in my ear. "Go on!"

I ate it and handed her one, watching as she chewed, amazed as the deluge turned back into a softer rain that slowed to a complete halt.

It was like magic.

We both laughed and shouted and hugged, and when we parted, Noni's expression switched from joy to panic.

I didn't have to wonder why. The strong grip on my shoulder and the sight of a meaty hand reaching over me to grip Noni told me all I needed to know.

I froze, like the Prisoner Of War I was, then slowly turned to face a very large head, belonging to a very large man. With a twist of his hands, he turned us around, our flashlight catching him dead in the face.

Security.

With a gun strapped to his waist and a long, club-looking object on the ground beside him.

The man didn't have a name tag, but if he had, it would have said BUTCH, BRUNO, or something intimidating like GRIDLOCK. Bald head, bulging muscles, and a handlebar mustache big enough to make a fur coat for a baby pig.

"Nice evening for a walk," he said, dripping sarcasm.

"Yes, sir," I said, trying to sound innocent. Lord knows why I even tried. There was zero possible explanation for our whereabouts.

"You two going somewhere?" he asked.

Noni had clammed up and was staring at the man like he'd broken her heart.

"Um . . . We were thinking we'd go get some auto-graphs?" I squeaked like a cornered squirrel. I was feeling about as twitchy as one too. "Thought we'd see if any of the boys in the Crow's Nest were still awake. That's the room in the clubhouse where amateurs get to stay during the tour-nament."

"I know what the Crow's Nest is. It's not open to visitors, especially the late-night-kiddie-fan variety."

My eyes were waist level with him, and I saw that my startled glance had been playing tricks on me and his gun was just a flashlight. And the club was an umbrella. "You're not security?"

He shook his head. "Extra night maintenance, brought in for the tournament. Forecast said chance of storm, so I got the lucky job of staying up. Saw the lightning and came to check out the greens to make sure they didn't have any major debris fall on them."

"Well," I said. "I guess we'll just get going, then."

"Not your lucky day, kids. There's some people awake in the security office. We're gonna need to have a visit with them."

"Did Hobart Crane make the cut?" Noni asked, finally breaking her silence.

The man seemed surprised. "He did. He's playing great. You a fan?"

She pointed to me. "Our daddy is. Can't you let us go?" Her voice was trembling. She looked like a lost soul, and anybody with a heart would have wanted to help her.

He shook his head, a little sadly. "Sorry. I get a bonus for catching intruders during the tournament. I got mouths to feed, kid. Now, who should we call to come get you? Or do you prefer I drop you at the local police station?"

If he called Mama, the trip might be over. No, there had to be a way to stay in Augusta. There *had* to be. When the solution came, I weighed the betrayal of going against Daddy's orders against the certainty of failure. I shook my head. "We're staying with our uncle. Luke Putter. I don't know his phone number, but he lives here in Augusta. You can look it up." I pointed to the trees. "I need my backpack."

His voice softened. "All right. Let's grab it and get moving. I imagine your uncle has rules against sneaking out of the house and won't be too happy to hear from me. You've broken a lot of rules tonight. If your uncle is anything like my daddy was, boy, I don't envy your backside."

My backside was the least of my concerns. There were only a handful of hours until the second-to-last day of the Masters started. I could only hope that Uncle Luke would help us find a way to make a miracle happen and get us back on Augusta's grounds.

"Sir, I mean no disrespect to adults in general or you in particular," I said, "but I think maybe the people who make the rules don't always know what's best."

He considered me. "You may be right, son, but this golf club's rules aren't meant to be challenged. Not tonight, anyway." He chuckled. "I mean, Good Lord, you'd have better luck getting into this course during the Masters by hopping a ride with one of the players." Shaking his head at his joke, he blew out air. "Now, let's get you out of here."

Twenty minutes later, at eleven o'clock at night, the door to the security office opened. A short man casting a long shadow walked inside, and his resemblance to Daddy was enough to make me lurch against Noni. I straightened the pack on my shoulder, not sure what to expect from a relative I'd rarely seen.

"Hello, nephew. I dozed off and didn't realize you'd run off until I got an unpleasant phone call, you rascal."

Uncle Luke nodded at Noni. "And hello, my dear *niece*."

Was that a wink he'd thrown my way? It was. He was playing along.

He tipped his hat to the security man we'd been passed along to. "Much obliged, sir." After a few minutes spent talking about his days on the PGA tour, Uncle Luke knuckled my head and assured Augusta's head of security that I'd be properly punished. Then he placed a hand on the back of Daddy's pack and pushed me toward the door. "Come on, you two."

I held up Daddy's urn. "There's three of us."

Uncle Luke stopped. He stared at the urn. One hand went up to rub his chin. To scratch his head. To flop against his side. "Well," he said, blowing out a deep breath and walking out the door, "come on, you three."

Mr. Bobby Jones said that you swing your best when you have the fewest things to think about. Of all the Big Five quotes Daddy'd hammered into me, that one bothered me the most. Every time I'd been on a golf course with my daddy, I had about a million things running through my mind. And right then I had a million and one things, starting with not knowing if my uncle was on my side and Daddy's side. Not knowing if he was going to drive us to his place or straight back to Hilltop.

As Noni and I got in the car and drove through the entrance separating us from the golf paradise Bobby Jones had founded, I stared out the window. Thoughts, circling like vultures, reminded me that whether or not Uncle Luke decided to help us, this journey would end the same way. With Daddy being gone forever. Augusta's raindrops had left my shirt soaked, but it was my mind that felt flooded, spilling over with echoes of the same word:

Goodbye

Goodbye

Goodbye

Goodbye

Goodbye.

Family, Understanding

My uncle came into the world six years after Daddy, but they look almost the same. Same one-eighth inch regulation golf green haircut, same Putter ears, and same nose long enough to be able to sit on the couch and smell when barbecue outside the house is just about done. From my view in the passenger seat, I might have been driving alongside my father again, other than the silence. Daddy always had something to say about golf or meat or life or what a man should be, but it was only when we pulled in the driveway of a shingle-sided house at eleven thirty that Uncle Luke managed another word.

"Explain," he said, not leaving the car.

"Yes, sir." Just like you feel before puke comes spewing out of your mouth, I had a nervous feeling that a big mess was about to be made. Trying to hold it back just made me look crazier, so I spilled my guts about everything that'd happened in the last several days, praying that he didn't call the local loony truck to pick me up.

"So, am I to understand," he said slowly, "that you were trying to sneak into Augusta National Golf Club because . . . Bogey told you to do it?" His face was sober, fingers still clutching the steering wheel tight.

"Yes, sir," I answered.

"I see," Uncle Luke said, turning off the engine. He turned to face Noni. "And who's this?"

"Wait, whose voice is that?" Daddy said, groggy-voiced and slow. "That's not—"

Noni stuck a hand over the backseat. "*This* is Noni. I'm helping," she said.

"I see," Uncle Luke said again, covering his face with both palms, then rubbing his eyes. "Helping to do what? Oh, God, that's right. Look, everybody out." He got out of the car and marched up the walkway to his quiet house on his well-groomed street, which had more cement on its side-walks than Hilltop had altogether.

"*Benjamin!*" Daddy's voice boomed. "Tell me I didn't just hear—"

"We didn't have a choice, Daddy. Just hush. He might help us. Good to hear you sounding stronger."

"Hmph," Daddy said. "You just let me be in charge, you hear me?"

I dug him out of the backpack. "Okay, Daddy. You're in charge."

Noni and I got out of the car and followed Uncle Luke inside the house. He tapped something beside the door. It was a hand-size metal box with a bunch of black buttons along the bottom.

"It's an alarm system," Uncle Luke said. "If I have it turned on and someone opens the door and doesn't know how to turn it off quick, it puts out a heck of a shrieking noise. If they press the wrong button, same thing happens. The neighbors called the police when I tested it out. Would give a deaf man a headache, so don't touch it."

"Why do you need an alarm?" I asked.

"I run a side business doing regrips and angle adjustments on clubs. Got about twenty thousand bucks' worth of golf equipment in the house that folks wouldn't appreciate being stolen." He pointed down a narrow hallway. "Stay outta my workshop."

We passed a sitting room that had about a million books scattered around and a beautiful framed watercolor of Augusta National Golf Club hanging on the far wall. If I squinted my eyes, the eighteen holes and surrounding trees blurred together, the sand bunkers becoming beige lily pads in a sea of green. It was almost like a version of the poster in Miss Stone's art room that made me fall in love with painting back in first grade. I felt my spirits lift a little. Maybe we'd come to the right place. I hoped so.

"Have a seat, kids."

The kitchen was big and open with another Augusta

wall painting, a large table covered in bright yellow clothes and sewing stuff, and a small television sitting on the counter. There was a single club leaning against a kitchen chair. Sliding glass doors opened to a patio and backyard that was bigger than the house. I saw a putting green and a driving net.

There was a big bowl of oranges on the table, the normal big ones and little ones, too. Uncle Luke motioned for me to take a seat, moving a glue gun, scissors, a dress and a sweater, a frilly hat with a huge cloth daisy in the center, a bunch of cloth, shoes, spools of thread, and about ten key chains off the table and onto a chair by the patio door with an embarrassed look on his face.

"That's my girlfriend Trisha's sewing, not mine. She brought over some kind of frock she's making for her niece." He opened a cabinet and reached for the highest shelf. There must have been twenty plastic bottles up there. He popped the lid on a blue one and shook it into his hand, then noticed me looking. "I seem to have developed a headache," he said. "Imagine that." Looking down at the three pills in his hand, he glanced at the bottle, shrugged, and threw them all back. "These things make me a little sleepy, so let's get to talking."

"What are the key chains from?" Noni asked, picking one up.

"Trish and her sister took a road trip." He turned back to us and rolled his eyes. "She got me a key chain from every gas station they stopped at. I hate key chains." He wrinkled his nose at the pile.

"I hate frocks," Noni said.

He eyed the backpack and the urn. "Put your stuff down."

He turned and shoved several papers next to his sink into a drawer, gripped the counter, and looked into the back-yard. "So, that's him?" he asked, not turning around. "That's his urn?"

"Yes, sir." Instead of traveling to Hilltop for Daddy's ser-vice, Uncle Luke had sent a bunch of azaleas and a note that was glued shut. On the outside he'd written instructions to burn it, so it'd meet up with his brother's ashes. I'd forgotten about that note until just now.

"You mad at me for not coming to the memorial service?"

I wasn't sure which of us he was talking to, me or Daddy, so I didn't say anything.

He nodded to himself, reached for a cookie jar and pulled out a golf ball. He turned and tossed it high in the air, catching it neatly before throwing it to me. "You know your daddy could have gone pro. He could beat the pants off me back when we were kids. He was a better caddie, too, and brought the tips home to our mother to prove it. But he quit playing and caddying and school at fifteen and got a solid job to help out. Made enough that I could keep playing and enter tournaments. He should've been on the PGA tour with me. But he traded his dream for us like that."

He snapped his fingers. "He didn't have a choice, really. You knew that about your daddy, right?"

I didn't know that. I didn't know that at all. Daddy'd always kept quiet about his growing-up years, and I'd never asked.

"Son," Daddy said a little quietly. He coughed again. "You don't need to hear this."

Uncle Luke stared at the urn. "Bogey always hated part of me, I think. He had to take the place of a husband and a father when he was nothing but a kid himself."

Back in the orchard, Daddy'd talked about responsibility getting shoved on him. Was it possible that he meant Uncle Luke, not me?

That's right, Uncle Luke stole his life, answered a phone number marked TRISHA taped to the refrigerator. *Lived his dream.*

"Never mind that," Daddy said. "Don't listen to that, Ben. The reason we fought was something he said, not what I had to do back then." Grit made his voice gravelly, like sandpaper rubbing against my ears. "In my home, he had the nerve to say something that I should have beat him solid for."

"Please help us get back in, Uncle Luke," I said. "Please."

Grim-faced, Uncle Luke gave me a nod. He turned to the refrigerator and reached inside for a bottle of Coca-Cola. "Ya'll want one?" At our silence, he reached in a drawer for an opener and yanked off the lid. "Suit yourself." He lifted the bottle toward the words on Noni's T-shirt. "Cheers. I know it's late, Ben, but we need to have a serious talk." He opened the sliding glass door. "Let's have a fireside chat."

"Is this a planning session?" Noni asked. "Are you gonna help us?"

"I'm going to help the situation, yes." He tipped his head toward the glass sliding doors. "There's a fire pit out back. Just you and me, Ben."

"Noni can hear anything you want to tell me."

"Fine. Say, Bogey," he said, patting Daddy's urn, "mind if we leave you inside while I have a chat with this painter boy of yours?"

Out of nowhere, the walls felt closer and the lump rotated in my throat. I tried to swallow. Daddy stayed quiet and Uncle Luke hummed something that sounded a lot like "You Are My Sunshine." It didn't sound anything like Noni's hobo song.

Uncle Luke scratched at his ears as he walked outside, and something prickled along my neck. A warning of some kind. Like a golf course sand trap was about to appear out of nowhere.

Watch out, said the glue gun.

Might want to have a backup plan, said the hat.

This could be a tricky hole, said the dark sky out the window.

Hush Now

It was close to midnight as Noni sat on the edge of a lounge chair that she'd moved near the fire pit, the backpack resting on the ground beside her along with a fallen nine-iron club and a putter. She was curved over a stick, poking a marshmallow onto the tip she'd sharpened with her pocketknife. "Hope you don't mind," she said to Uncle Luke. "The bag was just sitting out here."

"Not at all. I'll take one myself. Bought those for my girlfriend's kid when she came to visit. I don't eat marshmallows much, so have at it." He picked up a stick and reached for the half-full bag.

"She will," I warned him. "She does magic, and her specialty is disappearing acts. This whole bag'll vanish right before your eyes."

Noni grinned and handed me a stick from beside her. I stuck a marshmallow on it. We sat around the low fire with stars overhead and, except for the neighbor's yard being just over his back fence, it felt like we were in the woods again, only with better provisions.

"Ben . . ." Uncle Luke opened and closed his mouth a few times, like he was trying to figure out what exactly he wanted to say to me.

Daddy, the fire poker said. *He looks just like your daddy when he . . . You remember.*

One time in third grade, Daddy came home three hours late from an afternoon on the course. It was nearly eight o'clock at night and Mama and I had finally started eating the chicken and mashed potatoes she'd reheated for the fourth time. The lump of potatoes on my plate had developed a film on the top, and I was busy tapping the crust with my spoon, making little maps from the cracks, when he came in. Mama said nothing at first, and I thought maybe we'd just have a nice meal together, but then he came over and kissed her on the head.

"Sorry, honey," he said.

"Sorry?" she'd said back, in a whisper louder than any shout I'd ever heard from her. "You should be apologizing to your son there."

They started shouting at each other, one of the few times I'd heard them do that. When I tried to interrupt, they ignored me and kept yelling and yelling and *yelling*, about things that happened last week, last month, last year. It was getting to be my worst birthday ever, so I did what any boy looking for the attention to get back on *him* would do: I gently tipped the half-eaten chicken carcass off the table, followed by the dish of green bean casserole, and, last of all, my birthday cake.

Both of their heads snapped over to me, but I remember Daddy in particular. The look painted on his face was a blend of surprise, panic, and guilt.

That same look was on Uncle Luke's face. Like he'd messed with something important but couldn't do anything about it except feel bad and wait to see how much he'd be hated for it.

"Hey." Noni stood and waved her gooey stick in Uncle Luke's face. "Why don't you say something?"

Uncle Luke eyed her stick and leaned back. "Do you know that Ben here was named for a golfer?"

Bringing the stick back into less dangerous territory, Noni sat back down. "He already told me th—"

He tossed her the marshmallow bag again. "Hush, now. Eat your marshmallows. William Ben Hogan was one of the world's greatest golfers when he was in a terrible car accident. Threw his body over his wife and saved her life. Saved his own life by doing it, since the driver's side was destroyed. Nobody thought he'd walk again, let alone play golf. But two years after that accident, in 1951, he won the Masters."

Uncle Luke smiled at the fire. "That day in 1951 was imprinted on all golf lovers' minds, whether they were old enough to see it happen or just to hear about it later. Miracles and second chances were never laid out so clear."

"Hear that, Benjamin Putter," Noni said, a satisfied look on her face as she reloaded her stick. "Miracles happen there. So are we heading back there now, or what? What's the plan?"

"Years later, this Ben was born on April 8th, the same day as that 1951 win." He glanced at Noni. "Bogey probably wished his boy would fall in love with golf and be as good as Ben Hogan." His eyes swept over me. "But you can't force a passion on people any more than you can force them to give one up."

"Here," Noni said, passing him my paint box. "Here's what Benjamin Putter's passion is."

Uncle Luke opened it and flipped through my sketch-book, arriving at the unfinished one. I'd made progress, but it needed "polish," as Miss Stone said. He held it up in the firelight, looking surprised and pleased. "This is real good, Ben. I mean *real* good."

"It's amazing," Noni said, her voice soft.

Uncle Luke ignored her. "Ben, your daddy would've loved to see this. Is this who I think it is?"

"Yeah. Thanks. I was going to give it to him for his birthday, but then . . ." I didn't need to finish the sentence. Daddy'd died two weeks before his birthday, so there was no need to complete the drawing.

"Well, it's nice. He would've loved it."

"I don't know. Maybe. When I asked if I could draw him something, he just looked at me funny. Then he said, 'Okay. Out of all the people alive in this world, who do you think I'd most like to spend a day with? You think on it, then draw me that person.' So I did."

Uncle Luke's face pinched together like he was going to sneeze. He turned away, but no sneeze came. "Well, it's nice."

"Thanks."

Luke stood. "Listen, Ben." The hand he put on my shoulder was the same size as Daddy's, but softer, even with his golf calluses. Daddy's hands were rough, dotted with old burns and colored in places like his spice rub had become part of him. I liked Daddy's hands better.

"What?"

Uncle Luke breathed in slowly, then breathed out fast before letting his eyes meet mine. "Listen, son." He pressed my shoulder, then scratched at his chin again. "I know you loved your daddy."

Those words butchered me to pieces. I sat there while they sliced away at my insides, nobody but me knowing that I was being cut up. Nobody but me knowing how hard it had been to love Daddy and how impossible it was not to.

"I'm sorry, Ben," he told me.

"For what?"

"Your mama's coming to pick you up. You're not going back to Augusta. I told her it's a bad idea."

My stick dropped in the fire, the marshmallow along with it.

Told you, said the sky.

"You did not," I said.

"I did," Uncle Luke answered. He leaned close to me. "Men can sneak the stink out of a slaughterhouse easier than a man can sneak onto that course during the Masters tournament. There's a whole herd of people whose only job is to walk around and investigate every single person and every Masters entrance badge for authenticity. I don't know what you were thinking. Listen, your mama's not mad you ran off. She's not even mad you took Bogey with you. She just wants to know you're all right."

I scowled. Noni growled.

Uncle Luke shifted around like a nervous pigeon. "She wanted to drive over tonight with your neighbor's car, but I told her that you might need a little time and that you were fine. She'll be here tomorrow afternoon."

He tilted his head toward Noni but didn't look at her. "I'll call tomorrow to make an appointment to drop Miss Noni at a place that can help her. You can't go sneaking into the greatest golf tournament in the world, and you can't be scattering ashes on private property." He patted my back and grinned like I'd agreed with him. "Besides, we can watch the

Masters together on the television. Mr. Hobart Crane might just pull off a win! Talk about things that would make your daddy happy."

"Augusta belongs to the world," I choked out. "Daddy said that."

"Now, don't make a scene. This is a classy neighborhood." He gestured to the open air and the neighbors' houses. "If you wake up my neighbors, they won't hesitate to call about a noise complaint, and the authorities will find their way over here."

Noni threw the bag of marshmallows at his head. "That's why you brought us outside to break the news that you're a big fat traitor?" she said, using her very best cat-with-rabies hiss on him. "I don't care if you get a noise complaint!" she yelled.

"Quiet, runaway, or I'll gladly drop you at a homeless shelter right now. How about that?" He turned back to me. "Son, your mama said that you think you've got something stuck in your throat. Is that true? And now you're hearing your daddy's voice?"

Noni stood up. "Why won't you help your nephew?"

I stood, feeling dizzy. "This is what he wanted. How can you not know that?" I stepped forward and felt Noni stand by my side. "He's your brother. Don't you understand your own brother?"

He didn't answer, and for a second I thought of the boy

whose pig I'd butchered and the way he'd looked at me, his heart broken. I thought the words *I hate you* might fly out of me and smack Uncle Luke in the face. I swallowed, then let my hand rise to feel and cover the lump. "I thought you believed me."

Uncle Luke nodded. "I know, son. I believe that you're hearing something—your aching heart or your conscience, maybe." He stood. "We'll get you someone to talk to. You kids can stay up a little later, but you've got to come inside. Rules are rules." He uncovered a pot beside the fire and scooped out gravel, killing the flames. "I'm gonna go catch up on the tournament coverage in the newspaper. I'll be in my office. Can't believe tomorrow's already Saturday."

Uncle Luke swiped a few moths away from the back-yard floodlight and stepped inside. "Come on. Oh, and I'll be setting my alarm after ya'll get in here. So please don't go trying to run off tonight. Like I said, it'll wake up the neighborhood."

"Ben," Noni whispered while we both stood. "What are we gonna do?"

The stars above echoed her question, but I didn't have an answer. Uncle Luke closed the door behind us and blocked our view with his body while he pressed a button on his alarm system, securing the fact that we were locked in like prisoners, no better off than Daddy in his urn.

Stay Hopeful

The framed paintings of Augusta in Uncle Luke's house were all wrong. They were false comforts. They felt like lies meant to lure me in, and they'd worked, like when Ann Walter had offered that cupcake and then ruined May Talbot's dress on purpose. I'd sat there and let that happen. Now I was sitting back, fiddling with the camping rope and looking at Uncle Luke's refrigerator, my eyes flitting over magnets, a golf course ad requesting instructors, and a telephone number. Staring at nothing, watching Daddy's chances to get to Augusta be snatched away with the same kind of helpless feeling I'd watched May with.

May, who'd never been anything but a friend to me. May, who'd seen me for my insides. May, who'd come over with flowers after her mama called my mama on the telephone. May, who'd ... just given me an idea?

I looked again at the refrigerator, then stood and checked

the cabinet. I set the rope on the table and gave it my Considering look. Like a golfer inspecting his putt from every angle, I thought about the possibilities and consequences. I picked up an orange and gave it a good sniff. The citrus smell burned brightness into my nostrils. I knew what to do.

"Hey, Uncle Luke," I said, keeping my voice casual and catching his arm before he could disappear into his office. "I know it's late, but can I use your telephone to call Mama?"

He looked puzzled. "Sure you can. I'll be reading the paper if you all need me. Feel free to wake me if I doze off and you need something. Help yourself to anything but the beer."

I waited to respond to Noni's thick pinch until after my uncle had left the room. "*Ow.* Listen, Ben Hogan said to reverse every natural instinct and do the opposite of what you are inclined to do and you will probably come very close to having a perfect golf swing." I knocked against the urn. "Daddy, wake up."

"Stop talking in other people's quotes," Noni said. "What are we going to do? Ben, I *have* to get on that golf course tomorrow. The perfect sign is waiting for me there, I know it. I can't miss my chance."

"*Shh,*" I told her. "I'm thinking." Uncle Luke may have hijacked Daddy's dream life, but I wasn't about to let him steal his afterlife, too. It could work. The unlikely, impossible thing could work if I had enough faith in it. "We're gonna get to Augusta National," I said real soft. "I've got a couple of phone calls to make. If you want to help, grab the camping rope and practice your knots."

I shushed Noni's open mouth and dialed my home phone number. Mama picked up two rings later.

"Luke," she said, her voice hurried and higher pitched than normal. "I was just about to call. Can I talk to—"

"It's me, Mama."

Her silence was followed by several quivering inhaled breaths and exhaled choked cries of relief. "Are you okay?" she managed to say.

"I'm better than okay. I've got—"

"My God, Benjamin!" she shouted, the fast breaths changing from shaky to solid. "Do you know what you've done to me? Do you *know* how worried I was!" Her anger shot through the telephone line like it wanted to catch me around the throat and shake me. "How could you just—after all I've—how could, how could you—" The sound of crying cut off Mama's next words, and I let her sob, then sniff her way back to being able to speak. "You're okay," she said.

"I'm sorry, Mama. I'm sorry I worried you, but I've got a question and I need you to tell me the truth."

She sighed, sniffed, sighed. "All right. All right."

"What was Daddy's big fight with Uncle Luke about?" I had to know the answer before making a final decision about Augusta. To make sure I wasn't missing something important by trusting my heart over my uncle. Especially since my escape plan involved something not so nice where Uncle Luke was concerned.

She sighed. "Your daddy and Luke had a complicated history, Ben. There's some resentment on both sides, and an old argument came up. Both of them said things I suspect they didn't mean. Things that they'd kept inside for too long." She breathed in and held the air like she was waiting for something.

"What else?" I asked.

She let her breath out. I almost felt it, warm and mama-smelling against my ear.

"It's okay," I told her.

"I think the real reason your daddy kicked him out is that Luke said a few things about you."

My fingers traced shapes on Uncle Luke's kitchen table. Painter boy, my uncle had called me. "That I liked to paint and draw? Daddy got mad at him for saying that?"

"No, honey." She paused, and I saw her sitting in the kitchen all by herself. "He said you'd be better off without your daddy as a father, and that your daddy would have been better off without you for a son. He said you didn't have enough heart to become a real golfer, just like your daddy didn't have enough heart to become a real golfer. And your daddy"—her voice changed, and I heard a small smile go into it—"your daddy disagreed with all of that. Strongly."

I tried to let that sink in, not sure if it meant Daddy was more upset because Uncle Luke had said he wasn't cut out to be a golfer, or because Uncle Luke had said I wasn't cut out to be one either.

"Okay," I said. For the next fifteen minutes I told her what we'd been doing, where we'd been. And then I delivered the two words that were my last chance. I wasn't going to scatter Daddy without her permission. Not when she was right on the phone talking to me. I would need her vote to get through the rest of my time in Augusta. "Stay hopeful," I told her.

"What, honey?"

"Those were Daddy's last words to you. To stay hopeful."

She didn't respond.

"Mama? Isn't that right? He held your hand and told you to stay hopeful."

The phone dropped. I heard it smack the floor and roll. When she picked it up, Mama's voice shook so badly I could barely understand her. "How do you know that? That was a guess, wasn't it? You were at home, Ben."

"I was."

"You weren't there."

"I wasn't."

"Then how do you know what your daddy said to me?"

The whole truth was too big for her. I'd give her a little truth. If part of her needed to believe it was a guess, maybe other parts of her would need to believe otherwise. "I just know."

"You just *know*? Benjamin, I don't understand. I didn't tell anyone what Bo said, not a single—"

"I don't understand, either. Not all of it, anyway. But, Mama, I think I'm supposed to take Daddy to see the Masters. And I think I'm supposed to scatter his ashes there. I feel it more than I've felt anything in my life. It's where he belongs. Can I try? I'm not going to get hurt, I promise you that," I said.

I heard the hesitation in her voice. It was a good hesitation—one that meant her head's *no* was being battled by her heart's *yes*. "Your uncle won't allow it. He says it's impossible."

"Daddy and Uncle Luke didn't see eye to eye on everything."

She laughed for the first time since Daddy's memorial service. "You can try. I love you. Mrs. Grady's lending me her car, on the condition that I bring her with me. She said her husband, Richard, wants to come, too." Mama sighed. "I shouldn't play into her fantasies, but I needed the car. I said it'd be fine for him to come with us."

I looked at Daddy's urn and wondered if maybe Crazy Grady wasn't as crazy as all of us thought. "I like Mrs. Grady," I told Mama. "She'll be good company for you."

"We'll be there tomorrow afternoon, in time to get you a birthday dinner. Can't believe my baby's gonna be twelve. You're growing up too fast."

"Oh, Mama, growing up's a long way off." But it didn't feel that way. The last year alone had been full of changes, and there were more coming. I could feel and smell them somewhere just ahead, like a swollen river or an invisible barbecue scent, drawing me forward. There was no stopping things from changing.

"The bank loan came through, honey. We're gonna get the café back and start serving chicken. We'll keep some pork—your father would never forgive me if we didn't—but the overall menu will be more affordable for us. That means a lot of things for us. Maybe we'll get you better art supplies. Whatever you want, sweetheart."

"Thanks, Mama. That's good news."

When I got off the phone and told Noni the next part of my plan, she clapped her hands. "I like it. I'll figure out which knots will work best. What if he wakes up?"

"He took three of those pills—the bottle said two was the right dose. Add on the fact that when he stayed at our house, he and Daddy snored loud enough to block out a bear fight, and he'll sleep heavy, believe me. How are you at sewing?"

"Terrible." She looked at the needle and thread on the counter with suspicion. "Why?"

I turned the backpack over and showed her the rip. "Forgot to tell you. This got torn in the storm. Your dress did, too. I'll sew up the backpack, but it'll be ugly and noticeable.

We won't want to be noticed. I think you better wear that." I pointed to the frock that Uncle Luke's girlfriend had made.

Looking like she'd found a stinkbug in her dessert, she picked up the dress and held it against her, letting out a big sigh when it looked the right length. The thin sweater looked like a fit, too. Then she snatched up a yellow shoe and held it against her feet. "Fine," she said. "But I'm not putting that hat on my head. So if your plan works and we get out of here, then what? What about those badges your uncle talked about?"

I took a deep breath. The next part would be a leap of faith, something I'd been short on. "This may sound crazy, but I got the idea from the worker who caught us in the storm. He said we'd be better off getting a ride with one of the players."

Noni frowned. "How are we gonna do that?"

"We make sure we're right alongside the road where the players will go into Augusta. We make sure we look real sad, like we're in trouble and need someone to stop. Daddy always talked about how golf is a game of character and integrity—of doing the right thing. Masters players are the best golfers in the world. It's a long shot and we can try to think of something else, but if we get ourselves in the right place—"

Before I could finish, Noni's mouth opened and she snapped her fingers. "That's *it*." She began pacing around the table. "Why didn't I think of it? Superstitions."

"Superstitions?"

"Not wanting bad luck." She flashed me a grin so wide, I saw every tooth in her mouth. "Nobody's gonna want bad luck anyway, but especially not going into a day of the biggest golf tournament there is. He'll stop."

"Who'll stop?"

She pressed her lips together and snapped again. "Whoever. Somebody'll stop. Golfers are superstitious. I read it in that book." She tapped the backpack holding the Augusta book and gave me a serious nod. "It'll work."

It was the first time I'd seen her completely confident in one of my ideas. I liked it. And she was right. Golfers were superstitious. The best of them had been known to wear certain clothes on certain days of certain tournaments, and Daddy himself had ways he tried to avoid bad luck on the course.

"I think maybe it could," I said. "Sometimes the hardest thing about finishing is having the guts to show up. The strokes will take care of themselves or they won't, but either way, you've got to be there to find out what happens."

"Which golfer said that?"

"Me. I said it."

"Finally." Noni grinned. "I've been waiting for a Benjamin Putter quote. Hey, Benjamin Putter," she said in a soft, almost shy voice I hadn't heard from her before. "Can I try to paint something?"

"Sure. I'm gonna lie down on that couch in the other room. We'll leave in a few hours. Don't worry, I'm too wound up to fall asleep. What are you going to paint?"

"Not sure yet. I'm gonna rest for a little bit in that guest bedroom when I'm done. I'll leave the box on the kitchen table." She touched my shoulder. "Thanks for not giving up. We're so close."

"I know."

That's what I was afraid of.

Fears and Actions

An hour later, at three o'clock in the morning on my twelfth birthday, the first time I'd ever spend a whole birthday with my father, I stared at the ceiling and thought about fear. Back when we jumped off the train, Noni had told me that I had to face my fears, so at least they'd know I was up for a fight. But how can you be ready to fight something when you can't even pin down what it is?

Trying to think it out just made my head ache, so making sure I didn't creak too much, I stepped down the hallway to the kitchen and turned the oven light on. I needed to settle my mind with some paper and a pencil or a brush. Maybe make one more painting for May.

Why don't you paint her a pair of running shoes, runaway, said the faucet. *Bet she wishes she could run away from school, too, but she's not a coward, so she can't.*

How about a cupcake, suggested the half-wet drying towel. *For the one you watched get smeared all over her.*

No, no, no, it wasn't his fault, the refrigerator scolded them. *He's just a coward.*

Then they all started up, all of them. The cabinets, the dirty dishes in the sink, the sliding doors, the glue gun and dress and hat, all talking and accusing and crowding me and the ball stuck in my throat.

His daddy doesn't care about either of them, no he doesn't, golf, that's all Bogart Putter loves, oh hush, well, he doesn't care, golf balls, golf clubs, don't be mean, golf bags, golf course, I'm being honest, he's not good enough to love, heart of a golfer, be quiet, what's the heart of a golfer, he was never good enough, he seems so nice, not as nice as golf, why not, why what, why is he afraid, what is he afraid of—

"You all stop."

He's afraid of the space.

"Go away. Please go away."

He's afraid of the space between.

I gave up. "Between what?"

You know, yes you do, yes he knows.

"Between *what?*"

All of them got quiet, stayed silent, until one thing spoke. It was the golf ball in my throat.

The space between everything, it said. *The space between Hilltop and the world. Between the ground and the coal train. Between the train and the peach farm. Between you and May Talbot's lunch table.*

Between what your daddy could have been and what he was.

Between who you are and who you'll be.

"I don't understand," I told the lump. "I don't know what to do."

You do. You already said it.

"Said what?"

The strokes will take care of themselves or they won't, but either way, you've got to be there to find out. The space between you and your daddy. Fill it.

"I don't know how," I whispered. I opened my box and saw that Noni had taken the last piece of thick paper. I pulled out my sketchbook, wondering what she'd painted, and worked until I'd completely finished the sketch on the third-to-last page. I blew on it, and I could've sworn that the hair waved a little in the small wind I'd made.

I picked up the urn and put my mouth on the cool pewter, against a spot that felt right. I didn't care if he was the stars and I was a fool. Within twenty-four hours, Noni and I would be successful, or Mama would be taking both me and Daddy back to Hilltop. Either way, I knew this was the last of our time alone together.

"I love you, Daddy," I whispered, and gave him a kiss.

He didn't answer, but I took comfort in the low rumbling inside the urn.

Soft steps sounded, and Noni poked her head into the room. "I heard you rustling around." She sat on the edge of the table, putting down the Augusta book that had been tucked under her arm. Her eyes were bright. "I'm excited." She pointed to the camping ropes. "Your uncle is bound to be sleeping by now. His bedroom is empty."

"He's probably still in his office." I raised an eyebrow and slapped her on the back. "Let's get started. We'll leave him some water and a snack."

"Excellent." Noni frowned. "Just water. He doesn't deserve a snack."

Daddy woke and demanded an explanation. Leaving him cheering and snickering on the kitchen table, we crept down toward Uncle Luke's office with all the stealth we could manage. A low hum of something came from the room, its door open just a crack. The light was still on, and a cigar smell lingered around the hallway.

On my signal, we both dropped to our knees and inched forward. With nervous hands, I poked at the door and stuck my head in. I saw the back of Uncle Luke's armchair, facing a small television set. I crept forward.

"Dontchasdothat!" Uncle Luke blurted.

I backed out so quickly I knocked right into Noni. "*Retreat*," I whispered, expecting Uncle Luke to come charging. "Go, now, before—"

A loooooooong snore rang out, followed by mumbling. Hmm.

Noni pushed me aside and army crawled into the room.

A moment later, she waved me in. "Talking in his sleep," she whispered. "Snoring like a freight train. Time for some hog tying, pig boy."

It took both ropes to do it right. We tied his legs to the chair legs and his chest to the chair frame. He wasn't going anywhere when he woke up.

Just as we were leaving the room, Noni's face fell. "Benjamin Putter, we forgot one big thing. How are we supposed to beat the alarm?"

I smiled at her. "Third button from the left disables it."

"Huh?"

"We'll leave the front door unlocked so Mama can get in the house when she gets here." After our talk, I felt certain that Mama wouldn't be too mad, and I'd be sure to leave a note telling her that Noni and I would be home by sunrise on Sunday. "Hope Uncle Luke doesn't pee his pants before then."

Noni shot me a devilish grin. "I hope he does. But how do you know the right button? If you guess wrong, the neighbors will call the police, they'll untie Uncle Luke, and he'll tell Augusta's security what you're planning to do."

"His girlfriend. Trisha's phone number was on the fridge, so I called and told her Uncle Luke wanted something from the car, but couldn't remember the right button. She didn't seem surprised."

She laughed. "Congratulations, Benjamin Putter. You may not need me as much as I thought you did. I thought you were one of those sensitive artist types, not a trickster."

I bowed. "I may like a good flower to paint, ma'am, but I'm still a Putter. And Putters are men of action."

A Magical Ride

Georgia's spring heat still slumbered at five o'clock in the morning, but Noni and I were wide awake, slipping along the streets of Augusta, dodging streetlights like they were minefields. An hour later, we'd parked ourselves close to the entrance where players would drive through the gates of Augusta National. There was a separate entrance for people with tickets for the tournament, and we'd avoided that area. Nobody but players and official people drove down Magnolia Lane, and that's exactly who we were hoping to flag down.

Noni passed me a chunk of cloth that matched her dress, thread wrapped around it like a bow. "Happy birthday, Benjamin Putter."

"You got me something?" I was surprised and touched, and hoped she hadn't stolen anything more from the Marinos. But when the cloth fell open, it was her pocketknife. "I can't take this. It was from your daddy. Noni, no." I handed it to her.

She threw it back into my lap. "Take it. I know you probably prefer brushes to knives, but I want you to have it. You'll think of something to do with it."

I grinned. "Pick splinters out, maybe. Or gut a fish with the toothpick."

Noni smiled and gave me a salute. "Very funny."

"Thank you." I put it in my pocket.

"The players should arrive anytime now," Daddy said. "First tee time is in a couple hours, and they'll want to be here early. I can't believe we're gonna see the Masters!" He laughed. "Happy birthday, son. I didn't get you anything, but it's gonna be a good day. A great day."

Noni adjusted the fancy sun hat she wore, testing it at a low angle over her face, then taking if off again to rub her head all over and yank on her hair.

I felt bad for her. I'd forced her to wear the hat. "Sorry you have to wear that, but my ball cap wouldn't look right."

"It's not that. Well, it is, but it's also my hair. I *hate* pigtails. I've never worn pigtails in my life." She chewed on her bottom lip, staring down the road and tapping her toes.

"Take 'em out, then. You look twitchy instead of pathetic. We were going for pathetic, remember?"

"Don't tell me what to do." She tugged at her sleeves. "And this dress is ridiculous. And who puts a big plastic flower right on a shoe?" She eyed the barrier that surrounded the entire property. "You really think somebody's gonna pick us up?"

"You don't? I swear, you're the most faithless runaway I've ever met." I nudged her. "That's a Noni quote."

"I know my own quotes when I hear them. Maybe we should just hop this fence."

"Maybe not," I said, yanking her up with me. A slow car, lights shining bright through an early morning mist, came driving along. Black with white words shouting from the side. "Security," I whispered, pulling her behind a bush until it passed by. "Not a car we want to be stuck inside."

We got back in position after it was out of sight. "I'm sure we'll get in," I said, not sure of much. "You nervous?" I asked her, rubbing at the golf ball in my throat.

She nodded and wrapped her right hand around her left elbow, wincing.

"Are you finally gonna admit that nasty bruise of yours hurts?"

"It didn't before, not that it's any of your business." She glared, which made her seem more like herself. Poking lightly at the blue-black skin, she grimaced again. "I just hope everything works out."

A car approached, and we stood as rehearsed, stepping a few feet into the road. I pretended to take Noni's hand, and she pulled away dramatically, then curled into a ball. Fake-concerned, I bent down and was about to fake-comfort her when the car pulled around us and kept going.

The same thing happened three more times. My brilliant idea was looking less brilliant.

"Don't worry, Noni. We'll get the next one to stop."

But my false confidence didn't even fool me. My lump was heavy, and I didn't know if it was telling me I was making a good decision or the worst one possible. It was still hard to know whether to feel sad or excited about being so close to watching the Masters with Daddy. It meant spending an unimaginable day with him, but it also meant we'd reached the place where he would leave me. Right when I was leaning toward sad, a piece of gravel hit my ankle. A car had stopped.

It was a navy blue limousine, sleek and shined up like fresh quarters from the bank.

"Time for the show," Noni murmured low.

A window rolled down in the backseat, and a man popped his head out. "Are you okay, son?"

"Oh my God in heaven, I know that voice!" Daddy crowed. "Is that who I think it is?"

I looked at the ground to see if my jaw was there on the road. Felt like it'd fallen a good ways. Then I looked back to the man's face in wonder. "*Hobart Crane*," I said in a strange, garbled voice, my knees turning to jelly and dropping me to the dirt.

"Son? Are you all right?" he repeated. He looked over at Noni, who seemed to have frozen solid with her head down. "Are you okay?" he asked her, then fiddled with a plastic device on his ear. "This thing is acting up on me again. Honey, you're gonna have to look at me if you're whispering or I won't know what you're saying."

"She's my sister, sir," I said. "She doesn't talk. At all." Noni'd thought that having one of us be silent would get more sympathy, and she'd volunteered since she'd made me be a non-talker back at the bus station.

"Oh?" he said. "Is that right? And what are ya'll doing here?"

"Well, Mr. Crane. Our Daddy, well, our Daddy . . . You're his favorite player, sir, and he, well, he . . ." I trailed off, then started in with the fake sobbing Noni and I had practiced, hoping Hobart Crane couldn't tell that I was licking my fingers to get them wet before rubbing my eyes. *Stick to the plan*, the back of my eyelids reminded me, but in the presence of Mr. Hobart Crane, the details of my plan had turned into something like mush.

"Just hold on, now," Mr. Crane said, motioning for the driver to turn the engine off. "What happened?"

"Our Daddy"—I sniffed—"he died last month. We've been here all week, trying to find a way into the tournament." Noni elbowed me and handed me the urn, not raising her gaze from the ground. "This is him. We're off school this week, and Mama's got to work." I took a deep breath. "It was his biggest wish to see the Masters tournament. We thought we could show him, but we can't get in, and the security people won't let us inside without one of those badges," I moaned, dry-sobbing into my arm. "It was his dying wish."

"Son, just slow down. Is that really your daddy? Well, Lord, I'm so sorry."

He didn't need to be sorry. Daddy was more than okay. In fact, he was shouting praises to the Ol' Creator and laughing like a crazy man. "Holy rivers and streams, *Hobart Crane,* ha-ha! We're getting escorted into Augusta by Hobart Crane! Kill me now and I'd die a happy man, I tell you what!"

The front door of the car opened and the uniformed driver stepped out. "Mr. Crane, if you want some personal time before you hit the driving range, we need to get going."

"Right, thank you." Hobart Crane looked us over. Noni still hadn't looked up. She was playing her role to perfection, shaking slightly. Mr. Crane walked over to her. "You want to take your daddy to see some golf, sweetie?"

Very slightly, very slowly, Noni moved the rim of the hat up and down, not showing her face. The rest of her was arranged neatly, her hands held behind her back and her legs straight together.

"She went silent when Daddy died," I said, letting my voice waver. "Started with fewer and fewer words, and now she doesn't say anything at all. She and Daddy . . . Well, golf was their special thing. I've been praying that this would help her heal up." The lie felt wrong, but true somehow.

"Is that right?" His lips twisted to the side, and I believe I saw moisture in his eyes. Mr. Hobart Crane, bless his heart, not only bought the story but let me keep the change. Noni and I were inside the car within two minutes. The backseat was the hugest I'd ever seen, with two full seats that faced each other.

"My sponsor sent it," Hobart said, looking a little embarrassed. "I don't travel like this all the time." He told his driver to take it nice and slow. "After all," he said to me, "a man doesn't get a chance to drive down Magnolia Lane every day."

Just like in the Augusta book, the road leading into the golf club's grounds was lined on both sides by tall magnolia trees, all of them bursting flowers like it was a day to dress up and celebrate.

I sat next to Noni, who sat stiffly across from Mr. Crane, not looking out the window at all, sticking to her role as a child who couldn't talk after losing her father. A box turtle with her head pulled in, the rim of her hat pulled down so low she looked like her neck was sprouting a daisy.

Daddy was hooting and hollering and making such a stink about it that it was tough to keep up my sad/concerned/grateful appearance. Well, the grateful part was easy enough, but the rest of me was annoyed and worried that with Daddy's carrying on, I was gonna blow our cover.

"Thank you, Mr. Crane," I said.

"You're welcome," Hobart answered. "What's your name? And your sister's?"

I was all out of Big Fivers, other than the one I'd been named for. The truth would have to do. "My name is Ben Putter," I said. "Ben Hogan Putter. My sister's named Noni."

Mr. Crane stiffened a little, like his back was bothering him, then shifted in his seat. He bent down to retie one of his shoes, taking a long time. "That's a nice name for a little girl," he said real quiet, sitting up with a sigh and fingers that scrunched in and out of loose fists. He shook off some thought and raised an eyebrow. "And Ben Hogan Putter, what a name that is. Your daddy did love golf, didn't he?" His eyes crinkled, catching the sunlight shining between the line of trees we passed. He looked at the hat covering Noni's head and face. "Did you play much golf with your daddy, Noni Putter?"

Noni said nothing, keeping her legs nicely crossed at the ankle. If I didn't know better, I'd say she was a very quiet, well-behaved, graceful little girl, which was the opposite of the loping, shouting, skipping, pushing, smacking runaway I'd gotten to know.

Mr. Crane cleared his throat and looked at me. "So your sister can't talk? How about something other than golf? What else does she like?"

I shook my head. I didn't really know what Noni liked. "She used to sing. And she can do magic tricks."

"Hey, Noni Putter, do you like magic?"

Noni wouldn't look at him, but Hobart Crane chatted to her in a gentle voice and waved a coin and told her to pick.

Without raising her head, Noni picked a hand time after time. Hobart opened his empty hands and then found the coin somewhere new—behind her ear, underneath her shoe, in the car cushion just behind her shoulder. She played along and must've been following the movements of his forearms because she sure as heck wasn't looking up. Then she reached down toward the backpack. I watched her slip something from the outside pocket, and the next time Hobart Crane had her guess which hand, she stopped him from opening his left fist.

Slowly, with playful stealth, she grabbed his fist between her hands and started rotating it back and forth. When she finally peeled his fingers back, covering his palm with her own, Hobart Crane let out a bark of surprise. Daddy's ball-marking quarter sat there in the middle of his hand.

"Hoo! What's this? Tricking the trickster? I think I like you, Noni Putter." Hobart tapped the top of her head with his free hand and laughed, but it sounded choked.

"That's my daddy's special quarter," I said, another truth. "He used it as a ball marker. You can have it. He'd like that."

I held the urn tight between my hands while Hobart Crane met my eyes and nodded. "I'll use it. Thank you." He put the ball marker in his pocket and took one of Noni's hands in his own. "Thank you," he said. "I'll take good care of it. I promise."

Noni said nothing, but I noticed that her fingers curled around Mr. Crane's for a moment instead of pulling right away.

"So you all need day passes?" Hobart asked.

"I guess we do." I struggled to come up with something that didn't sound like begging. "We didn't bring any money to buy them."

"I'll make sure you get two. All the players get a few, but I left mine at home. I didn't think I'd have anyone to give them to. And why don't you take these." He let go of Noni's hand and reached into his pocket, pulling out two twenty-dollar bills as the car came to a halt. "So you can buy a couple souvenirs on me. Food's cheap during the tournament, so that should keep you fed on the course too. And if you show the badges I'll get you to the folks in the clubhouse restaurant, they should let you eat there. Just tell them to put it on my tab."

Noni kicked me, then jerked her head toward the backpack. When I didn't respond, she took out the paint box and flipped to the third-to-last page of my drawing pad, the one that was supposed to be Daddy's birthday present.

"Oh," I said, realizing what she meant. "We'd like to give you this. As a thank-you." Carefully, I ripped out the drawing and handed it to him.

He stared a long time at the paper, and Noni finally lifted her hat a tiny bit, taking a quick peek at his fascinated expression before ducking her head again.

"It's me," Hobart said. "Who drew this?"

"I drew it," I said. "It was for my daddy. But I didn't finish it on time."

"This is incredible." He looked at me a little hesitantly as the car came to a halt. "If I sent you a photo of someone, do you think you could get her down on paper like this?"

"I could try."

"Well, write down your address, son, and I'll get in touch." He took a notepad from a small duffel bag and handed it to me along with a pen, then stepped out of the car. Noni got out behind me, and he gave us both an awkward pat on the shoulder.

I handed him my address. "Thank you, sir."

"Call me Hobart."

"Don't you dare!" warned Daddy.

"I couldn't, Mr. Crane."

"Well, okay. Come on, Ben Putter and Noni Putter. I'll get you some passes, and then I've got to swing the club enough to digest the food in my belly." He rubbed his stomach. "There's a diner down the road that makes a great big omelet sweet and spicy enough to marry."

We walked into the fancy clubhouse, and everyone we passed smiled and said hello to Mr. Crane. We weaved around a few hallways until we came to an office.

"Kids, meet Rachel Reilly, the kindest Masters secretary ever to grace the halls of this clubhouse." Mr. Crane explained what he wanted, and before we knew it, Noni and I had specialty badges that said we could go anywhere we wanted.

Mrs. Reilly dug through her desk. "Ya'll want a picture? I know I put that camera somewhere."

"Sure. Thank you, ma'am," I said. While I got Mama's photograph out of the backpack, Noni squirmed beside me.

Mrs. Reilly searched drawers, finally lifting her head and hand in triumph. "Got it."

Hobart Crane put his arm around me and Noni. I held Daddy in one arm and Mama's picture in the other.

"Look up, little girl," the woman told Noni, who was looking at her shoes.

"That's okay. Noni Putter's perfect just the way she is," Hobart said. "Go ahead and take the picture." Right after she clicked, Noni bolted out of the office.

Mr. Crane watched Noni go, then turned to me with raised eyebrows.

"Bathroom," I said, figuring that had to be it. Either that, or she was dying to yank that hat off.

"Okay, I've got to warm up." Hobart handed Mrs. Reilly a piece of paper. "That paper is this little boy's address. Can you copy it down quick and send him a copy of that photo,

Mrs. Reilly? And send me one, too, if you would."

She wrote down my address in Hilltop and handed the paper back.

"I hope you smiled big. And tell him good luck," Daddy demanded.

"Good luck, sir," I obliged. "Hope you win. Thank you for helping us."

"You bet. It's never a good thing to turn down a child in need." He tipped his hat, then walked away.

"Mr. Crane," Daddy sighed, "I wish I was there to shake your hand."

I found Noni down the hallway, her pigtails pulled out and her hair hanging down free for the first time since I'd known her. It was only when she looked up that I realized she was crying. "What's the matter? Didn't you like Mr. Crane?"

She didn't answer.

I looked at her elbow, the sweater's sleeves covering the bruise there. I wished I could heal it. Help her stop hurting.

I thought of her hand holding Hobart Crane's in the car. "Are you missing your daddy?" I asked her.

"I am," she whispered. "I miss him so much."

I weaved my fingers into hers and squeezed. "I bet he's missing you, too. Come on, sister. Let's watch some golf."

"Let's watch some *golf*!" Daddy repeated in a croaky shout, and in spite of the fact that I was hours away from scattering my father's ashes, I felt my smile go all the way to my big Putter ears. Noni thought that Augusta National had the power to make miracles.

Maybe, just maybe, a day on this golf course could do more than make my father proud of me.

Maybe it could make him stay after all.

Maybe there was still a chance I wouldn't have to say goodbye.

The Sistine Chapel of Golf Courses

In the back corner of the art room at Hilltop Primary School, a poster of a painting used to hang. Once a week, when we had class with Miss Stone, I would soak it in. Blue water with green lily pads and pink flowers. Swirls and movement. *Jump in*, the lily pads used to tell me. *The water feels so fine. You'll float like us.* The first day I saw it, I asked Miss Stone how somebody could make a picture that told you to come inside it and live there for a time. She didn't know the answer, but she'd always tell me something new about the artist if I lingered after the rest of my class walked out.

This one is a watercolor painting, she said, *but he also used oils and pastels.*

He spent twenty years of his life painting water lilies.

He liked to be outside and paint things from real life.

His father wanted him to join the grocery business, but he wanted to be an artist.

Augusta National Golf Club was like that Claude Monet painting. Just knowing something so incredible existed in the world made me feel changed.

Noni and me and Daddy leaned on the railings of the clubhouse porch, so far from the split-rail fences of Hilltop. The scents of grass and flowers and possibility mingled with the grounds workers and pockets of reporters. Noni put her elbows on the white wood and cupped her chin in both hands. I let my hip be cushioned by the rail and stared, soaking in Augusta National Golf Club's eighteen-hole course, feeling warmth settle into me, like a flower must feel when it opens to let the morning sunlight nestle inside.

I could see why Daddy might confuse the grounds of a golf course with church. Augusta National looked and felt like a place where a person could come to pray, like a wide open cathedral dotted with loblolly pines stretching straight toward heaven. I knew this was a place I would never capture on paper. It couldn't be put down. It was a living, breathing, rounded, moist piece of earth that burst with the most beautiful shades of color I'd ever seen. Greener green grass and trees and bushes, pinker pink flowers, whiter white flowers, bluer blue sky than I thought possible.

I poked Noni's shoulder. "Can you feel it?"

She smacked my arm and adjusted the sun hat on her head. "Feel what?"

"This place feels like magic. Let's go explore."

"While we're exploring, we better think of a magical place to hide out tonight."

"Right." To be real honest, I hadn't been certain that we'd even get on the course, so I didn't have a hint of a plan for where we'd wait after the day was over. All the sneaking, all the leaping over fences and sprinting from security I'd envisioned, all the distractions Noni and I had talked about . . . We didn't need any of them. All those barriers had been swept away by Hobart Crane.

We looked over the clubhouse, flashing our special badges at anyone who glanced at us with a slight side eye. Strolling to areas we shouldn't, we walked around the Par 3 course near the tournament course, crept along the edges of the fishing pond named after a president, and generally made ourselves at home.

We watched as play began. More and more people filled the grounds, but there was a grace to it all. While the people walking around the Masters were mostly white, not everyone was. Crowds formed in places, mixing together, watching the players, watching the Masters, brushing past each other, standing right next to each other like their skin colors didn't matter. Or like, if they were the kind of people who carried protest signs, for a few hours they could turn off whatever made it matter to them. Or maybe, for some of those people, it really didn't matter. It was hard to tell the insides of people just by looking at them.

Television cameras were there, and we stood for a while near a few of them, hearing three reporters talk about who they thought might win this year's Masters. Hobart Crane, Jack Nicklaus, and Homero Blancas were their favorites.

"Hey, think we should stand behind the cameras and wave to Uncle Luke?" Noni asked me.

It was tempting. The thought of my tied-up uncle watching golf news and seeing us saluting him from Augusta National was a satisfying one. "Maybe later."

The tournament may have been the hottest ticket in town, but Mr. Crane had been right about the food being affordable. Stations were set up selling sandwiches, moon pies, candy bars, cola, you name it—all for less than two dollars. I got a pimento cheese sandwich, which Daddy said was the specialty of the Masters.

"Like drinking mint juleps during the Kentucky Derby," he said. "Only cheaper and better on your liver."

I used Hobart's money to get a shirt for me and Noni and a key chain for Uncle Luke. Noni occasionally ticked off information she'd read in Daddy's Augusta book.

"Lots of people," I said.

"Up to thirty thousand people walking around on Saturdays and Sundays during the Masters," she shot back.

"How do you think they get the flowers to bloom right on the exact week of the tournament?"

"They put ice under the azalea bushes if they start to bloom early."

"Everyone's so calm around here."

"Rules, Benjamin Putter. No running, no shouting, no cameras, no food from outside, no—"

"I get the idea."

We wandered as we saw fit and clearly Augusta had found us worthy after all, because when we returned to Amen Corner, the turn that spanned holes eleven, twelve, and thirteen, the great Sam Snead himself was just about to hit a tee shot off twelve. The sight of him swinging his club, walking across the famous bridge named for Ben Hogan, and finally standing alone on the twelfth green, sheltered between Rae's creek and a wall of flowering azaleas . . .

Well, it took my breath away.

Daddy was overwhelmed when I told him who we were watching.

"My God," he said, when he was finally able to speak. "All the Masters winners get invited back for life, but most of the legends don't show up to play after they stop being competitive. Mr. Snead must've made the cut, and he's almost sixty." His invisible hand clutched the side of my arm, pulling me toward him. "Take a picture in your head, Ben," Daddy told me, his voice hushed to a reverent whisper. "Living legends are traveling this course today. Legends-to-be are walking it too. Breathe, son. Soak it in. You tell your children about this moment, you hear me?"

A single bead of sweat dripped down my temple. I

wiped it away, knowing that if I ever had any children, this moment and place would be nearly impossible to describe. I had the strangest feeling, like I was standing inside one of my father's dreams. Sam Snead was playing golf right in front of me. Ben Hogan, not playing, was probably placing his feet on Augusta National somewhere, watching the tournament. And the ghost of Bobby Jones was here, too.

This was the first year Bobby Jones wasn't alive to be at Augusta National during the Masters, but I felt certain that his spirit had found its way here. I could feel that sure as I felt my father leaning close. I could almost smell the soft hint of barbecue smoke that always flavored the air around him, lingering beneath the Old Spice cologne he used to wear on special occasions.

"Yes, sir," I said. "I'll try to tell them."

We walked along the course, stepping behind the crowds lined up along the fairways. They were called galleries, which brought to mind places people went to stare at art and think about it. And that's kind of how it felt to me, being at the Masters. Like I was seeing the biggest painting in the world—like it was so big and I was standing so close that I'd been able to step inside. It was hard to tell where the Masters ended, and me and Daddy's urn began.

Certain holes were more magical than others, carved

into the landscape like perfect golf glens that had been there since time began, but we saw them all.

Three pimento cheese sandwiches into the day, midway down the fairway on hole number eight, the crowd gasped and a wide shot came down two feet from where I stood, chewing. Noni jumped, but I couldn't take my eyes off the ball, let alone move. The crowd shuffled, and Hobart Crane marched through like Moses, parting the gallery of people like sea water. His face was all business as he looked for the ball.

"There, sir," said Noni, then ducked behind a group.

Hobart jerked around like he'd been shot. Then Mr. Crane stood still, his head tilted, eyes wide and seeking something. He looked lost. His caddie gently told people to stand back, then set down Hobart's bag, waiting patiently to pull the next club out as directed.

I'd noticed the caddies throughout the morning. Each man was dressed neatly in white coveralls. The white uniforms made the caddies look professional and serious and important and courteous. Each man walked behind their assigned player, carrying his load and picking out clubs. Each man was colored.

When I whispered a question to him about it, Daddy said Augusta National had a Negro-caddie-only policy, and while other professional tournaments allowed players to bring in their own caddies, this club required use of Augusta

National caddies during the Masters. Though Daddy only made saints out of golfers, he had a special spot for caddies, and I'd heard enough here and there from Daddy to know that some of Augusta's caddies were becoming legendary in their own right.

Mr. Crane's caddie cleared his throat. Hobart broke out of whatever spell had grabbed him and stepped to the man, exchanged a few low words, nodded, and accepted a four iron.

"But why not have white caddies, too?"

I saw Daddy's shoulders rise and fall. "It's tradition here. White club members, colored caddies. Just the way things are, Ben. The caddies are well respected here. Some of them form real close relationships with their Masters players."

So colored men were good enough to give advice to Masters players and club members, good enough to carry equipment, but not good enough that the people running Augusta National would ever let them join their club. Something wasn't right about that.

"Augusta National is a private club," Daddy said. "They've got the right to do whatever they want."

It reminded me of the school protests. "Like in Hilltop," I said.

"How's that?" he asked.

When our school integrated, the parents who took their kids out said it was their right to do that. They said they weren't going against the law by building a private school that shut out colored students. I looked down at Daddy. "Just because something's allowed and it doesn't break any laws, I don't know if that makes it right." I didn't expect him to answer and I didn't need his opinion. I just wanted to tell him mine.

A crowd roared approval of some shot at the golf green ahead of us.

"What was that?" Daddy stood on his ashy tiptoes, looking this way and that. "Who shot what?"

"Must have been a good putt, Daddy."

"Well, get over there and tell me what's going on."

He listened while I narrated our path, then told me background on holes and great shots that happened there long ago. But part of my mind drifted, not sure if I felt heavier or lighter.

Just concentrate on your daddy, the lump in my throat said. *For as long as he's here.*

Noni seemed to have settled into a quiet daze. We followed Hobart Crane for much of the day, and I kept hoping he'd look our way and wave, but he was all business. Daddy loved his swing, and when I stopped to really look and could see it right there in person, it was a beautiful thing. Easy and effortless.

"They seem confident, Ben, but even professional golfers

constantly question their swing. They're on a quest."

"For what?"

"For the one swing that defines them. A swing that comes easy and natural and fits them perfectly. One they can be proud of." He paused, then cleared his throat. "The best I can say is that I tried, son. I didn't find my swing in the time I had. I don't know that I'd ever have found it. But I tried."

He'd spent more time at the golf course than at home. His hands always seemed to be full of either clubs or barbecue equipment. I thought back and couldn't remember a time when his hand had held mine. He'd been on a quest to find his swing. "I know you tried, Daddy."

"Do you understand what I'm saying, son?" He coughed. "I'm not talking about golf anymore. I'm talking about . . . being your father. I never quite got there. I know that. Do you see what I'm saying?" His voice was soft and faint, like a golf ball hit high in the sky that you tried to follow, lost in the sun, then found again.

I didn't really know what he was talking about, but I could glimpse it, like an abstract watercolor where you couldn't define the picture, only know that it made you feel something. I saw how some parts of his life had gotten tangled around him like Spanish moss, beautiful and strangling at the same time. And I saw how he was like the Spanish moss, too. It wasn't his fault; he just didn't know how else to grow.

Abbott's Tree

It wasn't until four o'clock or so that I remembered that we needed to figure out where we'd wait while Augusta shut down for the night. The golf ball stuck in my throat pressed against its prison, rolling around like it was getting ready to make a break for it.

"I need a solid meal before we decide where to hide," Noni told me. "Let's eat in the clubhouse."

"Sounds good to me."

"My son, eating in Augusta National's clubhouse," Daddy said, shaking his head. "Man alive, of all the inconvenient times to be stuck in a cremation urn."

We ordered fried chicken in the clubhouse restaurant and were the only children in the whole place. I put Daddy's urn on the table as an authority figure, right by the window view. I could picture his face perfectly while I gave him every detail of the room, the server, the menu.

Halfway through her plate of chicken, Noni reached out

and clutched my hands, a worried look on her face. "Wait," she said. "Something's wrong."

"What?"

She pointed to a man across the room, eating a piece of cake. "We forgot to get you a birthday dessert." And with that, Noni grinned and ordered the biggest ice cream sundae the kitchen would make.

When it arrived, she sang me a soft happy birthday with her beautiful, low voice. And after she'd polished off most of the dessert like it was the last ice cream she'd ever get, we got serious about figuring out where to wait for nightfall.

After getting soaked the night before, having a roof over our heads would be nice. The clubhouse closets and bathrooms were out. Too much security and chance of getting caught. The maintenance sheds were out since they'd have people going in and out long after the crowds left. We were running out of options, and I can't say that a piece of me wasn't thinking maybe we should just go back to Uncle Luke's with Daddy and see what happened. Maybe Daddy was wrong about being out of time.

No.

It was a more forceful *no* than most objects would give me. *Don't go.*

I couldn't be certain, but I think that voice was coming from outside the window. From Augusta National itself.

If I squinted my eyes, the grass, the trees, the flowers, the hills, the water . . . it was all breathing. What better place to hide on Augusta National than to become part of it? What better floor and roof than Augusta itself? It wasn't going to rain again. That storm had already come and tested us. No, Augusta was calling to me, letting me know that it would keep us safe this time.

Earlier, the course had looked like a painting I could step inside. I scanned the possibilities, then remembered the perfect spot. I pushed a finger against the window, pointing far across the land and sky, past a crowd that watched a cad-die hand a club to a player putting on the eighteenth, past all the people who loved golf and straight to a spot where it couldn't be played at all. "Abbott Meyers," I said.

Noni held a hand over her eyes and looked in the direc-tion I'd pointed. "What? Where are we hiding?"

"The boy from my daddy's goodnight stories. He used to hide out in trees after caddying so he could sneak down and play golf courses at night. We're gonna pull an Abbott Meyers."

Beyond the window were acres of the most beautiful ground in Georgia, divided into yardages and challenges, tee boxes and holes, hills and hazards. Most of the big trees on the grounds had tall trunks and pine needles, but there was one that might work. An oak with low enough first branches and plenty of leaves. "That one," I said.

Never the Hard Part

Noni sat in a branch opposite mine. She looked out over Augusta with a blank expression. The temperature on the course had dropped steadily since sundown, and it was chilly. I'd put on a pair of pants and two extra shirts, but she'd refused the extra clothes of mine from the backpack and had her jeans and Coca-Cola shirt back on, like she wanted to feel as much of the world as she could, even if that meant being uncomfortable.

That bruise of hers was the worst I'd seen it. Whenever I'd bumped her left side throughout the day, she'd clearly been in pain. The rest of her was pale, like the more that bruise hurt, the closer she was to fading away. I had a horrible feeling that she'd disappear on me. She'd been so quiet. Thinking about her daddy, I guess.

"Did you hear that?" Noni turned in her perch, glancing beyond Augusta National's property.

"Hear what?"

She frowned and held her elbow bruise. "Maybe nothing. I thought I heard a train. Are there any rail yards or tracks around here?"

"I don't know. You thinking of stealing my backpack and hopping another train?" I felt my smile fall when her face didn't change.

"Noni, where are you from?"

"Alabama," she replied. "You need more?"

My fingers traced a leaf. I was about to pluck it, but didn't. Looked nicer there on the tree than in my hand. "Don't need more. I'm glad you came to Hilltop."

"Me too." Her leg reached out to tap my shoe. "And just because you don't *need* more doesn't mean you don't *want* more. Or deserve more. You've been a good friend."

"Did you find your sign?"

"Not yet. I feel like time's just about up." She closed her eyes. "I thought I'd find it by now."

"We can look somewhere else," I said. "Where are you going after this?"

Her big eyes stared right into me, the way May's did. "I'm not sure."

I hoped whatever happened in the next hours, she would come home with me. Noni'd said she didn't want to, but I couldn't believe that was true. I was sure I could convince Mama to keep her. We'd been pretending to be brother and sister for just a few days, but it felt like it was meant to be. We fit together somehow, I was certain.

As for what was about to happen with me and Daddy, I felt the opposite of certain. I'd had seconds and thirds and fourths of both happiness and heartache that day, and now I had the happiness-heartache meat sweats.

"Did you have a good birthday?" Daddy asked.

"The best," I told him, which was true. But it was a shadowed best, with What-I-Have-To-Do-Next standing over it and blocking a good part of the light. I didn't want to say goodbye. I didn't see how I could.

"You need anything else from me?" he asked. "Words of wisdom for your future, like why it's a bad idea to drink a lot of beer or reasons not to get a tattoo on April Fools' Day? You want some advice about girls? How to throw a right hook without breaking your hand?"

I hugged him close. "I guess I'll figure that stuff out. But thank you for asking."

Daddy didn't talk much more as we sat up there, keeping track of time on a watch we'd borrowed from Uncle Luke, waiting for Saturday to become Sunday. That was okay. We'd had more talking and listening between us in the last week than in my life altogether. Any idea I had about keeping Daddy for myself seemed nothing more than selfish now.

I had so many memories of my father. The good ones were there, but the painful ones outweighed them, and for a moment I wondered if that's what made the golf ball in my throat so heavy. The lump in my throat was the heaviest it'd been. If only I could find a way to let the dark, heavy memories go. Watch them drift away like colored balloons that would fade and disappear into the midnight sky.

It was one o'clock in the morning when we hopped down. Noni buttoned her father's shirt around her and we stayed among the trees as much as possible. The air was moist, and clumps of fog drifted here and there along the course. I nearly stopped myself once, my feet not wanting to walk forward, choosing instead to trip me so I landed straight on top of the urn.

It knocked the breath out of me, and I felt like I'd gotten sucker-punched in the belly at the school yard. Rolling onto my side, I pushed Noni's hand away. "I'm fine," I told her, trying not to let my voice tremble. "Daddy's just nervous, I think."

She moved to let me stand by myself. "I'll bet he is."

Hurrying between pockets of cover, islands of brush and trees that dotted the course, we made our way to the length of trees along the right side of the eighteenth fairway and tucked ourselves far within, walking north to the final hole. The plan was for me to walk out of the masked area and take care of Daddy while Noni stayed in the trees, ready to scream and provide a distraction in case anyone tried to stop me.

"Okay," Noni said. "If I have to hide and you come to

find me, walk around and whisper the password and I'll pop out. Password will be—"

"'It's a fine night for trespassing,'" I supplied.

"That's not a word."

I squeezed her hand. "No, it's not."

Underneath dropped pine needles, a small group of flowers still had their purple blooms opened to the moonlight. They weren't four inches high, but stood thin-stemmed and straight. Other blossoms around the course had closed up when nighttime approached, but these tiny things looked good and awake.

Noni plucked two and held them out to me. "For your father."

I picked two for her. "For yours."

She took the ones from my hand and twisted the four together, knotting them loosely near the flower base and the ends. "Whenever my daddy and I got in fights, I'd always make him a flower wreath like this," she told me softly. "He'd say 'I forgive you,' and then I'd say, 'No, I forgive *you*,' and then he'd say, 'Are we okay?' and I'd say, 'We're okay.'" She set the little wreath on the ground next to a tree root, then stood, looking at it for a moment. "Leave it there." Digging in her pocket, she came up with a wrinkled newspaper article. She tucked it in my pocket.

"What is it?"

"Read it later. It's the whole truth," she said. "For luck."

Noni stepped closer to me, her eyes shining. Her father's shirt moved in and out from her chest with soft breaths. "Benjamin Putter," she whispered, lifting her hand toward my neck, "tell me what's stuck in your throat." Her fingers reached and gently pressed against my skin, right over the lump.

I swallowed and felt it move. "A golf ball."

She let out a long sigh, lowered her hand and head and smiled at the ground. "You have a golf ball in your throat?"

"Yes."

"Benjamin Putter, when you get it out, can I have it?"

"You believe me? And you actually want the ball?"

"I told you I was looking for a miracle." She stared out at something beyond the course. "Huh. There it is again. I could swear I heard a train whistle." She reached out to squeeze my hand. "I believe you. And I believe *in* you. Now, go and set your daddy free."

I stepped out of the bushes, holding my daddy's urn. The sky was covered with stars that whispered among themselves, saying words that I should have known all along.

Getting onto Augusta National was never the hard part.

Daddy, Me, and the Whole Truth

The eighteenth hole of Augusta National Golf Club was named Holly. It shared a name with my mama. I must've seen the word a hundred times over the last few days, looking in Daddy's Augusta book and checking the course map, but it hadn't hit me until I was walking to the final green. It hadn't sunk in that those 420 yards could be more than a golf hole to Daddy. Or that a golf course could be far more than just a place where a game was played. I'd heard those words from Daddy time and time again, but they'd always belonged only to him. I felt a shift inside me as I walked, like something moving over to make room so those words could belong to me, too.

There was a clear path to the hole, not a security man in sight to slow me down. I almost wished one would appear, just to take away my chance of doing what I came all the way from Hilltop to do.

"Hey, Daddy, you didn't marry Mama because her name

was part of this golf course, did you?" I was only half-joking. Nervous joking, really.

"No, Ben," he replied, a coarse, unshaven noise coming from his throat. "Do you know why I named you after Ben Hogan?"

"Because you didn't like the name Byron or Bobby or Sam or Walter?"

He didn't laugh. "I named you after Ben Hogan because when you came into the world, it was like winning my own personal 1951 Masters. You were my miracle. My second chance to do something important. To become something that was bigger than myself, something that would live on."

Well, the fairway asked me, *how are you doing?*

I wasn't ever going to be a bigger or better version of my father. The things he was good at weren't the things that my heart wanted, and I'd come to realize that there were other ways we weren't the same. It was like we were staring at the same painting, just from a different place in the room, so we each got our own view.

I ran for a tree a hundred yards from the green, his words echoing in my ears. *You were my second chance.*

"You still there, son?"

"Yeah." I sniffled.

"I know you don't understand, son, but to me, you and this place are connected. Hey, are you crying?"

"No." I hadn't cried since he died. But wetness was there

now, just behind my eyes. I hunched down and tucked him under my armpit, not wanting his urn to see me weak. Daddy had never seemed weak, not even when he knew he was dying. He'd been strong in ways I'd never known. I thought of the things I'd learned about my father in the past few days, both the good and the troubling. His ability to listen. His feelings about golf, which were deeper and more meaningful than I'd ever realized. His views on the world and its hard parts. The childhood that maybe made him the man he turned out to be. "Daddy, you're Abbott Meyers, aren't you?"

His breath smiled. "I wasn't born and raised in Augusta, but I sure would've loved it if that were the case. And I didn't get to eat those Georgia peaches that Abbott was so fond of. But, yes, I'm pieces of Abbott Meyers. I never shared much about myself with you, Ben. I was never good at that kind of talking. I guess those stories were my way of trying to show you parts of me."

And now I'd never hear another. "Oh," I managed to say.

"What's wrong?"

I didn't answer. It was too big of a question.

"Ben, I said before you were born, if I had a child, I would be a real father. Mine ran out on me and my mama and your uncle. I promised myself I would never do that to my child. Ben, you were the most important thing in my life. I've always known that, even if I haven't shown it right."

I didn't answer. Couldn't answer.

"That's why I'm still around, I guess. Thank God I didn't leave without you knowing, that you, Ben. . . ." He had tears in his voice now. "You're what's left of me. You're what I'm leaving behind in the world, and I couldn't be prouder of that. You're a good boy."

I moved him to my chest.

Wind murmured through the leaves and needles and grass of the most beautiful place I'd ever seen, and a fog bank emerged from behind me. Then one from the right. They began a strange dance, gathering at the corners of the dimly lit clubhouse.

Slowly, methodically, a white curtain was forming along the edge of the eighteenth green, creating a gift. A barrier of protection for me.

For Daddy.

All the world's colors were inside me. Shifting. Changing. Purple flames of disappointment. Orange flashes of neglect. Yellow flickers of loneliness. Blue bursts of sadness and longing and love. "I don't want you to leave again," I said. "I wish you could stay. I can be a barbecue man and a golfer. I can be whatever you want."

"Ben," Daddy whispered. "Listen to me, now."

Listen to him, the far-off rustling trees told me. *Listen.*

"There are about a million things you can choose to do in this world, Ben, and there are only two things that I knew enough about to teach you. So that's what I did. That's what

a father does. I don't know anything about painting or drawing or art. But you say you're good and you love it? Then you
go after it. Call that teacher and let her help you. Ben Hogan
wasn't great because he wanted to be the greatest golfer in
the world. He was great because he wanted to be the greatest
golfer he could be. He wouldn't settle for less. I want you to
be your own best, that's all. I got you those canvases to paint
on, didn't I?"

"What?"

"I went to Mobile. Found an art store, and brought those
home. I left them on your bed."

Those words were like a golf ball to the head. Knocked
over, I stood there while the world went spinning sideways
and backward in time, making a good part of my past different. Those words unhinged me. Something I'd assumed was
true my whole life suddenly felt like a lie. My daddy hadn't
hated my art. He'd tried to show me that. I felt dangled
upside down in front of a portrait I'd been seeing all wrong.

"That was *you?*" I stared at the urn. At a daddy I hadn't
known existed. "Why didn't you tell me?"

"I thought you knew. And when you didn't say anything,
I figured you didn't want me busting into something that
was yours and yours alone. Ben, I want you to do whatever
your heart tells you."

I shook my head, confused. "You want me to have the
heart of a golfer."

"What?"

"Uncle Luke said that I didn't have the heart of a golfer. That's part of why you kicked him out. Because that's what you want me to have. It's okay, Daddy. I'm not mad."

"No. Ben, *no*." I saw Daddy shake his head, and a thin line appeared where his lips pressed together. "That had nothing to do with golf. I kicked him out because you have the biggest heart I've ever seen. It's so big . . . Ben, it's so much bigger than mine that I couldn't understand it all the time, son. I'm sorry for that. But that doesn't mean I didn't know it was there, just waiting for you to find out how to use it. I kicked your uncle out because any man who says my son doesn't have enough heart is a man I don't want to know. Ben, I swear, I was never trying to make you a golfer. Or a barbecue man."

I kept quiet.

He let out a choked chuckle. "Well, maybe a little. But mostly I was showing you things you can use anywhere. Patience. Hard work. Focus. Not giving up if things don't turn out how you planned. I should've done better, though. I should've just loved you."

I felt glued to the ground at those words.

The colors inside me softened to a neutral shade, almost clear. They whispered that I was forgetting to say something important. "I missed you," I told him. "So much."

"I know. I know you'll miss me."

"No, Daddy," I said. "I missed you when you were alive."

His silence seemed infinite, and when he did speak again, he sounded different. He sounded smaller. He sounded almost like a small boy standing on a golf course somewhere. A small boy who just wanted someone to understand him. But the same way he said he couldn't understand my whole heart, I don't know that I could ever understand all of his.

"What, Daddy? I didn't hear you," I told him.

He cleared his throat and tried again. "I said that I'd change things if I could, but I can't, Ben. I'm sorry."

He didn't say anything else.

Everything in me, everything I'd seen and done the last few days, felt hallowed and haunted, beautiful and disfigured, right and wrong. All of it was dying along with the ashes in my hands, and I could only watch. There was no stopping any of it.

Maybe me and Daddy had been a dying breed from the start of our time together. As much as being a father might have choked him at times, I'd felt the same way. We were two different ropes, facing different hard parts and not knowing the best way to hang on to each other.

And maybe we were both like the Spanish moss hanging off trees all over the South. Maybe there'd never been anything to do except for us to get tangled up during life, not knowing if we were hugging tight or strangling each other's dreams or just trying the best we could to keep living. And maybe golf was in there, too. Me and golf and Daddy, all struggling together, not knowing how else to grow.

I thought about all that until, without warning, the color in me turned back to blue. The cracks in my seal broke, and then tears were rushing down my face like they were trying to win a race. They just kept coming and coming, like a bunch of crazed runners, jostling for space. I stood there holding my father, crying like no boy has ever cried. All the pain I'd been keeping inside poured out of my body, and the release forced me to my knees.

I knelt there and cried for my father and me. For the time we'd had and for the time that we'd lost forever. I let myself cry until I was done. Then I tried to remember how to breathe again.

It took a small forever to come back to myself and to Augusta.

"Benjamin," said Daddy. "I don't want to go either."

"I know, Daddy. I know that."

"Will you say it?"

"Say what, Daddy?" But I knew what he was asking. It was the same thing that I'd been needing. I think I'd known all along. My neck lump knew it too.

"Please, Ben."

It wasn't about missing him when he was dead and gone. It wasn't about needing to say goodbye. I'd needed to tell him how I felt for once. Back in the orchard, I'd needed to yell and scream and tell him how much I'd hurt.

And now I needed to do one more thing.

"All right." I wiped a small dot of my spittle off the urn and brought him close. We were forehead to forehead.

"Please, Ben."

I concentrated hard until I felt my daddy's arms around me. Only then could I say it. "I forgive you," I told him.

That's why he'd come back. So he could be forgiven and so I could do the forgiving. My daddy'd come back for *me*, not for himself. To give me that chance. To let me say everything I needed to.

He sighed, and I heard a faraway echoing wind-of-change within the urn. "It's time to go, son. Go ahead, now. Before anyone comes."

Slowly, sheltering the ashes from the night breeze, I unlocked the lid and cracked it open. I looked at his ashes and took a slow, deep breath. "It's gonna cut me up to do it," I told him.

"I know. But the hurt'll fade and change. Go on, now. Set your daddy free."

I stepped to the middle of the perfect grass, not concerned about being seen. The fog wall was still there, a thick layer of mystery-sent camouflage. It was only when I turned around, facing the tee box 420 yards away, that I saw the sky. It was completely clear when I faced away from the fog.

Stars twinkled and blinked in the midnight canvas, and a sliver of moon gave me a lopsided smile of encouragement.

The golf green was smooth beneath my feet, welcoming me to the task ahead. I'd eaten a piece of Augusta's grass. Noni said it was part of me. And Daddy would be part of Augusta. So maybe we wouldn't be as far from each other as it seemed.

It was time.

A strong wind came out of nowhere when I raised Daddy's urn high in the air. I spun fast in circles, seeing him shimmer like foxfire dust in the moonlight. I felt something lift from me. Daddy hung there for a moment, whipping around in the wind, whispering goodbye. Then I watched him vanish into Augusta National's eighteenth green.

"Bye, Daddy," I whispered.

The wind brushed against me gently, sending a sensation of the unknown into my body. I knew Daddy was home, and for some reason, some prickle or inkling, I found myself walking to the eighteenth hole itself. It was nothing but a dark, round hole where the flag would be put back in the next day. That hole should have been empty, but with every step I took, I felt certain of what I would find inside. When I was close enough, I didn't even look in the hole, just reached in and pulled it out.

The golf ball.

Not a soul would believe me, but I knew exactly where that ball came from because as I lifted my fingers to my throat, I could tell.

The lump was gone.

. . .

When I walked back to her waiting spot, Noni was gone, too. In her place was a single piece of paper, folded. I opened it slowly, looking at the watercolor painting she'd done.

It was a crude set of parallel lines with a train just coming into view, wisps of smoke coming from the top. Along the bottom of the page were two figures, shown from the back. They were holding hands. A big figure and a little one. The big one held a stick—no, a golf club. The small one held a ball in her free hand. They looked like they were waiting for something. I studied the picture and turned it to read her words on the back.

Dear Benjamin Putter,

When I returned to my backyard, I knew I'd been given a chance to find my father. It was a miracle—the kind of thing you can't explain, only believe. When I saw that nobody was home and I started following the train tracks, I thought I would be alone on my mission. But then I came in your kitchen for pie and heard you say a magic word. A word that told me where I needed to go. I heard you say AUGUSTA.

I thought the wandering rules that echoed inside me were warnings of what not to do. I was afraid of what might happen if I broke them. I thought the whole truth was mine and mine alone. Now I realize that wasn't it at all. Or at least that wasn't all of it.

You were here to help me. I think I knew in my heart that you were the one person in the world who could bring me back to him one last time. And I was right.

Please put the ball in the middle of the wreath. That's where it belongs. It's my sign to him, Benjamin Putter— the one I was looking for. I'll bet you didn't know, and I didn't know it either, but you were carrying it for me.

You were carrying it all along.

Your friend,

Noni

I looked at her painting and read her letter again, looking for what was hidden inside her words and wondering if she'd really run off. When I reached in my pocket to see what she'd given me for luck, it was a golf article on Hobart Crane entitled WILL THERE BE A MIRACLE FOR HOBART "HOBO" CRANE? It was dated Wednesday, April 5th. It was the piece of newspaper I'd seen tucked in her pocket back at the café we'd crashed into.

I read the reporter's words, blending them with the letter and image I'd just looked at. Hobart Crane was from Mildred, Alabama, it said. A small town just down the tracks from Hilltop. He hadn't been home since his daughter's funeral two months before, her death caused by a tragedy that the article said must be haunting him. This would be his seventh appearance at the Masters.

I'm a wanderer and lucky to be one, Noni'd told me.

I thought of her secrecy when it came to details. *Never tell anyone the whole truth.*

I pictured her telling me about her past. *I went away after the funeral, then came back.*

Her telling me about her father. *My daddy went to Georgia six times for work.*

Her silence in Mr. Crane's car. *Don't talk to people you shouldn't be talking to, or your wandering time will be up.*

An empty space where I thought she'd be waiting for me. *When it's time to leave, leave.*

Noni'd never said her father was dead. *Lost*, she'd said. *Missed.* When she asked if I believed in getting signs from a dead loved one, I'd assumed she wanted to get a sign from her father. But I was wrong. The whole time I'd known her, she wanted to get the right sign *to* her father. When Noni's message made sense, when who Noni was became clear, I felt like I was ringing all over, like when I'd gotten shocked by Daddy's golf club.

There was so much I understood, but so much that I never would, so many questions answered and so many I'd never had time to ask. But all of it made me glad to be alive and in a world where I had time left—a world where things were impossible, until they weren't.

A world where maybe I could say more than I'd thought was allowed and do more than I'd thought I could do and be braver than I'd thought I could be and take what my daddy'd taught me and use it to be any kind of Putter I wanted to be. Be a man of action my own way.

A world where Miss Stone was right and mistakes led to a better way of going about things when you were given a second chance. A world where you could change. Decide to stop keeping your head down. Decide to be a better friend. Decide to call a teacher and tell her that making art made you feel like you'd found your heart's home.

A world where, suddenly, I was less alone. I was Benjamin Hogan Putter, and I was a barbecue man and an artist and a Big Five quoter and a runaway and a thinker and a man of action and a knot tyer and a listener and a talker and a friend.

All of those things were part of me. I didn't have to choose between them. The spaces I thought had always existed, the barriers and dividing lines that held me back like a boy at the edge of his bed . . . those weren't there anymore. They'd never been there at all. And if they were, they were like the fences around Hilltop, Alabama, which didn't keep a thing in or out.

Yep, said a bush, *that one'll be all right.*

That's right, he did real good, said a star.

Good boy, said Augusta.

I wiped my eyes, put the ball in its rightful place, and went to find my mama.

The Rest

Hobart Crane didn't win the Masters that year. Nobody was surprised. People didn't understand how a man could play the biggest golf tournament in the world just two months after his daughter died. Some thought he was heartless. Others thought he was punishing himself, wallowing in his grief by playing the game that had taken him away from a girl who'd already lost a parent. I think maybe he played the Masters because he didn't know what else to do, and maybe part of him thought he would find her there, nestled somewhere inside the only thing he had left on earth to love.

He played horrible on Sunday, right up until the eighteenth hole, when he sliced his tee shot deep into the trees. It took forever for him to find his ball, and when he did, he sat there in the bushes for close to ten minutes with the officials. And that's when Hobo, as people called him, hit the shot of his life and saved par for the hole. An impossible shot out of the rough that didn't have an equal. A miracle shot. It was a shot from the same place that Noni and I hid the night before.

I only know because there was an article the following day detailing the drama of the shot and shedding some light on Mr. Crane's long time spent in the trees. It seemed that two balls were found in the rough of the course, close together. Neither ball was allowed to be touched until it was pointed out, by Hobart himself, that one of them was a brand of ball he hadn't used in years, let alone during the tournament. His caddie confirmed the fact. Apparently Mr. Crane had then kneeled down by the ball and stared at it for a good minute before getting real emotional and asking to keep the rogue ball, a request so odd that it made it into the article. The officials saw no reason to deny the request.

A photograph of Mr. Crane on the eighteenth green, tears running down his face after his final putt, was included with the article. People said he was sad about losing or sad about his daughter, but I think they were wrong. He was crying because he felt better. I'm sure nobody else noticed it, but if you looked closely at the photograph, a weedy-looking circle with a few limp flowers on it was hanging out of his pocket.

The photograph Mrs. Reilly sent me sits right beside Daddy's ashless urn on the kitchen shelf: Hobart Crane with one arm around me while I held Mama's photograph and

Daddy's urn. His other arm was around a small girl in a dress and pigtails, who kept her head down, her right hand gently squeezing his pants leg. I wrote down the return address for Mrs. Reilly at Augusta National before throwing away the envelope. I figured I could send her the drawing Mr. Crane had requested in the car, along with the pocketknife he'd given to his daughter, and she could find a way to get those things to him. He hadn't said who he wanted me to draw, but I knew. In the five days I'd spent with Noni, I'd come to know just about every freckle on her big-eyed face.

I kept everything to myself, telling Mama that I'd never thought Daddy was talking to me and that Uncle Luke must've heard me wrong and that I guessed Noni had just run off again because that's what runners do.

Mama said she only wished she'd been with us. I told her how the eighteenth hole had her name and how I'd had her picture, so she sort of had been there. After apologizing to Uncle Luke for the excessive knot tying, I did work up the nerve to ask him if he knew how Mr. Crane's daughter had died. She'd died two months before I set out to scatter Daddy. Right around the time that lump showed up in my throat.

Train accident, he said. The coroner said it looked like her hand somehow got stuck in the tracks behind their house. Train ran over her arm, right at the elbow. She bled to death beside the tracks. Hobart Crane was at home, but he didn't hear her yelling for help. They'd found a golf club next to her, but nothing else. A polished trophy board, where Hobart's championship golf ball had been mounted, was found in the backyard, thrown haphazardly next to the burn pile, emptied of its prize.

I didn't ask whether his daughter's nickname had been Noni. I didn't need to. I knew when Uncle Luke told me about her death that Wynona Crane had somehow come back to the world for a brief time, and she'd helped me. But she'd also gotten her own wish. We'd been flung together, both of us waiting for Augusta to offer forgiveness. To help me forgive my father and to let Noni find a way to help her father forgive himself.

I think second chances show up more often than we notice. During the journey to Augusta, I'd run into my life over and over, the farther I went from home, like the quote Noni'd told me from her father. And maybe that's all life is. Like a big game of repeat, with people running into the same things, the same situations, just against a different time and landscape. Like people are brushed into paintings over and over, being given new chances to act different. To maybe be a better version of themselves.

And I think Fate or the Ol' Creator or Mama Nature or Whatever sometimes brings two people together to help each other. To carry each other's burdens and dreams. To ease the hard and strengthen the good in life. To help each other get where they need to be.

I don't know much for absolute certain except what I believe. I believe with all I've got that the ball stuck in my throat was the one that Noni hit onto the tracks. The one that she'd been reaching for when her arm got stuck. I believe that something wiser than us put Noni back at her house beside the tracks instead of taking her right to Augusta, so that we would meet. So we could help each other. The whole time we were together, she'd helped carry me to the place I needed to go so I could make peace with my father. And I'd been carrying the thing she needed most to help heal hers.

It makes me wonder if maybe I'm carrying other things inside me that people need. Maybe good things. Maybe brave things, just waiting for me to find the right place to let them out.

Ben Hogan said that the most important shot in golf is the next one. When I got home from Augusta on Sunday evening, my next shot had been to take the paintings I'd made for May over to her house. I wrote a long letter to go with them, and since it was too late to knock on the Talbots' door, I left all the papers on their front porch, along with a paint palette of different shades of green that I'd asked Mama to buy before we left Augusta. Then I rode my bike home. The next day at school, I found a note in my locker.

It was a short note. It said *Now do more water. With lots of lily pads.*

. . .

I never found out the last thing Daddy said to me before he died, but I decided I could choose which brushstrokes filled that space. It didn't have to be a golfer quote or instructions to take care of Mama or telling me that I'd be okay or even him saying *I love you*. Or it could. Daddy never said those words out loud to me, but I know they were inside him somewhere.

I feel like he wanted to be the father I needed. And I think he did the best he could. What I know for sure is this: When he came back, my father chose me to take him to his final resting place. He had faith in me, and maybe that's what I was looking for all along.

I didn't tell anyone the whole truth about Noni or Daddy or what happened that night at Augusta National. I didn't need anyone else to believe me.

Some things are true whether other people believe you or not.

ACKNOWLEDGMENTS

My character Ben Putter talks about people coming into your world—people who help to carry you where you need to be, who ease the hard and strengthen the good in life. This is the third book of mine that's had the benefit of Kristin Ostby's editing skills. I say "editing skills," but I think what I really mean is "editing heart." Her total commitment, acute observations, plot/content guidance, and staunch support helped carry me on the journey of completing this novel, which started as an unconventional love story about a son and father finding a mutual sense of understanding, and evolved into something more. Thank you, Kristin. I'm also thankful for the editorial eyes of Mekisha Telfer.

To my wonderful literary agent, Tina Wexler, thank you for encouraging me through this story's writing and revision process. I'm so grateful for you.

Thank you to wicked-talented cover/book designer Lizzy Bromley for all of her work and brilliance. Cover artist Kenard Pak, I feel so lucky to have your art nestling these pages. Huge amounts of gratitude belong to Justin Chanda and the entire team at Simon & Schuster Books for Young Readers for all that they do for readers and writers.

To critique partners Joy McCullough-Carranza, Tara Dairman, Ann Bedichek, and Becky Wallace—you ladies are appreciated more than you know. A big thanks to Shelby Bach for reading/critiquing a version of this story years and years ago.

Thanks to Rebecca Petruck and Patrick Robinette for their help in matters of pigs/hogs, Tom Fletcher of Capital/Colonial/Southern Trailways for bus route/fare information, and Nancy Glaser at the Augusta Museum of History. Thank you Mom and Dad for your fact-sleuthing assistance. The 18th hole's yardage is a historical one that is not reflective of today's course. Fictional liberties were taken in places to aid the novel's plot, but any/all missteps in regard to pigs, barbecue, or Augusta National Golf Club's course can be attributed to me, not the helpful folks listed.

The protest scene in this book is based on an actual television clip that shows a group of people protesting elementary school desegregation in Augusta, Georgia, in mid-March, 1972, just weeks before Ben Hogan Putter would have arrived there. The fight for school integration in the United States carried on well into the 1970s, particularly in areas of the South mentioned in this book. "Segregation academies"—private schools formed in response to enforced integration of schools—were very much alive at the time. They still exist in certain forms.

Finally, thank you to my husband, who loves golf—I'm hoping you'll go to Augusta to watch the Masters one day and that you'll get a chance to play at the Old Course in Scotland as well. To my brother-in-law Evan—I'm thankful for the day you stood in my kitchen and declared that, given the choice, you'd want your ashes scattered at Augusta National Golf Club's 18th hole. Pretty crazy idea, brother.